A Treacherous Engagement

GENTLEMEN *of* LONDON

Laura Beers

Chapter One

England, 1813

GROWING UP, Nathaniel Calvert, the Earl of Hawthorne, had always wanted to be a spy or a pirate. Each would have given him the adventure he craved, but being a pirate was a good way to get a noose around one's neck. So, he was grateful he'd been recruited out of Oxford to be a spy.

It had helped fill a void in his life these ten years, one that he hadn't even realized he had. He enjoyed being an agent of the Crown, even though he knew things that could easily get him killed. He recognized that he was therefore living on borrowed time.

Nathaniel's reflections on his occupation came to a crashing halt as he was hit squarely in the jaw and stumbled back towards the wall.

His friend, Mr. Aaron Berkeley, shook his head. "You left yourself open."

"It won't happen again," Nathaniel said, pushing off the wall.

Berkeley put his hands up in front of him. "We shall see."

Nathaniel advanced towards Berkeley, his posture slightly bent and his footwork nimble. He pulled his fist back and swung at Berkeley, hitting him in the face.

"Nice hit," Berkeley acknowledged begrudgingly, rubbing his jaw where he was hit.

Nathaniel lowered his fists. "On that note, I should be going."

"So soon?"

"I'm afraid I will be late for a meeting if I do not leave soon," Nathaniel replied, stepping out of the chalked area.

Berkeley followed him out and waved off the bottle-holder.

Nathaniel removed the cloth that was wrapped around his hands, then reached for a towel on the bench to wipe the sweat from his forehead. "Are we still on for White's this evening?"

"I hope so," Berkeley said. "Everyone will be there."

He nodded approvingly as he dropped the towel onto the bench. After he unrolled his white sleeves, he reached for his cravat and made quick work of tying an intricate knot.

"We should try to get them to join us here at Gentleman Jackson's Saloon," Berkeley remarked.

"Perhaps," Nathaniel said, picking up his blue jacket. "It would give me a chance to knock some sense into Hugh."

Berkeley chuckled. "Hugh is a lost cause."

"I don't believe that."

"You are only saying that because he is your brother."

"Don't remind me," Nathaniel said good-naturedly. "Good day, Berkeley."

Nathaniel exited Gentleman Jackson's Saloon, leaving the smell of rancid sweat behind. He enjoyed starting his morning off with a boxing match. It kept him limber, knowing that he always had to be prepared for a fight. One wrong misstep could mean the difference between life or death for him.

He hailed a hackney and shouted the address up to the

driver. As he stepped inside, he felt his boots stick to the floor, and a pungent odor filled the air. It was a far cry from the smart coaches he was used to, but where he was going, it wouldn't be wise to draw attention to himself.

Nathaniel stared out the window and watched as they headed towards the unsavory part of London. The buildings shifted from large and spacious to narrow, darkened structures that gave the appearance of being structurally unsound. The men and women walking down the pavement all seemed to be lost in their own thoughts.

The hackney came to a stop and Nathaniel exited. He reached into his waistband pocket and removed a few coins.

The driver's nervous eyes roamed the street. "Are ye sure ye want to be here, mister?"

"I do," Nathaniel replied, extending the coins to him.

"This ain't no place for a gentleman," the driver pressed.

Nathaniel took a step back. "You do not need to concern yourself with that."

"Suit yourself," the driver said as he urged his team forward.

Tucking his hands in his pockets, Nathaniel walked down the pavement, being mindful of all the eyes on him. He would be a fool to dismiss the men that no doubt had pegged him as an easy target.

Nathaniel carried only an overcoat pistol in his right boot and a dagger in his left, easily accessible if he was called upon to defend himself. It wouldn't be the first time that he had been forced to fight himself out of a dangerous situation, and he was confident it wouldn't be the last time, either.

As he approached a two-level, nondescript brick building, he saw two familiar men sitting in front of it, both wearing tattered clothing. They appeared to be down on their luck, but he knew it was only an act. These men were poised for a fight as they guarded the building from any potential threats.

The thin, dark-haired agent held up a cup as he

approached. "Do you have any coins to spare, mister?" Talbot asked.

Nathaniel reached into his pocket and removed a sixpence. "I do," he replied, dropping it into the cup.

Talbot nodded, lowering the cup. "Thank you, mister." He looked inside and frowned. "I expected better from you, Hawthorne."

The other agent spoke up as he brushed his red hair to the side. "Why are you dressed so fashionably?" Worsley asked.

"Not that it is any of your business, but I had something I needed to see to across Town," Nathaniel replied.

"It's a good look on you," Worsley said, holding up his cup. "I believe you forgot something."

Nathaniel shook his head as he retrieved another coin from his pocket. As he dropped it into the cup, Worsley advised, "You'd best get inside before you draw any more attention to yourself."

Nathaniel tipped his head as he moved to open the door. He stepped inside and saw an older man behind a desk, his white hair slicked to the side.

The man brought his gaze up, but his hands were hidden behind the desk. "What business do you have here?"

"The countryside is idyllic in the spring."

The man visibly relaxed at his coded message. "Very good, sir," he said, gesturing towards the back door with a pistol in his hand. "You may go back now."

"Where is Mostyn?" Nathaniel asked as he approached the back door.

"His wife is sick," the man replied. "Merritt asked me to fill in for him today."

Nathaniel opened the door and stepped inside the hall. Desks filled the space and agents were busily working, giving him little heed as he headed towards the rear of the hall.

He stopped outside of Merritt's office and knocked.

"Enter," Merritt ordered.

4

Nathaniel opened the door and stepped inside. The chief spymaster was sitting behind his desk, an annoyed look on his face. His black hair was heavily streaked with grey, accentuating his wrinkles. Merritt may be advancing in age, but he was still a man who was not to be trifled with.

The chief spymaster's critical eye swept over him and announced, "You are late."

"I assure you that it couldn't be helped."

Merritt closed the book in front of him and moved it to the side of his desk. "I expect my agents to be punctual."

"Duly noted," Nathaniel said as he came to sit down in front of the desk. "Your note indicated that it was urgent."

"It is," Merritt responded. "I have a new assignment for you."

"But I am already working on a case," Nathaniel responded. "Two, in fact."

"Not anymore," Merritt said. "I want this assignment to take priority."

"I understand."

Merritt grew serious as he gave him his full attention. "There has been some alarming chatter about the prince regent."

"There is always chatter," Nathaniel replied, unconcerned. He couldn't think of a time when there wasn't an active threat against the prince regent's life.

"That may be true, but I would like you to take these threats seriously and investigate them," Merritt said, reaching for a file on his desk. "There is a group starting to garner strength in the rookeries."

"That is not surprising. Crime has always been rampant there."

Merritt nodded in agreement. "Their hatred seems to be concentrated on the prince regent, and I worry that they might do something rash." He extended him a file. "The group is known as the Red Ravens, and they are growing in numbers. The file will give you some basic information about them."

"This assignment sounds easy enough," Nathaniel said, rising. "I shall infiltrate them and have a report to you by morning."

Merritt gave him a displeased look. "I do not believe this assignment will be that easy," he remarked. "You will not be the first agent who has tried to infiltrate the group. The last agent I assigned to this case is still unaccounted for."

Lowering himself back onto the chair, Nathaniel dreaded the answer to his next question. "Who?"

Merritt's jaw clenched. "Rutledge."

Nathaniel felt like he had been punched in the stomach at that unexpected news. It took him a moment to recover. "When did he disappear?" he asked.

"He failed to check in last week."

"And I am just finding out about this now?" Nathaniel asked, his voice rising. "I should have been out there looking for him."

"I had a few agents make some inquiries, but they were unable to turn up anything." Merritt grew solemn. "It isn't entirely uncommon for Rutledge to disappear for a week or two, only to appear later unharmed."

"No, it isn't."

"I want you to proceed with extreme caution," Merritt advised. "I don't want to lose two agents on this assignment."

Nathaniel rose from his seat. "I will find Rutledge and bring him home."

"Hawthorne—"

"I don't believe that Rutledge would have succumbed to his fate without a fight," Nathaniel interrupted.

"We don't know what that fate is," Merritt remarked. "For all we know, Rutledge is deep undercover and was unable to get a message out."

"When has that stopped him before?" Nathaniel questioned. He walked to the door with the file in hand but was stopped by Merritt's voice.

"Do not let Rutledge's disappearance cloud your judgement," he said. "You will need all your wits about you to solve this case."

"You need not concern yourself with that. I can complete this assignment and find Rutledge," Nathaniel stated before he opened the door and stepped out into the hall. He quickly exited the building and started down the pavement. There was no point in trying to hail a hackney in this part of town; they weren't foolish enough to pick up fares here.

Nathaniel half-hoped for a fight, growing increasingly agitated that his mentor and friend had disappeared without a trace. That didn't sound like the man who had recruited him out of Oxford and taught him everything he needed to know to be an agent. No; he refused to give up on Rutledge, just as his friend would not have given up on him.

A man stepped out of the alleyway with a dagger clutched in his hand. "Give me yer money," he demanded, his beady eyes perusing the length of him.

"No."

"No?" the man repeated back in disbelief. "But I have a dagger."

Nathaniel shook his head. "That dagger is not sharp, and it would cause little damage, assuming you even know how to use it properly."

"I do," the man claimed as he stepped in front of him.

"Not likely," Nathaniel said. "Now, let me pass before I get angry."

The man's eyes narrowed. "I think not," he replied. "Ye are the one at a disadvantage."

Nathaniel took a moment to size up his opponent. His clothing was threadbare, his cap was crooked, and his shoes had holes along the top. This man was robbing him out of desperation, and that made him dangerous.

In a swift motion, Nathaniel reached into his boot, pulled out his overcoat pistol, and pointed it at his attacker. "It would now appear that you are at a disadvantage."

His attacker looked unsure. "Who carries a pistol in their boot?"

"A man who is prepared for the unexpected."

Lowering his dagger, the man said, "That pistol only has one shot, and ye are far from home."

"Perhaps, but I like my odds."

"Ye won't make it far," his attacker insisted. "If I don't kill ye, someone else will have the pleasure."

"You underestimate me, and that is your biggest mistake."

Nathaniel had just spoken his words when a coach pulled up alongside of him. The door opened to reveal Lord Grenton.

"Get in," Grenton ordered.

"Gladly." Nathaniel approached the coach, keeping a close eye on his attacker.

He sat across from Grenton, who gave him a look of disbelief before asking, "What in the blazes are you doing in the rookeries?"

As the coach jerked forward, Nathaniel set the file down next to him and slipped his overcoat pistol back into his right boot. "I had an errand that I needed to see to."

"In the rookeries?" Grenton asked.

"Yes."

Grenton gave him a look that implied he didn't believe him. Not that it mattered; Nathaniel had no intention of revealing the truth. "Why were you pointing a pistol at that man?" Grenton pressed.

With a shrug of his shoulders, Nathaniel replied, "He was attempting to rob me, and I turned the tables on him."

"I see," Grenton muttered. "You must think me a fool."

"Not particularly."

Grenton huffed. "You have always been one to have secrets."

"That is true," Nathaniel replied, seeing no reason to deny it. "Not that I am complaining, but why were you in the rookeries?"

"I was visiting my mother's orphanage on Tryon Street," Grenton revealed, his voice growing reflective. "The orphanage meant a great deal to my mother, and I am going to ensure that it thrives."

"That is good of you."

"It is the least I can do to honor her memory," Grenton remarked, dismissing his praise. "But I am having a hard time hiring someone to run it."

"Why is that?"

"There have been many applicants, but I wonder if my expectations are too lofty."

"What are you looking for?"

"A lady," Grenton revealed.

"A lady?" Nathaniel questioned.

Grenton nodded. "My mother wanted a lady to run the orphanage, giving it credence amongst members of high Society."

"What lady is foolish enough to accept the position?"

"That is the issue."

Nathaniel glanced out the window, then asked, "Are you still joining us at White's tonight?"

"I wouldn't miss it," Grenton replied. "It has been far too long since I have gone out."

"We have missed you."

A pained look came to Grenton's face. "I'm afraid I haven't felt like celebrating since my mother's death."

"That is understandable."

Grenton forced a smile, attempting to mask the sorrow beneath. "Enough of that talk," he started, "I would much rather discuss how you intended to get yourself out of your predicament earlier."

"I wasn't worried."

"You weren't?" Grenton asked. "You were walking through the rookeries, alone."

"I had a pistol on me."

Grenton shook his head. "Your cockiness has always astounded me."

"I shall take that as a compliment."

"I must have said it wrong, then," Grenton joked.

Nathaniel smiled as the coach came to a stop in front of his three-level whitewashed townhouse. "I do thank you for the ride."

"You mean 'rescue'," Grenton corrected.

"No, I said it correctly," Nathaniel smiled as he opened the door. "I had the situation in hand."

"You are an idiot, Hawthorne."

Nathaniel chuckled. "I shall see you this evening," he said as he exited the coach.

As he approached the main door, it opened, and his butler, Balfour, stepped to the side to allow him entry.

"Good afternoon, my lord," Balfour greeted.

Nathaniel stopped in front of the lanky butler. "I shall be eating at White's tonight," he informed him.

Balfour tipped his head in acknowledgement. "Very good."

"I will be in my study until I depart."

"Your mother was looking for you."

Nathaniel resisted the urge to sigh. He had a fairly good idea of why his mother was seeking him out. "Understood."

He walked towards his study with the file in hand. He wanted to learn all he could about the Red Ravens and their leader. If they had anything to do with Rutledge's disappearance, they would pay dearly.

Nathaniel stepped into his study and walked around his desk. As he sat down, he dropped the file onto the desk and opened it.

It appeared that the leader of the Red Ravens was a man known as John Abrams. He owned a shop near the rookeries, and there was a basic description of his appearance.

It wasn't much to go on, but it was a start. He would go meet this John Abrams, and with any luck, the man would be in Newgate by the end of the day. It was where he deserved to be. Any threat to the Crown had to be dealt with swiftly.

His mother walked into the room purposefully. "There you are," she declared.

Nathaniel closed the file in front of him and put it in one of the desk drawers. "How can I help you, Mother?"

"Hugh didn't come home again last night."

"You sound surprised."

His mother stopped in front of the desk. "He is spending all of his time at that gambling hall, and I am worried about him."

"As am I."

"Your father is of little help," his mother said.

"Why do you say that?"

"He believes that Hugh will come around on his own."

Nathaniel leaned back in his chair. "He might not be wrong. Eventually, Hugh will run out of money, and he will come home."

"But what respectable girl will want to marry him, given his reputation?"

"He is the son of a marquess," Nathaniel replied. "I have no doubt that many young women will be willing to overlook his flaws."

His mother sat on a chair that faced the desk. "I suppose you are right, but I do wish that Hugh was more like you."

"In what regard?"

"You have embraced your role within this family, whereas Hugh just seems adrift."

"If it helps, I will speak to Hugh tonight, assuming he shows up at White's."

A relieved expression crossed his mother's face. "I would greatly appreciate that."

Nathaniel smiled and asked, "How are you faring?"

"I would be much better if I had grandchildren to dote on," she responded with a tilt of her chin.

"In due time, Mother."

"When?" his mother pressed. "You don't even seem interested in matrimony."

"That is not true," he replied. "I have been busy as of late."

"You rarely attend social events, and I can't recall the last time you joined your father and I at the opera."

"I'm afraid social events hold little appeal for me."

"That is most unfortunate. How else will you find a bride?"

"The right woman will come along eventually."

His mother looked displeased. "You don't want to wait too long. If you do, I might be too old to play with my grandchildren."

"You are still young."

"Only in your eyes, dear."

His father's voice came from the doorway. "Do stop pressuring our son to wed," Lord Montfort chided lightly.

"You are finally home," his mother said, rising.

His father approached her, kissing her on the cheek. "I told you that I would be home for dinner."

"You did, but I know the House of Lords often exceeds their scheduled time."

"Not today," his father replied. "I just want to spend the evening with my lovely wife."

Nathaniel watched as a look of love passed between his parents. He had been blessed to live in a home with parents who loved each other dearly.

His father turned his attention towards him. "Where have you been all day?"

"I've been out."

"Did you have a chance to review the ledger that I left for you?"

Nathaniel reached for the ledger and placed it in front of him. "I will review it before I leave for White's this evening."

"See that you do," his father replied. "You need to be acquainted with all of our properties and investments."

"I understand."

"One day, this will all be yours, and I won't be around to coddle you anymore."

"You are hardly coddling me, Father," Nathaniel remarked dryly.

His father frowned. "I just wish you wouldn't spend your time on..." he hesitated, "how exactly do you spend your time?"

"I enjoy the usual pastimes for gentlemen."

His father eyed him warily. "It is time for you to accept your responsibility and manage your inheritance."

"I shall think on that."

His father opened his mouth to respond but closed it when his wife laid a hand on his sleeve. "Why don't we leave Nathaniel to his work, and we can go take a turn in the gardens before we dress for dinner?" she suggested.

His father's face softened as he turned his attention towards her. "That sounds far preferable to yelling at our son."

"I would agree," his mother replied.

Nathaniel caught his mother's eye and mouthed, "Thank you."

She placed her hand in the crook of her husband's arm,

and they started towards the door. Nathaniel's father spun back around. "This conversation isn't over, son."

"I assumed as much."

Nathaniel watched as his parents departed before opening the ledger in front of him. His father did make a valid point; he needed to be more involved in managing their investments. Doing so would take away from his job as an agent, though—which his parents knew nothing about.

Nathaniel just wished that there were more hours to the day.

Chapter Two

Miss Dinah Ashmore had a problem. Her older sister, Evie, had gone missing nearly three days ago, and little was being done about it. Now she was forced to endure the endless chatter of a large, rounded constable. She highly doubted that Mr. Burns had ever successfully found a missing person because he spent far too much time boasting about his abilities.

She watched as Mr. Burns brought his cup up to his lips and slurped his tea. Dear heavens, did the man have no manners at all?

Her Aunt Nancy must have sensed her rising irritation because she met her gaze and offered her a weak smile.

Mr. Burns lowered his teacup to his protruding belly. "You two must not worry. I shall ensure Miss Ashmore returns home."

"How can we not worry, Mr. Burns?" Dinah asked. "My sister left our home three days ago and she has yet to return."

"Most likely, Miss Ashmore eloped to Gretna Green and will be returning shortly with a husband in tow," Mr. Burns remarked.

"My sister has shown no favor to any man."

"It is not uncommon for someone to keep secrets from their family," Mr. Burns attempted.

"I can assure you that is not the case."

Mr. Burns reached for a biscuit on the tray. "I mean no offense, but you are young and obviously naïve as to the ways of the world."

"I don't dispute that, but—"

"I have seen countless cases where a young woman goes missing and returns a week later after a visit with the anvil priest," Mr. Burns said, cutting her off.

"This is not one of those cases," she asserted.

Mr. Burns gave her a look that could only be construed as pity. "I know that you may doubt me, but you shall see that I am right soon enough." He looked around the drawing room. "You may want to inform your cook to plan a celebration for when she returns."

"Mr. Burns—" Dinah attempted.

He put his hand up, stilling her words. "Nothing can be done until Miss Ashmore has been missing for at least a week."

Dinah pursed her lips together, knowing that no good would come from fighting with the infuriating man.

Her aunt spoke up. "We do thank you for your time, but as you can imagine, we are both extremely worried about Evie. This is so unlike her."

Mr. Burns bobbed his head, causing the fat under his chin to jiggle. "I understand, but this is an all-too-common plight for young, sheltered women."

"What if Evie does not return after a week?" Dinah asked, fearful of the answer.

"Then I shall make some inquiries," Mr. Burns said, leaning forward to place his empty cup onto the tray, "but I do not believe that will be necessary."

"My sister left in the middle of the day to go shopping for

flowers," Dinah pressed. "She mentioned nothing of meeting a potential suitor."

"Most likely, she snuck into his awaiting coach," Mr. Burns explained. "I'm afraid I have other cases that take precedence, but if you have no objections, I shall return in a weeks' time to confirm my suspicions."

"You are always welcome in our home, Mr. Burns," Aunt Nancy said.

Mr. Burns rose awkwardly. "I do appreciate that, Mrs. Carter. Good day, Miss Dinah."

Knowing what was expected of her, Dinah responded with a tip of her head. "Good day, Mr. Burns."

After the constable left, Dinah put her cup down and walked over to the window. She watched Mr. Burns walk down the street, appearing as if he didn't have a care in the world.

"Insufferable man," she muttered under her breath.

"He means well," her aunt said.

Dinah rested her shoulder against the windowsill. "He is adamant that Evie has eloped to Gretna Green, and he refuses to listen to reason."

"He does make a valid point."

"Not you, too?" Dinah asked, turning back to face her aunt. "Evie disappeared while she was shopping with her maid for flowers. If she had gotten into an awaiting coach, don't you think Sally would have seen something?"

"I suppose so."

Dinah frowned. "Evie did not disappear on her own accord, I'm sure of it."

"I'm of a mind to agree with you, but we cannot convince Mr. Burns to investigate her disappearance until she has been gone for at least a week."

"Then we need to search for her."

Her aunt's eyes grew large at the suggestion. "You cannot

be in earnest," she said. "Where would we even begin looking?"

"At the shop she went to before she vanished."

"You have already spoken to the shopkeeper, and he didn't remember Evie even visiting the store that day."

"But I didn't interview all the workers."

Her aunt set her teacup aside. "I know you are worried, but there is little we can do right now."

"I refuse to give up."

"I'm not suggesting we do so," her aunt responded, "but London is a big city. It is not as if we can go knocking on people's doors to see if they have seen Evie."

"We could hire a Bow Street Runner to investigate her disappearance," Dinah suggested.

Her aunt looked unsure, and her voice was low and soft. "How would we even go about doing such a thing?"

"We could visit their offices at number four on Bow Street."

"How do you know where their offices are located?"

"From the newssheets," Dinah replied. "I have read countless stories of their bravery and exploits solving crimes."

"Those stories might be vastly exaggerated to sell morning newspapers."

"Perhaps, but don't you think we should at least try?" Dinah asked hopefully. "For Evie's sake?"

Her aunt pressed her lips together. "I know you are anxious for Evie's return, but I don't believe hiring a Bow Street Runner would be the solution to our problems."

"Why not?"

"They have a reputation for being uncouth."

"That hardly matters to me," Dinah said. "I don't care how they act, assuming they bring Evie home."

"I propose we wait, at least for another day, to see if Evie returns."

Dinah's shoulders slumped. "I don't know what I would do if I lost Evie, too."

Her aunt rose and walked over to her. "You won't," she said. "I am confident that Evie will return to us."

"How can you be so sure of that?"

"I'm not, but I have faith in her."

"And what if your faith is misplaced?"

Her aunt slipped her arm over her shoulder. "Your sister would do anything for you, and I believe she is fighting to return home to you, as we speak."

"What if she is not in a position to return?"

"I do not know," her aunt murmured.

Tears came to Dinah's eyes, but she blinked them away. Crying did no good, and she had shed far too many tears over her sister's disappearance. It was time that she did something about it, and that meant she needed to take matters into her own hands.

"I think I just need a distraction," Dinah said.

Her aunt removed her hand. "I agree."

"Would you care to go shopping with me?" Dinah asked.

"I have a meeting with my solicitor this morning," her aunt replied, smoothing back her fading brown hair. "We could always go this afternoon."

"I would prefer to go this morning."

"I don't know…"

Dinah knew she needed to convince her aunt without drawing any suspicion to her true motives. "I will take Julia along with me."

"And two footmen," her aunt said firmly.

"I can agree to that."

For a moment, Aunt Nancy looked as if she might refuse her request, but she nodded slowly. "Do be careful," she urged. "I don't know what I would do if I lost you, as well."

"I will be." Dinah felt guilty for lying to her aunt, but she refused to sit back and do nothing; not when so much was at stake.

Her aunt glanced down at her white gown. "If you are going to Bond Street, you should change into something more appropriate."

"I believe I shall," Dinah said as she walked over to the door.

After she departed from the drawing room, she saw the butler standing in the entry hall. She approached Barnes and smiled at the tall, bald man.

Barnes returned her smile. "How may I be of service, miss?"

"Will you see to bringing the coach around front?" she asked. "Also, I will require two footmen to accompany me to do some shopping."

"That can be arranged."

"Thank you," she replied.

Dinah headed towards her bedchamber on the second level. As she reached the top of the staircase, she saw her lady's maid, Julia, walking down the hall.

"I need to speak to you," Dinah said.

The petite blonde nodded. "Of course."

Dinah hurried into her bedchamber and waited for Julia to do the same, closing the door behind her.

Julia eyed her curiously. "What are you about?"

"I need you to come with me."

"Where?"

"To hire a Bow Street Runner."

Julia blinked. "Pardon?"

"I need to hire a Bow Street Runner to investigate Evie's disappearance," Dinah explained.

"How does one go about hiring a Bow Street Runner?" Julia asked.

"I'm not entirely sure, but I plan to go to their offices on Bow Street. Fortunately, it isn't far from Bond Street."

"What does your aunt say about this?"

Dinah winced. "She doesn't know. I told her I was going shopping."

"Why didn't you tell Mrs. Carter the truth?"

"Aunt Nancy believes I should wait another day before we do something drastic."

"She isn't wrong, you know."

"Please," Dinah pleaded. "I cannot in good faith sit around and do nothing to help Evie."

Her lady's maid grew silent. "I am not going to be able to talk you out of this, am I?"

"No," she replied swiftly.

"Fine, but you must promise not to take any unnecessary risks," Julia said.

"I can agree to that."

Julia rose and walked over to the armoire. "What does one wear to speak to a Bow Street Runner?"

"I'm not entirely sure, but I need to give the appearance that I am going shopping."

"Yes, miss."

Dinah felt awful for lying to her aunt, but it was for the best. She would go to Bow Street, hire a Runner, and be back before her aunt would even suspect a thing.

Nathaniel walked down the pavement as he headed towards John Abrams' shop. He didn't want to draw attention to himself, so he wore an unassuming brown suit with a burgundy waistcoat, a worn brown cap pulled low over his face. He paused to read a sign in front of a brick building.

J.B. ABRAMS, PLUMASSIER

He opened the door and a bell above it chimed as he

stepped inside. Fancy feathers and silk flowers were stacked neatly next to one another throughout the room.

A pleasant-looking woman approached him with a smile. "How may I help you, sir?"

"I was hoping to speak to Mr. Abrams," Nathaniel replied, removing the cap from his head.

The woman's eyes roamed over him. "Are you looking for work?"

"I am."

She nodded her understanding. "If you will wait here, Mister…"

"Collier."

"I'll be back shortly," she said.

She disappeared into the back room. Nathaniel's eyes landed on large ostrich feathers, and he wondered what kind of woman would wear such an ostentatious thing. He would never understand women's fashion.

A man's voice came from the back door. "How may I help you, Mr. Collier?"

Nathaniel turned toward the dark-haired, burly man. "I am looking for work," he replied.

Mr. Abrams perused the length of him. "When I put an advertisement in the newssheets, I must admit that you were not the person I was hoping would respond."

"No?"

"I am looking for someone who can trim hats and help sell feathers and flowers," Mr. Abrams replied. "Can you trim a hat?"

"I cannot."

"Then I'm afraid this conversation is a waste of time," Mr. Abrams said.

Nathaniel fidgeted with the cap in his hand. "Please, sir, I really need the work," he begged.

Mr. Abrams considered him for a moment. "I could hire

you to unpack the crates in the back, but it is menial work, and I'm afraid it isn't much."

"I will take any work you are willing to give me."

"Then I shall see you in two days at sunrise."

"Yes, Mr. Abrams."

"I do hope you won't disappoint me," Mr. Abrams said.

"No, sir."

Two women stepped into the store and Mr. Abrams smiled and stepped towards them. "How may I help you ladies?" he asked.

Nathaniel knew he'd been dismissed, so he exited the store. He hadn't planned on being hired to work for Mr. Abrams, but it would allow him to have a look around the back room. Perhaps there would be some clues that would lead him to the Red Ravens.

He hailed a hackney, but to his surprise, a black coach came to a stop in front of him. The door opened, revealing a young woman with blonde hair, high cheekbones, and a pointed chin. She had a beauty so severe that at first it was startling.

As she exited the coach, she surprised him by saying, "I need to hire you."

He stared at the woman, not quite sure what she was about. "I beg your pardon?"

"You are a Bow Street Runner, are you not?" she demanded.

"Why would you think I am a Bow Street Runner?" he asked, taken back.

"Because Runners wear red waistcoats."

Nathaniel glanced down at his waistcoat. "But this waist-coat is burgundy."

She made a face. "It has more of a reddish hue to it."

"Regardless, I am not—"

"I am in desperate need of your services, and I will pay whatever I need to pay for you to take my case." She reached into the reticule around her wrist and held out a handful of coins.

Nathaniel quickly covered the proffered hand. "Put that money away," he ordered. "You don't want to attract attention to yourself."

She did his bidding, but her wide eyes remained fixated on him. "Please, sir, I need your help." Her voice was soft, a stark contrast to the commanding tone she'd previously used.

The plea in her voice was his undoing. Before he could second-guess himself, he said, "It isn't wise to be standing on the street. It would be preferable if we took a walk to discuss what is distressing you."

"Thank you," the woman sighed in relief.

Nathaniel watched as a maid exited the coach and stood behind her mistress. The woman who'd stopped him was dressed in a fine blue gown, indicating she was a woman of means. Her blonde hair was piled atop her head, though a few strands had escaped and curled around her forehead. Why was this woman so desperate to hire a Bow Street Runner?

They walked along the street, and he watched as the young woman clasped her hands in front of her, her whole person tense.

"You might want to start from the beginning," he suggested.

The young woman turned her blue eyes towards him. "My sister has disappeared," she informed him.

"How long has she been missing?"

"Three days," she said, "and I know what you are going to say."

"You do?" he asked, amused. "Pray tell, what am I going to say?"

Her chin tilted stubbornly. "That my sister ran off to Gretna Green with a suitor."

"Why would I say such a thing?"

"Because the constable believes that my sister eloped and

refuses to investigate her disappearance until she has been gone for a week."

"It has been my experience that constables are useless."

"I would agree," the young woman replied. "My sister went shopping for new flowers for her hat and never returned."

"I assume she went to Bond Street."

The young woman shook her head. "No, she prefers the plumassier just around the corner."

Nathaniel came to a stop on the pavement and turned to face her. "Which one?"

"J.B. Abrams," came her reply.

"Your sister went missing after visiting John Abrams' store?" he asked in disbelief. Surely that couldn't be a coincidence.

"She did."

He glanced over his shoulder at her maid. "Was she accompanied by a maid?" he asked.

She nodded. "Yes, but the maid lost sight of her after she exited the store."

"How is that possible?"

"I'm not sure, but the maid said that she just disappeared."

"And you have reason to believe someone abducted her?"

The young woman shrugged. "I do not believe my sister vanished of her own accord, if that is your question."

Nathaniel resumed walking down the pavement, his mind reeling. He wasn't one to believe in coincidences, and he couldn't shake the feeling that this missing girl might have something to do with his investigation.

"Will you take my case?" she asked as she kept pace with him.

"I have a few more questions for you," he replied.

"Which are?"

He glanced over at her. "How do we know with certainty that your sister didn't elope to Gretna Green?"

"Because she has showed favor to no man."

"That doesn't mean she didn't fancy someone."

"True, but if that had been the case, she would have told me," the young woman asserted. "We tell each other everything."

"Clearly not," Nathaniel replied.

"Why do you say that?"

"Women of your station do not just disappear in the middle of the day," he said. "Which leads me to believe she may have planned her disappearance."

"That is impossible," she asserted. "She never would have left me willingly."

"She might have had a good reason to do so."

The young woman reached up and tucked a piece of errant hair behind her ear. "My sister loves me—"

He spoke over her. "I am not disputing that. I am merely pointing out the possibility that your sister may not want to be found."

"But why?" she asked.

"I don't know," he said, "but I intend to find out."

"Does this mean you will help me?"

His boots ground on the loose stones as he turned to face her. "I believe it does."

"Thank you, sir!" she gushed, her face instantly transforming into a bright smile.

"You may want to hold off on your gratitude until I have found your sister," he suggested.

"Yes, quite right," she replied, but her smile remained intact.

He gestured back the way they'd come. "May I escort you back to your coach?" he asked.

"You may."

As they started walking down the pavement, he said, "I'm afraid I did not catch your name, miss."

"I am Dinah Ashmore."

"Ashmore?" he repeated in surprise. "Are you by chance related to the late Lord Gladstone?"

"He was my father," she replied.

Nathaniel clasped his hands behind his back. "I was saddened to hear about your parents' passing."

"Thank you, but it has been more than three years since they died."

"That doesn't mean having them gone gets any easier."

"No, it most assuredly does not," she agreed. "Now do you see why I can't lose my sister, as well?"

Nathaniel came to a stop next to her coach and waved off the footman. "I do," he said, "but I can't promise anything."

"I understand."

"I shall call upon you tomorrow to discuss the case."

"I appreciate that, sir."

"I would prefer if you would stop calling me 'sir'," he said.

"What would you have me call you, then?"

Nathaniel opened the door and held his hand out to assist her. "You can call me by my name," he encouraged. "Mr. Collier."

"Thank you, Mr. Collier," she murmured as she slipped her hand into his.

Once Miss Dinah was situated in the coach, he took a step back and said, "Until tomorrow."

Chapter Three

Nathaniel watched as Miss Dinah's coach merged into traffic before he started walking down the pavement. He thought her actions rather brazen but understood the reasons behind it. People tended to do desperate things when they were at their wit's end.

After walking a few blocks, he stopped in front of the two-level, brown brick boarding house where Rutledge was renting a room. He opened the door, stepped inside, and headed down the hall towards the rear of the building.

An older woman emerged from a room, a set of keys jingling around her waist. Her white hair was tied tightly at the base of her neck, accentuating the wrinkles on her face. "May I help you?" she asked, her critical eye sweeping over him.

"I'm here to see Rutledge."

"I'm afraid he is not here," the woman said in an exasperated tone. "In fact, he hasn't been here for nearly a week and missed paying his rent. I will have no choice but to evict him if he doesn't return soon."

Nathaniel removed a pound from his pocket and extended it towards her. "This should cover his rent."

The woman snatched it from his hand. "It will, but I won't be holding his room forever. People want to live in a respectable boarding house, and I expect my tenants to behave accordingly."

"I shall pass along your wishes once I see him."

"I would appreciate that." The woman gave him an expectant look. "Will there be anything else?"

"Would it be permissible for me to see his room?"

The woman shook her head. "I'm afraid not," she replied. "I value my tenants' privacy most ardently."

"I see," Nathaniel said, removing another pound from his pocket. "Even if it was just for a moment?"

The woman glanced over her shoulder before she put her hand out for the money. "I will make an exception in this case, but only because you appear to be an honorable man."

"Thank you."

The woman started down the hall and asked over her shoulder, "Is Rutledge in some kind of trouble?"

"Why do you ask?"

"You are not the first person to come looking for him."

"I'm not?"

"I sent the other man away, and I have yet to hear from him again," the woman shared as she stopped in front of a door.

"Can you describe this man?"

The woman reached for a key on the ring. "He was a burly man and had a long scar on his chin," she revealed as she unlocked the door. "You have five minutes."

Nathaniel opened the door and saw that the room was in complete and utter shambles. The mattress was slit open, clothes and papers were strewn all over the floor, and the desk drawers were ajar. Someone had already been here.

The woman gasped behind him. "Dear heavens, who would have done such a thing?"

"That is what I intend to find out," Nathaniel said as he

started picking up papers off the floor.

He glanced at the papers as he gathered them, but saw nothing that would indicate what Rutledge was involved in. He put the papers down on the table and started looking around. Rutledge wasn't a fool; he wouldn't have left anything of value out in the open.

Nathaniel scanned the room, his eyes stopping when they landed on the fireplace. Had it served a dual purpose? He approached it and ran his hand along the stones, looking for any loose ones, but he wasn't so fortunate.

Nathaniel crouched down and reached up the fireplace. His hand ran along the bricks until he felt something tucked into a crevice. He pulled it out, but it was only an advertisement for a rally in Winstead Square in four days. Why would Rutledge hide that?

He turned it over and saw "Evie Ashmore" scribbled on the back. He folded the paper and tucked it into his jacket pocket. As he rose, he heard the woman say, "Your time is up."

"Yes, ma'am."

Nathaniel exited the room and headed down the hall. He didn't quite know what to think about what he'd discovered, but it meant he had some questions for Miss Dinah when he met with her tomorrow.

After he left the boarding house, he hailed a hackney and drove towards his townhouse. He needed to get cleaned up before he headed to White's. The hackney came to a stop outside of his townhouse and he opened the door. He paid the driver and approached the main door.

"Welcome home, my lord," Balfour greeted him, opening the door wide.

Nathaniel stepped into the entry hall. "I require a bath."

Balfour tipped his head. "I shall inform your valet, and I will see to the water being heated up."

After the butler departed from the entry hall to do his

bidding, his brother, Hugh, stepped inside.

Nathaniel lifted his brow. "You look terrible," he said, "and you don't smell much better."

"I could say the same thing about you," Hugh stated, tugging down on his wrinkled blue jacket. "Where did you get that tattered suit?"

"From my closet."

"You should toss it," Hugh suggested.

"It serves a purpose."

"What for?" Hugh asked. "To look like a pauper?"

Ignoring his brother's question, Nathaniel asked one of his own. "Are you just getting home?"

Hugh smirked. "I had a good run at the tables."

"How much did you lose?" Nathaniel asked.

"Hardly any, but I won a small fortune against Lord Walton."

Nathaniel crossed his arms over his chest. "Why would you do such a thing?" he asked. "Lady Walton is a friend of Mother's."

"Not anymore," Hugh said, shrugging. "Lord Walton made a ridiculous bet, and he deserved to lose his thousand pounds."

"I daresay you took advantage of the situation."

"So what if I did?" Hugh asked defiantly. "It is not my job to cosset rich lords. Besides, if I don't take their money, someone else most assuredly will."

"You already have sufficient funds."

"But now I have more," Hugh replied.

Nathaniel gave him a disapproving look. "You should spend your time on more worthwhile pursuits."

"Like you do?" Hugh scoffed.

"What do you mean by that?" Nathaniel asked.

Hugh gave him a pointed look. "You disappear constantly, dress in old, tattered clothing, and no one is quite sure where you go."

"A man is entitled to his secrets."

"I won't disagree with you there," Hugh said. "I see no reason to start asking questions, assuming you stay out of my business."

Nathaniel uncrossed his arms. "You should know that Mother and Father are worried about you."

"They always are, but they will see I am a roaring success soon enough. I have acquired enough funds to buy a grand estate."

"Success is not always determined by the amount of money we have."

"It is by Father."

"That doesn't mean he is right."

Hugh walked over to the stairs and put his hand on the iron banister. "Is this conversation over? Because I would like to take a bath before we leave for White's." He started walking up the stairs, not waiting for a response.

As Nathaniel followed Hugh up the stairs, he asked, "Do you ever tire of going to the gambling hells?"

"I do not," Hugh replied. "It gives me a reprieve, even if just for a moment."

"Is your life so unbearable?"

A pained look crossed Hugh's face. "Life has not always been kind to me. I was cursed to be the second son, the spare."

"Is that so bad?"

"It is when Father constantly compares me to you," Hugh responded. "We are very different, yet Father wants us to be exactly the same."

"That is unfair of him."

"I agree, but Father doesn't seem to care about being fair. He only cares about being right," Hugh said curtly.

"Father can be rather difficult at times, but he means well."

Hugh huffed. "I don't believe that. I have been a grand

disappointment to him since the moment I was born."

"That isn't true," Nathaniel asserted as he stepped onto the top step. "Father loves you."

"No, Mother loves me," Hugh corrected. "Father tolerates me."

While they walked down the hall, Nathaniel remarked, "I had no idea that you felt this way."

"Why would you?" Hugh asked. "You are always gone when I return home."

"Would you like me to speak to Father about this?"

"It will do no good," Hugh insisted. "Father is set in his ways, just as I am."

Nathaniel stopped outside his bedchamber. "That doesn't mean I can't try."

"Suit yourself."

A line of footmen arrived with buckets of water, and Nathaniel opened the door. "It would appear that my bath has arrived."

"Enjoy," Hugh said as he continued walking down the hall.

Dinah sat on a settee in her bedchamber attempting to read, but her mind kept wandering towards the Bow Street Runner she'd hired only a few hours ago.

He wasn't at all what she had expected a Bow Street Runner to be. Mr. Collier was a very handsome man. He was tall and broad-shouldered with a square jaw, and blonde hair had peeked out from under the cap he wore. He may have been dressed in a worn brown suit, but he had an air of authority about him, a commanding presence that demanded respect.

There was something about him that gave her pause, but

she wasn't quite sure what that was. His eyes were wary, yet from the moment she met his gaze, they drew her in, enticing her to trust him.

A knock came at the door, breaking her out of her reverie.

"Come in," she ordered.

The door opened and Aunt Nancy stepped into the room. "I see that you are dressed for dinner," she said.

"I am."

"I just heard the most distressing news," Aunt Nancy declared as she came closer.

"You did?"

"I did," her aunt replied. "It was about a young woman who lied to her aunt about going shopping but instead met up with an unknown man."

Dinah hurriedly put her book down and turned to face her aunt. "I can explain," she rushed out.

"You can?" her aunt asked. "Because I am quite anxious to hear why you lied to me."

"I told the driver to drive to Bow Street rather than Bond Street."

"For what purpose?"

"To hire a Bow Street Runner, of course," Dinah said.

Her aunt sighed. "Is that who you met up with on the street?"

"It was," Dinah confessed. "I saw a man wearing a red waistcoat, so I had the driver pull over so I could speak to him."

"That was a foolish thing to do," her aunt said. "You can't approach strange men and speak to them. It is simply not done."

"I am well aware, but he was a Bow Street Runner," Dinah argued.

"That doesn't make it right, Dinah."

Dinah let out a sigh. "I had to do something, for Evie's sake."

Her aunt's face softened. "I know you are worried about Evie—we both are—but you can't put your life in peril."

"I was hardly in danger," Dinah said. "We spoke for only a few moments, and he agreed to take the case."

"He did?"

"Yes, and he will be calling here tomorrow to speak further about it."

Her aunt sat next to her on the settee. "I know you want to help Evie, but you must think of your own reputation. What if someone saw you conversing with that man?"

"No one did."

"Then how do I know about it?" her aunt asked.

Dinah winced.

"We are not in the country anymore," her aunt pressed. "The rules are much more stringent here in London."

"I am well aware."

"Let's hope your antics went unnoticed."

Dinah fingered the edges of her book. "I know I acted rashly, but I am scared that Evie won't return."

"I know, dear, but you must be strong," her aunt encouraged. "With any luck, this Bow Street Runner will discover Evie's whereabouts and bring her home."

"I hope so."

Her aunt smiled at her tenderly. "You must not give up hope."

"I won't."

"We both know that Evie would not want you to worry incessantly about her."

"No, she most assuredly would not."

Her aunt gave her a knowing look. "But that isn't going to stop you, is it?"

"No," Dinah replied. "I just want Evie to come home."

Her aunt glanced over at the window. "I was not blessed to have my own children, but you and Evie fill that void in my life. I don't know what I would do if I lost either one of you."

"You won't."

"After my Andrew died and I came to live with you, I watched you grow up to become a fine young woman," her aunt continued, "but sometimes your emotions can cloud your judgment."

"I am not reckless like Evie—"

Her aunt let out a slight huff, stilling her words. "That is an understatement," she said. "Do you recall when Evie wanted to join your father's hunting party, and you encouraged her to attend?"

"I do."

"She dressed up as a man and nearly caused Lord Fenton to have a fit when he saw her."

"Lord Fenton is a stuffy, old man."

"That may be true, but your father invited him to the house party," her aunt said. "It was your father's intention for you and Lord Fenton's son to wed."

"I could never have married George. We have been friends since we were young, and I view him more as a brother than anything."

"You said as much to your father, but he was still hopeful that a union would take place."

Dinah grew silent for a moment. "Had I known that house party would have been one of the last times I would see my parents, I would have acted much differently."

With an amused look, her aunt said, "No, you wouldn't have. You would have never agreed to marry George."

"You are right, but I do miss them, desperately."

"I know, dear," her aunt said. "I miss them too, but we must carry on, for their sakes."

Dinah shook her head. "I don't think I can, not without Evie."

"But we must," her aunt asserted. "We must give the appearance that all is well, or else the *ton* might discover that Evie is missing."

"That would be awful."

"I agree," her aunt said. "Evie is already in her ninth Season and has yet to agree to an offer of courtship."

"Which has displeased Cousin Robert greatly."

"That is because Robert is your father's heir and responsible for you."

Dinah frowned. "Robert only considers us to be a burden."

"He is letting us remain at the townhouse when we are in Town, and he stays at his other home."

"That is because he wants to reside with his mistress."

"Perhaps, but it could be much worse for us, considering you are only twenty," her aunt said. "Robert is only your guardian until you are twenty-one."

"I am well aware," Dinah muttered, "but my birthday is only a few months away. Then I shall receive my inheritance and can do as I please."

"You must be cautious, being an heiress."

"That is precisely why I carry a muff pistol in my reticule."

Her aunt gave her a disapproving look. "I do not think that is necessary."

"You need not fret," Dinah said. "Evie taught me how to care for a pistol properly, and I am quite a good shot."

"I have no doubt, but I hope there never comes a time when you need to use it."

"I feel the same way, but one never knows when they need to be prepared."

The dinner bell rang, beckoning them to come.

"It is time for dinner," Aunt Nancy said, rising.

"I'm not hungry."

"Neither am I, but you need to eat," her aunt encouraged.

Dinah reluctantly rose. "I suppose I could eat enough to avoid starvation."

"That would be sufficient."

Chapter Four

Dressed fashionably in a blue jacket, buff trousers, and Hessian boots, Nathaniel descended the stairs of his townhouse. His mother was pacing the floor in the entry hall, looking distressed.

"Whatever is the matter?" Nathaniel asked.

His mother stopped pacing. "It's your brother," she said. "Lady Walton came to see me and informed me that her husband lost a thousand pounds to Hugh."

"Hugh did mention that to me."

"What is to be done about it?"

Nathaniel shrugged. "I am not sure there is anything that can be done."

"He must return that money," his mother urged.

Hugh's voice came from the top of the stairs. "Why would I do something so foolish?" he asked as he started down the stairs. "If I returned the money, Lord Walton would only go on to lose it again."

"Lady Walton is one of my dearest friends, and I cannot condone you stealing from them."

"It isn't stealing, Mother," Hugh said, coming to stand in front of her. "It is gambling. There is a huge difference."

"Not to me," his mother replied. "One day, you will regret having ever gambled."

"That day won't be today," Hugh responded as he leaned in to kiss his mother on the cheek. "You should be happy that I am so successful."

"Gambling is a terrible vice to have," his mother insisted.

Hugh walked over to the door. "Only if you lose."

Their mother shook her head. "You are impossible, son."

Hugh went outside, and Nathaniel turned towards his mother. "I will speak to Hugh."

"Do try to talk some sense into him."

"I will try."

His mother let out a frustrated sigh. "Lady Walton confided in me that they may have to retire to the countryside early due to the loss of funds."

"Lord Walton should never have gambled away what he wasn't able to lose."

"That is easier said than done."

Nathaniel leaned in and kissed his mother's cheek as well. "I will see what I can do," he said before he headed out the door.

He stepped into the awaiting carriage and sat across from his brother. He had just opened his mouth when Hugh spoke first. "You should save your breath, brother."

"Why is that?"

"I know Mother wants you to talk some sense into me."

"And why do you suppose that is?"

"Because she does not condone my gambling."

"None of us do," Nathaniel said. "There are more honorable ways to earn a living."

Hugh huffed. "Not every one of us can be the golden child, the firstborn, the chosen one—"

Nathaniel spoke over him. "I get your point, but that isn't what this is about."

"No?" Hugh asked. "Then what is this about?"

"You are the son of a marquess, and there are certain expectations that come with that role," Nathaniel said.

"Now you are sounding like Father."

"At least one of us is starting to."

Hugh looked uninterested. "What is it that you want from me?"

"Take the money that you have acquired, buy an estate, and manage it," Nathaniel replied. "It is the respectable thing to do."

"It is boring."

"You could always go back to being a barrister."

A pained looked came into Hugh's eyes before he blinked it away. "I think not. Those days are long past."

Nathaniel shrugged. "Perhaps it is time that you take a wife, then."

"What of you?" Hugh asked. "Where is your wife?"

"I am not sure I want a wife."

"Whyever not?"

Nathaniel tugged down on his green waistcoat. "If anything were to ever happen to me, you would be Father's heir."

"I don't want to be a blasted marquess. It comes with too much responsibility," Hugh said. "Besides, nothing will ever happen to you."

"And you would know this how?"

"You don't take risks."

"Why do you say that?"

"You don't ride your horse at breakneck speeds, nor do you ever get into fights," Hugh commented. "Your life is entirely too predictable."

A smile tugged at the corner of Nathaniel's mouth. "I suppose you are right." He found it humorous that his brother thought his life to be so ordinary.

The coach stopped in front of White's, effectively ending

their conversation. Nathaniel waited for his brother to exit before he stepped out onto the street.

They proceeded inside, and his eyes roamed the crowded hall. In the corner, he saw Berkeley and Grenton already seated, drinks in their hands.

"I see them," Nathaniel said loudly so he could be heard over the noise in the hall.

Nathaniel led his brother towards the table and sat down. Once they were all situated, Grenton held his glass up and declared, "Raise a glass to Berkeley's freedom. I'm sad to say that it is something that he will never see again."

"You are a jackanapes," Berkeley stated. "I have no intention of marrying the chit."

"But your father arranged for this marriage," Grenton said. "You would defy your father?"

Berkeley nodded. "I would."

Grenton shook his head. "You have never defied your father on anything. Why start now?"

"Because I refuse to be shackled to a young woman as vexing as Lady Beatrice," Berkeley said firmly.

Hugh spoke up. "I do believe you protest too much," he joked.

Berkeley shook his head. "You have no idea how infuriating Lady Beatrice can be. She used to follow me around our country estate when we were little."

"Have you seen her since then?" Hugh asked.

"I have not, but it surely doesn't matter," Berkeley said. "She couldn't have changed that much over the years."

Nathaniel saw Lord Haddington step into White's wearing a bright purple jacket and tight buff trousers. He raised his hand in greeting when their eyes met.

"I see that Haddington has arrived," Hugh observed, following his gaze. "I have never understood why he dresses like such a dandy."

"There is nothing wrong with how he dresses," Nathaniel said.

Hugh chuckled. "Perhaps you need spectacles."

Haddington pulled out a chair and sat down. "Good evening," he greeted. "What did I interrupt?"

"We were just discussing Berkeley's upcoming nuptials," Grenton informed him.

"There will be no such thing," Berkeley muttered as he brought his drink to his lips.

"Leave him be," Nathaniel encouraged. "None of us wish for the parson's mousetrap."

Berkeley clunked his empty glass onto the table. "Thank you, Hawthorne."

Haddington pushed back his chair and announced, "Next round is on me, gentlemen." He turned towards him. "Will you assist me, Hawthorne?"

"I will," Nathaniel responded, rising.

As they walked towards the bar where the drinks were being served, Haddington said quietly, "Merritt told me about Rutledge."

"It is a most unfortunate situation."

"That it is," Haddington agreed. "Do you have any leads?"

"Just one. What do you know of the rally in Winstead square?"

Haddington stopped in front of the bar and replied, "It is supposed to be a peaceful one, with John Tilbury as orator."

"John Tilbury?" Nathaniel repeated. "I have heard he is quite well spoken."

"He is," Haddington said. "The people are in misery due to the high taxes, lack of jobs, and skyrocketing food prices. They want their voices to be heard."

"I'm afraid their cries will fall on deaf ears."

"We are both aware of that, but the people are discontent," Haddington responded as he caught the eye of the man serving the drinks. "This rally could easily turn to a riot if not handled properly."

"Have the Bow Street Runners been made aware of the rally?"

"I don't know," Haddington said. "I only heard about the rally from a drunk at a tavern in the rookeries. How did you hear about it?"

"Rutledge had an advertisement for it in his room."

A man approached them from behind the bar and asked, "What can I get for you, gentlemen?"

"We need five glasses of your finest port," Haddington ordered.

"Yes, sir."

As the man filled the glasses, Nathaniel asked, "What do you know of Miss Ashmore, the eldest daughter of the late Lord Gladstone?"

"She is a dear friend of our family." Haddington eyed him curiously. "Why do you ask?"

"Her name was written on the back of the handbill announcing the rally in Rutledge's room."

"I wonder why."

"Furthermore, she went missing after she visited a shop that has ties to the Red Ravens."

Haddington lifted his brow. "That can't be a coincidence."

"I agree," Nathaniel said.

"How did you discover she was missing?"

"Her sister mistook me for a Bow Street Runner on the street and offered to hire me to find her."

Haddington chuckled. "I would like to have witnessed that."

"I intend to speak to Miss Dinah tomorrow and get some clarity on the case."

The man behind the bar interjected, "Here are your drinks."

Haddington reached into his jacket pocket and pulled out some coins, then slid them towards the man. "Thank you."

They started back towards their table.

"Do you suppose Rutledge went undercover?" Haddington asked.

"It wouldn't be the first time that he just disappeared for a case that he was working on," Nathaniel replied.

"No, it wouldn't."

"I am not discounting anything yet," Nathaniel said.

Haddington nodded approvingly. "If you need anything, all you have to do is ask."

"That is assuming I can find you," Nathaniel teased.

"Just look for the brightly colored jackets," Haddington joked.

They arrived back at the table and passed out the drinks. As they sat down, Berkeley asked, "Why didn't you just wait for a server to pass by the table to order drinks?"

Haddington smiled. "I wanted everyone to see my new jacket as I crossed the room."

"No one can miss it," Grenton joked. "It is so bright that it practically glows."

"Then my tailor succeeded," Haddington said.

Nathaniel leaned back in his seat and smiled at his friends' banter. They had met in Eton and remained close over the years. He disliked keeping part of his life secret from all but Haddington, but it was much safer that way.

Dinah stared out the window of her townhouse as she anxiously waited for Mr. Collier to arrive. She slept fitfully, worried about the fate of her sister, and she hoped that the Bow Street Runner could help.

"What if he doesn't come?" she asked.

"Do not fret, dear. Didn't he say he would?"

Dinah nodded. "He did, but I never told him where I live."

Her aunt pulled the needle through her embroidery. "He is an investigator. I have no doubt he could ascertain where you live."

"Perhaps," Dinah muttered, unconvinced.

"Why don't you come and have some tea?" Aunt Nancy suggested. "It might soothe your nerves."

Dinah walked over to the settee and sat down, then poured herself a cup and took a long sip.

"Did it work?" her aunt asked.

Dinah lowered the cup to her lap. "It did not," she replied.

"It might be best if you took another sip," her aunt said, clearly amused.

"I don't think it will help."

Their conversation was interrupted when Barnes stepped into the room and announced, "Mr. Nathaniel Collier has arrived and has requested a moment of your time."

"Please send him in," Dinah requested, setting her teacup on the tray.

"Yes, miss," Barnes said before disappearing.

Dinah took a moment to smooth out her white dress.

"There is no reason to be nervous," her aunt advised.

"I know, but there is so much at stake."

Before Aunt Nancy could reply, Mr. Collier stepped into the room dressed in a grey jacket, white cravat, and dark trousers. His intense eyes met Dinah's and he bowed. "Miss Dinah," he greeted.

"Mr. Collier," she replied. "It is a pleasure to see you again."

"I wish it was under different circumstances," Mr. Collier said.

"I agree." Dinah gestured towards Aunt Nancy. "Allow me to introduce you to my aunt, Mrs. Carter."

Mr. Collier turned his attention towards her. "Good morning, Mrs. Carter. Thank you for receiving me."

"It is our pleasure." Her aunt leaned forward and set her needlework on the table. "Please have a seat, Mr. Collier."

"Thank you." Mr. Collier walked over to an upholstered armchair and sat down, his back stiff. "I was hoping to ask you a few questions about your sister," he said to Dinah.

"I imagined that would be the case," Dinah said.

"Miss Ashmore is your older sister, correct?"

"She is."

"Has she ever disappeared before?"

Aunt Nancy spoke up. "Never," she declared. "This is so unlike her."

Dinah bit her lower lip. "That isn't entirely true."

"It's not?" her aunt asked, turning to face her.

"Evie would, on occasion, sneak out to attend a lecture at Oxford," Dinah revealed.

Mr. Collier lifted his brow. "Women are not allowed to attend the lectures. How did she gain entrance?"

Dinah winced as she admitted, "She would dress as a man."

Her aunt gasped. "Please say that isn't true."

"I'm afraid I am unable to do so," Dinah responded. "She swore me to secrecy, but she always returned before dinner."

"How often did she attend lectures?" Mr. Collier asked.

"At least once a week," Dinah admitted.

Mr. Collier appeared to consider her words before asking, "Do you know how she traveled to Oxford?"

"She would take a hackney."

"Did she often dress up like a man?" Mr. Collier pressed.

"Only to attend the lectures."

"Do you know what the lectures were on?"

"Evie said they were about physics," Dinah shared.

"Dare I ask how many people knew of Evie's escapades?" Aunt Nancy interjected.

"Very few," Dinah replied. "She didn't want to get anyone in trouble if she was ever caught."

"Why didn't Evie just tell me the truth?" her aunt asked.

Dinah glanced over at Mr. Collier before saying, "Because Evie knew you would never condone her actions."

"She was right about that," her aunt said. "No respectable young woman should ever dress like a man and attend a lecture at Oxford. It is just a recipe for disaster."

Dinah turned to face Mr. Collier. "I know you must have a poor opinion of my sister…"

He put his hand up, stilling her words. "Quite the contrary," he said. "I applaud her ingenuity."

"You do?" Dinah asked.

"I do," Mr. Collier replied. "Miss Ashmore's ability to go undetected for so long is admirable, but I do worry that it put her at great risk."

"She is always very careful," Dinah said.

"I'm not sure that is true," Mr. Collier responded. "Do you know if your sister was involved in politics?"

"Heavens, no," Dinah stated. "Evie may have snuck out to attend lectures, but she never showed any favor towards politics."

"Did she attend any rallies that you know of?"

"She did not."

Mr. Collier didn't look convinced. "Do you not believe it was entirely possible that she attended a rally under the guise of going to a lecture?"

"She would have told me if she was going to do something so foolhardy," Dinah said.

"Would you have attempted to talk her out of it?" Mr. Collier asked.

"I would have."

"Perhaps that is why she didn't tell you," Mr. Collier remarked.

Dinah pressed her lips together. "My sister and I didn't keep secrets from one another."

"Sometimes people keep secrets to protect the ones that they love," Mr. Collier said.

"But that is not what is happening here," Dinah pressed. "Evie disappeared in broad daylight, in the middle of the street."

Mr. Collier shifted his gaze towards her aunt. "Does Miss Ashmore have access to funds?"

"She does," her aunt replied. "She received her inheritance when she turned twenty-one."

"I assume it is a substantial amount," Mr. Collier said.

"It is," her aunt confirmed.

Mr. Collier grew serious. "This does complicate matters some."

"How so?" Dinah asked.

"If she wanted to disappear, she has the funds to do so."

Dinah let out a frustrated sigh. "My sister did not want to disappear, and I wish you would stop speaking so."

Mr. Collier abruptly rose. "I believe I have enough to go on. I do not wish to keep you any further."

Rising, Dinah asked, "How will we contact you?"

"You won't."

"But will you at least keep us informed of your progress?"

"There is no need," Mr. Collier said. "I will find your sister and return her to you."

"How can you be so certain?"

Mr. Collier's expression grew smug. "I can assure you that I am very good at my job."

"That may be true, but I would prefer it if you kept us informed."

"I'm sorry," Mr. Collier said. "My time is very valuable, and I don't have any time to waste."

Her aunt interrupted, "I do hope you will be discreet when making inquiries."

"I shall be," Mr. Collier replied. "I understand what is at stake."

Dinah placed a hand on her hip, not ready to concede. "I must insist that you keep us apprised on your investigation."

"My answer is still no," Mr. Collier said firmly, "but you need not worry."

"How can you say such a thing?" Dinah asked.

"You must trust me on this."

"Trust is to be earned, Mr. Collier."

"Well said, Miss Dinah," he replied, "but, if you recall, you were the one that sought me out to help you. You must allow me to do so."

"I do not like to sit idly by," Dinah informed him.

"With any luck, you won't have to wait for too long," Mr. Collier said. "If you will excuse me, I should depart."

After Mr. Collier left the drawing room, Dinah went over to the window and watched as he walked down the street. Could she just stand back and let Mr. Collier investigate her sister's disappearance? That is what she was paying him to do, and it was evident that he was very confident in his abilities.

Aunt Nancy's voice came from behind her. "I know that look."

"What look?"

"You are plotting something," her aunt said, "aren't you?"

Dinah turned to face her aunt. "I am just concerned about Evie. How do we know we can trust Mr. Collier?"

"He seems competent enough."

"That he does, but what if he fails to find Evie?"

"I have more confidence in Mr. Collier than I do in the constable."

Dinah let out a slight huff. "I agree," she replied. "The constable is worthless."

Her aunt rested a hand on her sleeve. "Let Mr. Collier do his job, and with any luck, Evie will be home shortly."

"I hope so."

"Why don't you go on a ride?" her aunt suggested. "It might help clear your head."

Dinah bobbed her head. "I believe I shall."

"Just be mindful to take along two grooms," her aunt said, dropping her hand.

As Dinah departed, she couldn't help but attempt to formulate a new plan. She refused to sit back and do nothing, knowing her sister was out there somewhere.

Chapter Five

Nathaniel wondered how Miss Ashmore tied into all of this as he traveled across town. He had more questions than answers at this point.

The hackney came to a stop and Nathaniel opened the door, then stepped out and paid the driver. Once the hackney merged back into the traffic, Nathaniel started walking down the street.

As he approached his headquarters, he saw Talbot and Worsley hawking bread from behind a cart.

Nathaniel stopped in front of them. "What in the blazes are you two doing?"

"We're selling bread," Worsley said, putting the loaf he was holding down.

"I can see that, but why?" Nathaniel pressed.

"The constable came by yesterday and threatened to send us to a workhouse if we kept loitering outside the building," Talbot explained. "We decided that we needed to sell bread, after a failed attempt at selling socks."

"Socks?" Nathaniel shook his head. "May I ask why you decided on bread?"

"Because we can eat it if we get hungry." Worsley tore off a chunk and took a bite. "It is quite ingenious on our part."

"And Merritt agreed to this?"

"Who do you think bought the cart?" Talbot asked.

"Have you sold anything?"

Worsley picked up another loaf of bread and hit it against the side of the cart. "Unfortunately, most of the bread is inedible, but the constable doesn't need to know that."

"I wish you luck," Nathaniel said as he walked over to the door.

"We don't need luck," Talbot called out to him.

Nathaniel stepped into the building and saw Mostyn sitting behind the desk. He approached the older agent and asked, "How is your wife feeling?"

"She is feeling much better," Mostyn replied, rising. "Thank you for asking."

"Is Merritt here?"

Mostyn nodded. "He is, but I should warn you that he is in a foul mood."

"Why is that?"

"The usual reasons, I suppose."

"I shall have to take my chances," Nathaniel said, walking towards the back door. He opened the door, stepped into the hall, and walked towards Merritt's office.

He stopped outside of the closed door and knocked, receiving a gruff "Enter" in reply.

Nathaniel opened the door and greeted the spymaster. "Good afternoon," he said, closing the door behind him.

"What is good about it, Hawthorne?" Merritt asked curtly.

"We both are alive, are we not?"

Merritt huffed. "I daresay you have a low standard."

Nathaniel went and sat down in front of the desk. "Why are you in such a surly mood?"

Merritt waved a hand over the desk. "We don't have

enough agents to deal with all of the threats that are coming our way."

"Then hire more agents."

"It isn't that simple," Merritt said. "Besides, we don't have the budget to do so."

Leaning back in his chair, Nathaniel asked, "Is there anything I can assist with?"

"You can solve your case and find Rutledge."

"I intend to."

Merritt picked up a stack of files and moved them to the side of his desk. "Have you made any progress?"

"I went to Rutledge's room, but someone got there first. The place was ransacked."

Merritt bobbed his head. "Continue."

"I was able to find an advertisement for a rally in Winstead Square that was stuck up the fireplace." Nathaniel removed the paper from his jacket and extended it towards Merritt. "It's in two days."

"These blasted events are popping up all over England," Merritt grumbled as he accepted the paper.

"I did speak to Haddington last night, and he informed me that the orator will be John Tilbury," Nathaniel said. "He is known for his peaceful demonstrations."

"I will assign a few agents to attend the rally and hope it is not a rowdy group."

"I haven't found a connection between the Red Ravens and the rally, though."

"Perhaps there isn't one."

Nathaniel took the paper and turned it over in Merritt's hands. "There was also a name written on the back of the paper," he revealed. "Evie Ashmore."

"Ashmore?" Merritt asked. "Any relation to Lord Gladstone?"

"His eldest daughter."

"Lord Gladstone was a fine man," Merritt said. "He served in the House of Lords quite admirably."

"I have spoken to Miss Ashmore's sister, but I am still trying to determine what role she plays in all of this."

"It sounds like you have a lot of work ahead of you," Merritt said, giving the handbill back.

"That I do," Nathaniel agreed as he pocketed it. "I was hired to unpack crates at J.B. Abrams' shop."

Merritt gave him an amused look. "I do hope you won't mess that up."

"I won't. It'll give me a chance to look around his shop."

"That it will," Merritt said. "Do not disappoint me on this assignment."

"I have no intention to."

"Good," Merritt responded. "I do not have time for incompetence of any kind."

"I understand."

"Now, be off with you," Merritt ordered with a wave of his hand. "I have to get back to work."

"Make sure you buy some bread from those fools out front," Merritt said as Nathaniel reached for the door.

"I understand you purchased them a cart."

"I did," Merritt said. "They couldn't very well protect the building if they were taken to a workhouse."

"They seem happy."

"They are blasted idiots," Merritt declared, "but at least they are competent at their jobs."

"That is a good thing."

"Worsley is asking to go into the field," Merritt revealed, "but I haven't decided if he is ready yet."

"What are your reservations?"

Merritt grimaced. "I suppose I am a little more cautious since we lost Whitney. He went into the field too soon and lost his life because of it."

"You must not blame yourself for that."

"It was my decision, and he was my responsibility."

Nathaniel shook his head. "Whitney was a hothead, and he went into his assignment with pistols blazing."

"I should have anticipated that."

"You are being much too hard on yourself," Nathaniel said. "No one blames you for Whitney's death."

Merritt looked crestfallen. "I blame myself."

Nathaniel opened his mouth to argue, but Merritt spoke first. "That will be all, agent."

"Yes, sir," Nathaniel replied.

As he exited the building, Worsley held up a loaf of bread towards him. "Are you hungry, sir?"

"How much for the bread?" he asked as he approached them.

"Ten shillings?"

Nathaniel lifted his brow. "Ten shillings?" he asked. "Are you mad?"

Worsley shrugged. "I suppose it is a matter of how hungry you are."

"I'm not that hungry."

Talbot leaned into Worsley and exchanged a few words. After a moment, Worsley nodded and said, "We could let this bread go for eight shillings."

Nathaniel chuckled. "You two are halfwits."

"How dare you, sir!" Talbot shouted with a swipe of his hand. "No bread for you. Be off with you!"

"My pleasure," Nathaniel said as he walked away. Despite being amused by their antics, he had too much work to do to dillydally.

———

Dinah adjusted the puffy sleeves of her gown. She couldn't believe that her aunt had convinced her to attend Lady

Bannerman's soirée. How could she pretend that all is well when her sister was missing? They should be out there searching for her, not socializing with members of the *ton*.

Her aunt's voice broke through the silence. "We are almost there," she said as she sat across from her.

"Wonderful," Dinah muttered.

"It is imperative that we act as if nothing is wrong," Aunt Nancy advised.

"But something is terribly wrong," Dinah asserted. "Evie is missing."

Her aunt gave her a pointed look. "If word ever got out about Evie's disappearance, she would be ruined, and that could affect you."

"There are worse things than being ruined."

"Not for a young woman of your station."

Dinah clasped her hands in her lap. "I wish we could just have stayed home."

"We already sent word to Lady Bannerman that we would be attending," her aunt explained. "It would be rude not to."

"I am not in a jovial mood."

"I know you think me callous, but I am trying to protect you and Evie from harsh gossip," her aunt said. "It can be devastating to be on the receiving end."

The way her aunt spoke gave Dinah pause. "It sounds as if you are speaking from experience."

"Sadly, I am," her aunt admitted. "I was much too opinionated for members of Society, and I quickly became an outcast."

"That is most unfortunate."

"It was, but your uncle always appreciated that I spoke my mind. He cared little for what the gossips said about me."

"The gossips can be cruel and unyielding."

"That they can, which is why you must behave in such a way as to not give them anything to gossip about."

The coach came to a stop in front of a large townhouse,

and they exited the coach with the assistance of the footman. They followed the crowd of people into the entry hall, where Dinah saw Lord Haddington leaning against a column. He was dressed in an emerald-green jacket, yellow waistcoat, and buff trousers.

Lord Haddington straightened as she approached. "I am so relieved to see you," he said.

"Why is that, Reginald?" she asked as she stopped in front of him.

"My mother convinced me to come, but she has abandoned me to speak to her friends." Reginald turned his attention towards Aunt Nancy and tipped his head. "It is always a pleasure to see you as well, Mrs. Carter."

Her aunt gave him a chiding look. "I believe I have asked you to call me Nancy on multiple occasions."

"My apologies," Reginald said as he glanced between them. "Where is Evie this evening?"

"I'm afraid she wasn't feeling well," her aunt said.

"I hope it isn't anything too serious," Reginald responded.

Aunt Nancy shook her head. "Nothing that a good night of sleep can't cure."

"That's good," Reginald said. "You will have to send her my regards."

"I will," her aunt responded.

The sound of a gentleman's deep laughter reached Dinah's ears, and she turned her head to see Lord Barnwell. He was standing next to Lady Charlotte and her mother, Lady Bangor.

"Is everything all right?" Reginald asked, following her gaze.

"It is," she replied. "I am not quite sure why Lord Barnwell is speaking to Lady Charlotte. She is horrible."

"I heard he is looking for a wife," Reginald shared.

"Dear heavens, you cannot be in earnest," Dinah said.

"Lord Barnwell is my father's age, and he would be miserable with young Lady Charlotte as his wife."

"Some men might consider him fortunate."

"Are you one of those men?" Dinah asked, raising an eyebrow.

"I am not," Reginald responded. "Besides, I have enough sense not to argue with you."

"I knew you were a smart man."

Reginald chuckled. "Would you care to take a turn around the room with me?"

Dinah glanced over at her aunt for approval, who promptly nodded. "I would be honored to," she replied as she accepted his arm.

They walked away from Aunt Nancy, and Reginald leaned close and asked, "Do you want to tell me the real reason why Evie isn't here?"

"Why do you assume something is afoot?"

"We both know that your aunt wouldn't have let Evie miss Lady Bannerman's soirée for any reason," Reginald said.

Dinah glanced over her shoulder and lowered her voice. "What I am about to reveal must stay in the strictest confidence."

"I understand."

She took in a deep breath before revealing, "Evie is missing. She went out shopping and has yet to return."

"How long has she been missing?"

"Four days."

Reginald's jaw tensed. "Have you contacted the constable?"

"We have, but he is of the mind that Evie eloped to Gretna Green," Dinah said. "I did manage to hire a Bow Street Runner, but I do not have much confidence in him."

"Why is that?"

"His eyes are guarded," Dinah revealed. "I can't explain it, but he appears to be a man of many secrets."

"You can trust this Bow Street Runner."

"Why do you say that?" she asked. "You don't even know the man."

Reginald met her gaze. "Trust me. Bow Street Runners are usually quite competent at their jobs."

"What if the Bow Street Runner can't find my sister?" she asked, voicing her greatest fear.

Reginald opened his mouth to respond but closed it when Lord Barnwell approached them. "Good evening, Miss Dinah."

Dinah removed her arm from Reginald's and dropped into a curtsy. "Good evening, my lord."

Lord Barnwell acknowledged Reginald with a tip of his head. "Lord Haddington," he said. "I do apologize for barging in, but I wanted to see how Dinah is faring."

"I am well," Dinah replied. "I thank you for asking."

"I am pleased to hear that," Lord Barnwell said. "I'm afraid I haven't seen your sister this evening. Is she well?"

"I'm afraid not. She wasn't up to coming this evening."

"I am sad to hear that," Lord Barnwell remarked. "Evie is not one to have a delicate constitution."

"No, she is not."

Lord Barnwell's eyes crinkled as he spoke. "I saw you observing me as I spoke to Lady Charlotte and her mother."

"Was I that obvious?" Dinah asked.

"Only to me," Lord Barnwell replied.

"Please say that you are not considering Lady Charlotte for a wife," Dinah blurted out.

Lord Barnwell blinked. "Good heavens, she is young enough to be my daughter. Why would you ever suppose I would be interested in her?"

Dinah snuck a glance at Reginald before admitting, "I heard you were searching for a wife."

A sad look came to Lord Barnwell's eyes. "Not yet. I'm afraid I am not quite over my wife's death."

"I can understand that," Dinah said. "Lady Barnwell was always so kind to me."

Lord Barnwell gave her a weak smile. "We had a good life together," he remarked. "I was very blessed."

"I hope to have a love match one day."

"Your parents wouldn't want anything less for you," Lord Barnwell stated. "Your father said as much to me."

"He did?"

Lord Barnwell nodded. "We not only served in the House of Lords together, but your father was one of my most trusted friends. I miss him dearly."

"As do I," Dinah said.

Lord Barnwell cleared his throat. "I do apologize for the serious turn of the conversation. We must only speak of jovial things at a soirée," he said. "We wouldn't want to give the gossips anything to chatter about."

"No, we wouldn't," Dinah agreed.

Lord Barnwell placed his hand on her sleeve and smiled. "Have a good rest of the evening, Miss Dinah."

As Lord Barnwell walked off, Reginald remarked, "There is talk that Lord Barnwell may be the next prime minister."

"Why would anyone wish to be prime minister, especially after Spencer Perceval was assassinated just last year?"

"It is a position that many men aspire to."

"Foolish men."

Reginald gave her an amused look. "I won't disagree with you there," he replied, offering his arm. "We have tarried long enough. We should get you back to your aunt."

Chapter Six

The sun had yet to rise as Nathaniel walked to the plumassier shop, wearing a tattered jacket and an old pair of boots. He was acutely aware of the men loitering in the alleyways, but he pretended to give them little heed.

He came to a stop in front of J.B. Abrams' shop and knocked on the door. It was a moment before the door opened and Mr. Abrams ushered him inside.

"You mustn't tarry on the streets for too long or you might be robbed, especially at this hour," Mr. Abrams said, closing the door behind him.

"I don't have two coins to rub together."

"That will change, assuming you're not afraid of hard work."

"I'm not."

Mr. Abrams bobbed his head in approval. "Good," he said as he started towards the back door. "I need your help moving crates and unpacking."

Nathaniel followed him into the back room, where crates of all sizes were stacked up against the wall.

Mr. Abrams picked up a crowbar and pried open the lid of one. "You can start unpacking these feathers, but be careful," he ordered. "Any feathers you break will come out of your pay."

"I understand."

"Good," Mr. Abrams said. "Put the feathers on the table, and I will examine them for any defects."

Nathaniel picked up a large ostrich feather and held it up. "No offense, but I can't believe women buy feathers."

"You would be amazed at the price women will pay for fashion."

"I suppose so."

Mr. Abrams gestured towards crates in the corner. "These crates will need to be broken down and disposed of."

"Yes, sir."

Nathaniel carefully removed the feathers from the crate and walked them over to the table. He gently laid them down before he went back to retrieve more. After that crate was empty, he retrieved another crate and started unpacking it.

Mr. Abrams spoke up from the table. "I know you must think it silly that I became a plumassier."

"I thought no such thing."

"I'm afraid I did." Mr. Abrams turned to face him. "This was my father's shop," he revealed. "He wanted me to run it with him, but I wanted to fight in the war."

"That is commendable."

Mr. Abrams huffed. "Not according to my father," he said. "He couldn't seem to understand why I would leave a profitable business to serve in the Royal Navy, and we became estranged when I left."

"That is most unfortunate."

"I couldn't very well stand here in a plumassier shop as Napoleon slaughtered my countrymen. My conscience wouldn't allow it, which is why I had to fight." Mr. Abrams rubbed his left leg. "I just didn't expect to get injured the first time our ship took fire from a French frigate."

Nathaniel carried more feathers to the table and set them down. "May I ask what happened?"

"It is a day that I'd prefer to forget, but I can't seem to get the blasted memories out of my head," Mr. Abrams said, a haunted look lingering on his face. "It all happened so fast. The frigate started firing on us, and the next thing I remember, I awoke in the infirmary."

Mr. Abrams paused in recollection. "I was one of the lucky ones," he continued. "Many of my comrades died that day, and I was sent home because of my injuries. But my desire to fight has never quite been quelled."

Picking up a feather from the pile, Mr. Abrams studied it. "I'm fighting a different type of war now."

"In what way?"

"You would be mindful to remember that there is injustice everywhere," Mr. Abrams said with a pointed look. "You just need to know where to look."

Nathaniel picked up the crowbar and opened another crate. "I just want to earn enough money so I can afford bread," he said.

"The food prices are outrageous these days."

"That they are," Nathaniel agreed. "I shouldn't have to decide between paying my rent and eating for the day."

"No man should."

Nathaniel removed the crate lid and started unloading the silk flowers within. "The amount ladies probably pay for one of these flowers would feed me for an entire week."

"That it would."

"I'm tired of being poor," Nathaniel muttered.

"I would think that most people would agree with that sentiment."

Nathaniel put a handful of flowers on the table. "I have to hide from the press gangs every night."

"There are worse things than serving in the Royal Navy."

"I am far too opinionated to serve," Nathaniel said.

"They would whip that out of you."

Nathaniel shuddered. "I am well aware, and I would prefer to avoid being flogged."

Mr. Abrams held up a bright blue silk flower. "This was my older sister's favorite flower," he murmured. "She passed away last year."

Mr. Abrams turned towards Nathaniel. "Are you blessed to have a sister?"

"I am," he lied.

Mr. Abrams extended him the flower. "Every woman deserves to have something beautiful," he said. "Will you see that she gets this?"

"I will, and thank you." Nathaniel gently set the flower aside.

"My sister died unexpectedly," Mr. Abrams explained. "It is hard to lose someone so suddenly."

"Yes, it is."

"I am fortunate that I take care of my younger sister," Mr. Abrams said with pride in his voice. "With any luck, she will be able to work in the shop in a few years."

Someone pounded at the main door, abruptly halting their conversation, and Mr. Abrams went to answer it. The sound of muffled arguing could be heard in the next room, and Nathaniel stepped closer to the door with the intention of eavesdropping.

Mr. Abrams was intently conversing with a tall, finely dressed man in hushed tones. The newcomer suddenly thumped the floor loudly with his cane. "Do it, or else!" he shouted.

Mr. Abrams didn't appear cowed by the man's outburst. "It will take more time," he said.

"My patience is wearing thin."

"I haven't found the right man for the job."

"Then look harder," the man declared before spinning on his heel and leaving the shop.

Nathaniel hurried back to the crates and continued unpacking so Mr. Abrams wouldn't suspect he had been eavesdropping.

"Did you overhear that?" Mr. Abrams asked as he returned.

"I wasn't listening, if that's what you're asking," Nathaniel said. "It weren't any of my business anyways."

"No, it wasn't." Mr. Abrams waved his hand over the crates. "We'd better hurry to get these unpacked before the shop opens."

Nathaniel retrieved another crate. "Yes, sir."

Mr. Abrams studied him for a moment. "Why don't you come back tomorrow?"

"You mean it?"

"I do," Mr. Abrams said. "I think I might have found the perfect task for you."

———————

Dinah glanced over her shoulder as she reached for the handle and pushed open the door to her sister's bedchamber. She hurried inside and quietly closed the door.

Evie had secrets, and it was time Dinah knew what they were. She rummaged through the drawers of the dressing table but found nothing out of the ordinary.

Where would her sister hide something? Dinah's eyes landed on the bed. She stepped over to it and ran her hand under the pillows. When she found nothing, she lifted the corner of the mattress up from the frame, and a piece of paper fell out onto the floor.

She lowered the mattress down and reached for the paper. It was advertising a rally in Winstead Square. Why would Evie have this? Her sister had never shown an interest in politics.

Then again, it seemed that there was a side to her that Dinah knew nothing about.

Dinah folded the paper and slipped it into the pocket of her pale green gown, then walked over to the armoire and glanced at the dresses there. She was much more interested in the clothing she found at the bottom. That's where Evie had hidden the men's clothing that she'd made to fit her frame.

Removing the men's clothes and boots, Dinah closed the door to the armoire and headed to her own room, where she found her lady's maid organizing the dressing table.

Julia glanced up when she walked in and gave her a peculiar look. "Where did you get those clothes?"

"From Evie's room."

"But why do you have them?"

Dinah deposited the clothing on the bed. "I am not quite sure yet, but I think it's time I do more to find my sister."

"By dressing up as a man?"

"These clothes will give me the freedom to do as I please."

Julia gave her a disapproving look. "It sounds rather foolhardy."

"Perhaps. I haven't quite solidified my plan yet."

"Do you even have a plan started?"

Dinah shrugged helplessly. "It's just in the beginning stages."

Julia looked unsure. "You are not the type of girl to dress in men's clothing and engage in reckless behavior."

"But my sister is that type of person."

"That may be true, but it doesn't make it right."

Dinah sat down on the bed. "How was it possible that Evie was able to hide part of herself from me?"

"Everyone keeps secrets, even from the ones that they are closest to."

"But I'm her sister."

Julia's eyes held compassion. "I imagine she was trying to

keep you safe, in her own way. Your sister has always been fiercely protective of you."

"That she has," Dinah agreed, "which is why I must find her."

"How do you intend to do that?"

"I'll start by speaking to Sally," she said. "Will you inform her that I wish to speak to her?"

"As you wish," Julia replied, walking over to the door.

After her lady's maid departed from the room, Dinah laid out the men's clothing on her bed and ran her hand over the coarse material of the trousers. Could she truly don these clothes and pretend to be a man? Her sister appeared to have no qualms about it, but Dinah had never been as adventurous as Evie.

A knock at the door broke through her musings.

Dinah grabbed the blanket that was at the foot of her bed and draped it over the men's clothing. It wouldn't do well for her if her aunt discovered what she was plotting.

"Come in," she ordered.

The door opened and Evie's lady's maid stepped into the room. "You called for me, miss?" Sally asked.

"I did," Dinah replied. "Would you mind closing the door?"

Sally did as requested before turning back with an expectant look. "How may I be of service to you?"

Dinah decided that the best course of action would be to say what needed to be said and be done with it. "How often did my sister sneak out?"

Sally pressed her lips together before saying, "Hardly at all."

"Did my sister truly sneak out to attend lectures at Oxford, or was that a lie?"

Sally lowered her gaze. "I do not wish to betray her confidences."

"I know, but I need to know the truth."

"For what purpose?"

Dinah removed the blanket and revealed the men's clothing. "I intend to go looking for her."

Sally gasped. "But you mustn't!"

"Why not?"

"It's not safe."

"It wasn't safe for Evie, but that didn't stop her."

Sally unclasped her hands. "I tried to warn her that it was unsafe, but your sister can be quite stubborn when she wants to be."

"I am well aware."

A frown tugged at the corners of Sally's mouth. "At first, Miss Ashmore would sneak out to attend lectures, but then she started attending rallies."

"Do you know why?"

Sally shook her head. "I told her it wasn't safe, but she didn't give me much heed."

"How did she get out?"

"She would leave through the servant's entrance," Sally revealed. "If she left after dark, I would ensure the door was unlocked for her return."

"She left at night?"

Sally nodded. "On occasion, and sometimes she wouldn't return until morning."

"Do you know why she'd be out so long?"

"No," Sally replied. "Miss Ashmore was rather uncommunicative about where she had been."

"She didn't tell you anything?"

"Miss Ashmore used to confide in me, but she has been different as of late," Sally said.

Dinah glanced down at the men's clothing. "On the day she disappeared, did she give any inclination that she intended to do so on purpose?"

"She did not," Sally replied. "I was trailing behind her at a discreet pace, and she just seemed to vanish before my very eyes."

Dinah removed the paper from her pocket and held it up for the maid's inspection. "Did she mention anything about this rally?"

"I'm afraid not, miss."

Dinah slipped the paper back into her pocket and picked up the shirt from the bed. "I think it is time that I take a page from my sister's book."

"Why would you wish to do that, miss?" Sally asked.

Dinah held the shirt up in front of her. "I need to find my sister, and I'm tired of sitting around the townhouse doing nothing."

"Did you not hire a Bow Street Runner to investigate?"

"I did, but I'm not about to put all my faith in him."

"I do not think this is wise," Sally said. "You are a lady and have no idea of the depravity that is prevalent on the streets of London."

Dinah lowered the shirt and replied, "I have no intention of going into the rookeries. I believe I will start with the plumassier shop."

"Why there?"

"It's where Evie was last seen," Dinah responded as she put the shirt back down on the bed. "Will you help me dress?"

Sally didn't move to assist her and looked uncertain. "Your aunt will be furious if she discovers what you plan to do."

"That is why neither of us will tell her," Dinah said, giving her a pointed look. "Will we?"

Sally hesitated. "Your secret is safe with me, but I urge you to be cautious."

"I can promise that."

Sally's eyes perused the clothing on the bed and let out a resigned sigh. "Miss Ashmore always said that she preferred men's clothing over her gowns."

"Do you know if Evie was unhappy?"

"Miss Ashmore appeared to be happy, but she did seem to be burdened by something."

"Well, I intend to find out what that was."

"How?"

Dinah shrugged. "I'm not really sure."

"I wish you luck," Sally said. "There is one more thing that I think you should know."

"Which is?"

"After your sister disappeared, so did her extra set of men's clothing."

Dinah contemplated that. "Do you suppose Evie returned for them?"

"That's what I assumed, but I can't confirm it with any certainty." Sally stepped closer. "We should hurry and get you dressed so you can be home before dinner."

Chapter Seven

Nathaniel's muscles ached as he loaded the last crate onto the wagon and watched as it rolled off to make deliveries. He took the sleeve of his faded white shirt and wiped the sweat off his brow, wondering how people managed to do this day in and day out. He was exhausted.

The door opened and Mr. Abrams stepped out. "You did good today," he praised.

"I appreciate you saying so."

Mr. Abrams reached into his pocket of his white apron and pulled out two coins. "You earned this," he said, extending the coins.

Nathaniel accepted the two sixpences and clutched it in his hands. "Thank you, Sir. I will be eating well tonight."

"I do hope you will be returning tomorrow."

"I have every intention to."

"Very good," Mr. Abrams replied. "I shall see you bright and early tomorrow."

Mr. Abrams didn't wait for a response before he headed back into his shop. The sun was low in the sky, and Nathaniel turned to make his way home. He'd done what he set out to do today in earning Mr. Abrams' confidence. Time would tell if the effort proved fruitful to the case or not.

As he turned the corner, Nathaniel caught sight of a young lad out of the corner of his eye, his cap low on his head. His clothing didn't fit his thin frame, and he was leaning his shoulder against the side of the building, reading the newssheets in his hands.

But Nathaniel wasn't so easily fooled. The lad was watching him.

Nathaniel continued down the street and ducked into an alleyway, then stood in a dark doorway and removed his pistol from his boot.

The lad stepped into the alleyway and covered his nose at the foul stench he encountered there. As the lad walked further into the alleyway, he slipped on the slick stones and rested his hand on the wall to steady himself.

The lad didn't appear to be a threat, but Nathaniel had to find out what he was up to. He stepped out from the doorway and pointed his pistol at the lad. "Why are you following me?" he demanded.

The lad's head jolted up, and Nathaniel found himself staring into the eyes of Miss Dinah. He lowered his pistol and took a step towards her. "What in the blazes do you think you are doing?" he snapped.

Miss Dinah tilted her chin. "I could ask you the same thing," she responded. "I've been watching you, and you're working for Mr. Abrams."

Nathaniel put his pistol back in his boot. "How long have you been watching me?"

"A few hours."

"Why?"

"I hired you to find my sister, but you are wasting your time working for a plumassier instead," Miss Dinah said. "I should fire you."

"That is your right, but it would be foolish to do so."

"Have you even bothered to look for Evie?"

"Perhaps you should stop and ask yourself why I might be working for Mr. Abrams," Nathaniel said. "I am attempting to earn his trust."

"I hadn't considered that," Miss Dinah murmured. "Do you think he is responsible for Evie's disappearance?"

"I'm not sure." Nathaniel's eyes roamed over her. "Why are you wearing men's clothing?"

"To go undetected, of course."

"For what purpose?"

"This was the last place my sister was seen, and I was hoping to find a clue as to where she went."

He huffed. "You should know that your clothing is entirely too fine for this section of town, and you stood out by reading newssheets."

"I hadn't realized."

"Where did you even get men's clothing?"

"From Evie's closet."

Nathaniel shook his head. "It would be best if you returned the clothing and never do anything so foolish again."

"I don't think I will."

"No?" Nathaniel repeated. "Why not?"

"I am tired of sitting at home while my sister is out here somewhere," Miss Dinah said defiantly.

Nathaniel took a step closer to her. "Do you think this is some type of game, Miss Dinah?"

"No."

"Do you know the level of depravity that resides on these streets?" he asked.

"I am acquainted—"

He spoke over her. "You live a gilded life and can't understand the struggles that these men and women face every single day just to survive."

"But you do?"

"More so than you," Nathaniel said. "Life is not kind to

these people. They do not have a lady's maid to draw a bath for them, nor do they have time for games."

"I'm not playing a game."

"Then what are you doing out here?" he asked, crossing his arms over his chest.

"I'm trying to find my sister."

"By dressing up as a man and putting yourself in danger?" Nathaniel inquired. "That seems rather idiotic to me."

Miss Dinah held his gaze, uncertainty filling her blue eyes. "I had to do something, and I was tired of waiting."

Nathaniel sighed. "Your reckless behavior could have gotten you killed."

"I think not." She reached behind her and pulled out a muff pistol. "I have a pistol," she announced smugly.

Uncrossing his arms, he asked, "Do you even know how to use it?"

"I do," she replied. "My sister taught me how to shoot, and she is quite proficient at it."

"And you believe one pistol is sufficient against the ruffians on the street?"

"I do."

"Is it even loaded?"

"It is."

He held out his hand for the pistol. "May I see it?"

"You may," she replied, extending it towards him.

Nathaniel inspected the pistol and saw that it was in good condition. "Do you care for this pistol yourself?"

"Yes, I clean it myself."

"That is impressive," Nathaniel responded.

Nathaniel handed her back the pistol as she shared, "Evie brought it home for me one day and told me that I needed to know how to protect myself."

"Why do you suppose that was?"

Miss Dinah shrugged. "My sister has always done things her own way."

"I think I would like your sister very much."

"Most do," Miss Dinah replied.

The sound of a window opening on the third level drew his attention, followed by someone dumping a bucket of something foul into the alleyway.

Miss Dinah put a hand up to her nose. "That smells awful."

"I think that it is time that I escort you back home."

"That won't be necessary."

"I cannot in good conscience let you travel to your townhouse on your own."

Miss Dinah reached behind her and crammed the pistol into the waistband of her trousers. "My coach is not far from the plumassier shop."

"You brought a coach?"

"How else would I get home?" she asked innocently.

He gestured outward, indicating she should exit the alleyway first. "You could have hailed a hackney," he suggested.

"I've never been in a hackney before," she replied. "I heard they are quite unbearable."

"That they are. They make the smell in the alleyway seem pleasant."

Miss Dinah scrunched her nose. "That's terrible."

"It is a perfectly acceptable way to travel."

"I did not mean to offend you, Mr. Collier," Miss Dinah said.

"You did no such thing."

They walked towards her coach. "You hired me to do a job; now let me do it," Nathaniel asserted.

"I would like to help. I don't like being idle."

"Pray tell, how do you think you could aid in my investigation?"

"I could—"

"No."

"You didn't even let me finish."

"There was no need. That was a rhetorical question."

Miss Dinah glanced over at him. "I did find something in my sister's room that might be of interest to you."

"Which was?"

"An advertisement for a rally."

Now she had his full attention. "Which rally?"

Miss Dinah reached into her pocket and pulled out a folded piece of paper. "It's in Winstead Square," she replied, extending it towards him.

Nathaniel accepted the paper and reviewed the familiar words. "I've seen this before."

"Where?"

"It is of little consequence."

Miss Dinah stopped in front of a black coach, and a footman stepped down to open the door for her. "I intend to go."

"Absolutely not. It isn't safe for you to attend."

"If there is any chance my sister is attending this rally, then I want to be there," Miss Dinah replied firmly.

He frowned. "Is there any chance that I can talk you out of this?"

"No," she replied.

Nathaniel returned the handbill, already regretting his next words. "Then I shall accompany you."

"You will?"

"Yes, but the moment the crowd becomes too rowdy, we leave."

"I can agree to that."

Nathaniel assisted her into the coach. "I'll call on you tomorrow to discuss the particulars."

"I will be looking forward to it."

Once Miss Dinah was situated in the coach, Nathaniel stood back and allowed the footman to close the door. He wasn't quite sure what to make of this reckless young woman.

Her determination was admirable, but her naivete was on full display.

He was about to walk away when Mr. Abram called from behind him. "Collier," he shouted, holding up the blue flower. "You forgot this in my shop."

Nathaniel went and accepted the flower. "Thank you," he replied. "My sister will be thrilled when she sees this."

The door to the townhouse had scarcely closed when her aunt stormed out of the drawing room with a thunderous look on her face.

"Where have you been, young lady?" Aunt Nancy demanded as she perused the length of her. "And why are you dressed like a man?"

Dinah shifted uncomfortably under her aunt's scrutiny. "I went to try to find Evie."

"How?"

"I went to J.B. Abrams' shop, hoping to find a clue as to where Evie went."

"Were you successful?"

"I was not," she said dejectedly.

Some of the anger from her aunt's face dissipated, showing the worry that had been hidden before. "You can't be so reckless with your safety," she said. "Did anyone see you?"

"Just Mr. Collier."

"The Bow Street Runner?"

Dinah nodded. "He was working for Mr. Abrams to try to earn his trust."

"Does he believe that Mr. Abrams knows anything about Evie's disappearance?" Aunt Nancy asked.

"He doesn't rightly know," Dinah replied. "Although Mr. Collier isn't exactly forthcoming with information."

Her aunt stepped closer and put a hand on her shoulder. "You scared me, Dinah," she said. "You can't just leave the townhouse whenever you please, especially dressed in something so vulgar."

"I can't just stand by and do nothing to help Evie."

"I know this is difficult, but there is nothing that we can do to aid in her return," her aunt said, lowering her hand to the side. "You must accept that."

"I refuse to."

Aunt Nancy gazed at her with sorrowful eyes. "If I truly thought there was a way to find Evie on my own, I wouldn't rest until I found her."

"I believe that Evie wished to disappear."

"Impossible," her aunt replied with a swipe of her hand. "Evie would never leave you."

"I want to believe that too, but I don't think that is the case."

"Why is that?"

Dinah slipped her hand into her pocket but stopped. Did she want to tell Aunt Nancy about the rally? If she did, then she had no doubt that her aunt would forbid her from attending. It would be easier to attend and ask for forgiveness later.

She removed her hand from her pocket and replied, "It is just a feeling that I have."

"I do credit your feelings, but they can be muddled in times like this."

"I suppose you make a valid point."

Her aunt sighed. "It is nearly time for dinner. Why don't you go change and we can discuss this later?"

"All right," Dinah said.

She didn't get far, as a knock came at the door.

Aunt Nancy gave her a curious look. "Were you expecting anyone?"

"I was not."

Barnes stepped out of a side room and opened the door,

revealing Mr. Collier with a blue flower in his hand. He stepped to the side to allow the Bow Street Runner to enter.

"Is everything all right, Mr. Collier?" Dinah asked.

"It is," Mr. Collier confirmed. "I do apologize for the intrusion, but I came to make sure you'd arrived home safely, and to give you this flower."

Dinah looked at him curiously. "You wish to give me a flower?"

"Mr. Abrams gave it to me," Mr. Collier replied, "and I'm afraid I have no purpose for it. I thought you could use it for one of your straw hats."

"Thank you," Dinah said as she accepted the flower. "It is beautiful, but I do hope it wasn't too much of an inconvenience for you to bring it to me."

"Not at all."

Their gazes locked for a moment, and before the silence could grow awkward, Dinah asked, "Would you care to stay for dinner?"

"I... uh..." Mr. Collier attempted.

Dinah felt embarrassed by her brazen question. "It is all right if you are unable to," she rushed out. "I'm sure you have plans to eat with your own family."

Mr. Collier's eyes became guarded, and she waited for his refusal. To her surprise, he replied, "I would be honored to dine with you this evening."

"Truly?"

Mr. Collier looked amused by her response. "Truly," he repeated.

Dinah started backing up. "If you will give me just a moment to change into something more presentable, I will be down shortly."

Mr. Collier tipped his head. "I will be here."

"You could wait in the drawing room," she suggested. "I'm sure it would be much more comfortable than standing in the entry hall."

"That is a fine idea," Mr. Collier replied.

"You can sit on the yellow settee," she said. "It is quite comfortable. Many people have said as much, so it is not just me who believes it." Dinah wasn't quite sure why she added that last part. Why was she blathering on? There was no reason to be nervous around Mr. Collier.

Her aunt spoke up. "I will escort you to your bedchamber."

"Thank you," Dinah replied.

After they'd walked up the stairs and turned down the hall, Aunt Nancy fixed her with a pointed look. "Pray tell, why did you invite Mr. Collier to dine with us?"

Dinah hesitated. She wasn't quite sure why she had blurted out an invitation to dine with them, but she couldn't admit that to her aunt. "I thought it was the polite thing to do."

"Because he brought you a flower?"

"That was rather sweet of him."

Aunt Nancy frowned. "I fear that our table may make him uncomfortable."

"In what way?"

"He is not of our class, dear," her aunt replied. "Most likely, he eats most of his dinners at a tavern. He has no experience with a refined meal."

"I hadn't taken you for such a prude."

Aunt Nancy stopped outside of her bedchamber door. "I daresay that you are giving Mr. Collier too much credit."

"Or are you not giving him enough?" Dinah countered.

"We shall see," her aunt replied. "I need to inform Barnes that we will be having a guest dining with us."

Dinah waited until her aunt walked off before she opened her door and stepped inside. Julia looked up when she stepped into the room, relief etched on her face.

"You are finally home!" Julia exclaimed. "I was so worried about you."

"There was no need. I was perfectly safe."

Julia approached her. "Did you find anything that will help find your sister?"

"I did not."

"That is most unfortunate." Julia glanced at the flower in her hand. "That is a beautiful flower."

"Mr. Collier gave it to me," Dinah shared as she set it on the dressing table. "In fact, he accepted my invitation to dine with us this evening."

Julia furrowed her brow. "Isn't Mr. Collier the Bow Street Runner you hired?"

"He is."

"Then why would you invite him to dine with you?"

Dinah walked over to the armoire and started looking through her gowns. "Frankly, I am not sure why I extended the invitation, but I was pleased when he accepted it." She pulled out a jonquil gown. "I need to change."

Julia walked over and held her hand out for the dress. "I agree," she replied. "You can't very well wear men's clothing for dinner."

"I must admit that wearing trousers is quite comfortable. I can see why Evie liked wearing them."

"You'd better not let your aunt hear you say that."

"Will you launder these clothes and put them in my armoire?"

"Do you intend to wear them again?"

"I do."

Julia looked displeased. "Why?"

"I intend to go to a rally in Winstead Square."

"A rally is no place for a lady," Julia asserted.

"But I must go."

"Whatever for?"

Dinah removed the paper from her pocket. "I think Evie might be there." She extended the handbill to Julia. "I found this in her bedchamber."

"That doesn't mean she will be in attendance."

"Perhaps, but I can't risk not going."

Julia handed the paper back. "Are you going by yourself?"

"No, Mr. Collier will be accompanying me."

"Your aunt would lock you up in a madhouse if she discovered you went to a rally."

"That is why I have no intention of telling her," Dinah said. "I will leave from the servant's entrance, just as Evie used to do."

"Your aunt is not so easily fooled."

"We'll see."

Julia shook her head. "We should get you dressed before Mr. Collier grows tired of waiting."

"Thank you, Julia," Dinah said. "I'm not sure what I would do without you."

"I just wish I could talk you out of this madness."

"I know what I am doing."

"Do you?" Julia questioned as she stepped forward to assist her in undressing.

"I do," Dinah replied, hoping her words held some truth.

Chapter Eight

After the ladies had disappeared down the hall, Nathaniel stepped into the drawing room, a smile tugging at his lips when he saw the yellow camelback settee that Miss Dinah had assured him was comfortable. Her ramblings had been oddly charming.

Rather than take the offered seat, Nathaniel walked over to the window. Why had he brought over the blasted flower? When Mr. Abrams had given it to him, his first thought had been that Miss Dinah might enjoy it. Now he was regretting his decision. He had no desire to dine with her and be peppered with questions that he couldn't answer truthfully.

Miss Dinah was a beautiful woman, there was no denying that, but no good could come from forming an attachment to her. Besides, he had no intention of ever marrying. He couldn't risk having any more distractions in his life. His loyalty was to the Crown.

Nathaniel stared out at the gardens and sighed. He had so much he needed to accomplish, and he was wasting his time with Miss Dinah. Time was of the essence, and he didn't have time to become more acquainted with her. What was it about her that fascinated him? Her beauty may have first drawn him in, but it was her goodness that made him want to stay.

He tugged down on his worn ivory waistcoat as he thought of Rutledge. Where was he? He hoped that he was working on the case and had gone undercover. His mentor had always told him that, to truly understand a case, one must cast aside all pretenses and get to work. Is that what Rutledge was doing? Or was he truly in danger?

Blazes. Nathaniel had made no progress on this case, and he was fraternizing with a silly young woman who didn't think through the implications of her actions.

Nathaniel heard someone enter the drawing room and turned back around. Mrs. Carter stepped further into the room, a frown marring her features.

She sat down and pointed to a chair. "Would you care to sit, Mr. Collier?"

"I would," he replied as he went to do the woman's bidding.

Once he was situated, Mrs. Carter watched him with a critical eye. "What are you about, Mr. Collier?"

"I beg your pardon?"

"Your mannerisms and speech mark you as a gentleman, but your clothing," she hesitated, "looks contrived."

"Contrived?" he asked, glancing down at his jacket.

"It makes me wonder if you are who you truly say you are."

"Who else would I be?"

"I'm not sure." Mrs. Carter sat back in her chair. "Why are you calling on my niece?"

"To give her a flower."

"Gifts are typically reserved for suitors," Mrs. Carter remarked. "Are you hoping to become my niece's suitor?"

"I am not."

"Either you are lying, or you are a fool."

Surprised by her bold speech, he asked, "Why is that?"

"Dinah is an heiress and is quite desirable amongst the *ton*."

"I am well aware, but I have no interest in her money or her status in Society."

Mrs. Carter clasped her hands in her lap. "Then what are you interested in, Mr. Collier?"

"Nothing more than finding Miss Ashmore and bringing her home."

"Yet, instead of searching for Evie, you are dining with us," Mrs. Carter said with a lifted brow. "I would think you would be more interested in collecting the reward money for my niece's safe return."

"I had not intended on dining with you, but I didn't dare refuse Miss Dinah." There. That was the truth.

Mrs. Carter looked as if she wanted to ask more questions, but as she opened her mouth, Miss Dinah stepped into the room, wearing a yellow gown. Her blonde hair was piled atop her head, and she looked like the epitome of perfection.

Where had that thought even come from?

Miss Dinah stopped next to her aunt. "I do apologize for the delay."

"You have no reason to apologize," Mrs. Carter replied. "Mr. Collier and I were having a lovely chat."

"You were?" Miss Dinah asked, glancing between them.

Nathaniel nodded. "Yes, we were."

"Shall we adjourn to the dining room to continue the conversation?" Miss Dinah asked. "Barnes informed me that dinner is served."

"That sounds like a wonderful idea," Mrs. Carter said, rising. "I'm afraid I have many more questions for Mr. Collier."

Miss Dinah watched as her aunt departed from the room before turning towards Nathaniel with a curious look. "Is everything all right?"

"It is," he replied. "Why do you ask?"

"You appear tense."

"I assure you that this is how I normally am."

Miss Dinah smiled. "If you say so." She motioned towards the door. "Allow me to show you to the dining room."

Nathaniel approached her. "Your aunt is quite…" His words trailed off as he attempted to think of the right word.

"Intimidating?"

"Yes, that describes her perfectly."

As they exited the drawing room, Miss Dinah said, "You will have to excuse her, she is quite protective of us."

"That is admirable."

"It is, but you do not want to get on the wrong side of her," Miss Dinah expressed. "I fear she has a list of people she doesn't like."

"Surely she doesn't make a list."

"She is so fiercely loyal to her loved ones that my sister and I have long since suspected that she has."

"I do hope I don't make the list."

"As do I."

Miss Dinah stepped into the dining room, and he followed behind her. He pulled out a chair for her before claiming the seat across from her. Mrs. Carter sat at the head of the table, keeping a watchful eye over him.

Nathaniel took his napkin and laid it on his lap. It was evident that Mrs. Carter viewed him as a threat to her niece, and he knew that it would take some work to win her over.

"This townhouse is lovely," Nathaniel said.

"Thank you," Miss Dinah responded. "My cousin has graciously allowed us to remain here for the Season."

"That was most generous of him," Nathaniel acknowledged.

"This townhouse has been in our family for generations," Mrs. Carter shared as she reached for her glass. "It was a shame that Alfred had no sons, so his title passed to a distant cousin."

"Alfred was my father," Miss Dinah explained.

"I suspected as much," Nathaniel responded.

Mrs. Carter leaned to the side as a footman placed a bowl of soup in front of her. "How long have you been a Bow Street Runner?"

"Quite some time," Nathaniel said vaguely.

"Are you proficient at your job?" Mrs. Carter asked.

"I would like to believe I am."

Mrs. Carter picked up her spoon. "That didn't answer my question."

"Yes, I am proficient at my job," Nathaniel responded.

"That bodes well for us," Mrs. Carter said before taking a sip of her soup.

Miss Dinah gave him an apologetic smile. "Do you have any siblings?"

"I do," Nathaniel replied. "I have a younger brother."

"Are your parents alive?"

"They are."

Miss Dinah turned back towards her soup. "They must be proud of all that you have accomplished."

"Why do you say that?"

"To be a Bow Street Runner is quite a feat."

"I suppose it is, but they are just pleased that I return home safely every night," Nathaniel said. "The streets can be a dangerous place, as I'm sure you are aware."

Mrs. Carter placed her spoon down. "What made you want to become a Bow Street Runner?"

Nathaniel considered his response for a moment, knowing he had to be careful to skirt around the truth. "I suppose I am interested in the adventure of it all. I want to do all I can to protect the Crown."

"That is an honorable response," Mrs. Carter said.

"It's how I feel."

Mrs. Carter's eyes shown with approval. "Not everyone has the Crown's best interest at heart."

"No, they don't," Nathaniel readily agreed. "I have seen the sordid underbelly of the streets, and it is not a desirable place to be."

"Yet you freely mingle with those people," Mrs. Carter commented.

"Someone has to," Nathaniel responded.

Miss Dinah picked up her glass and took a sip. As she returned the glass to the table, she said, "Perhaps we should stop interrogating Mr. Collier, since he is a guest."

Mrs. Carter gave her niece an innocent look. "I was doing no such thing," she asserted. "I was merely making conversation."

"Quite frankly, I find Mrs. Carter's candor to be quite refreshing," Nathaniel remarked. "I know precisely where I stand with her."

"That you do, Mr. Collier," Mrs. Carter said with a wry smile.

Miss Dinah gestured towards his soup. "You must eat before your soup gets cold," she encouraged.

Nathaniel picked up his spoon and took a sip of the soup. "This is delicious," he remarked.

"It is our cook's own creation," Mrs. Carter shared proudly, "an adaptation of the classic white soup."

"I shall have to get the recipe," Nathaniel said.

"I'm afraid she will not share it," Miss Dinah informed him. "Mrs. Lorraine is very secretive when it comes to what is in her food."

"That is a shame."

Miss Dinah smirked. "Not for us," she responded. "We get to partake of her food, day in and day out."

"You are most fortunate."

"That we are," Mrs. Carter agreed. "I would imagine your dinners would be much simpler than this."

"They are. I mostly eat at taverns."

Miss Dinah's eyes twinkled with excitement. "What is that like?"

"It is not nearly as exciting as you would think," Nathaniel replied. "The tables are notoriously sticky, the food is bland, the company is terrible, and the ale is watered down."

"That sounds awful," Miss Dinah acknowledged.

Nathaniel put his spoon down, and a footman promptly came to remove the empty bowl. "It is, but it isn't all bad."

"In what way?" Miss Dinah asked.

"People tend to let information slip when they are drunk," Nathaniel shared.

A footman stepped into the dining room with a tray of meat and placed it into the center of the table.

Nathaniel rose and said, "Allow me to serve you lovely ladies."

Mrs. Carter nodded in approval. "It might be best if we discuss more pleasurable things for the remainder of the meal."

"I couldn't agree with you more," Nathaniel remarked as he set about to dish them food.

Nathaniel sat in the darkened hackney as it rolled down the street. He was trying to focus on the case, but his thoughts kept straying towards Miss Dinah. To his surprise, he had enjoyed dining with her and Mrs. Carter. He had politely refused their request to remain at their townhouse and play cards. He didn't have time to dawdle. He had a job to do, and he already wasted too much time.

The hackney came to a jerking stop, and he put his hand through the window to open the door. As he paid the driver, he noticed a figure lurking in the shadows a short distance away. He retrieved his pistol, not knowing if this was a friend or foe.

He cautiously approached the man and was pleased when he saw a bright purple jacket. "Haddington," he greeted. "May I ask why you are loitering in the shadows?"

"I didn't want to be seen," Haddington informed him. "Merritt wants an update on the case."

Nathaniel returned the pistol to his boot. "I'm afraid I haven't made much progress."

"He won't be happy about that."

"I am well aware, but I still have more questions than answers."

Haddington nodded. "That is the plight of being an agent."

"Why don't you come inside and have a drink with me?"

"Unfortunately, I need to return to Lady Lucinda's ball," Haddington said. "Where have you been this evening?"

"I had dinner with Miss Dinah and her aunt."

Haddington lifted his brow. "You had dinner with Miss Dinah?"

"I did."

"How did that come about?"

"After I gave her a flower—"

Haddington interrupted. "You gave her a flower?"

"I did, but you are reading too much into it," he said.

"I don't think I am," Haddington responded. "I have known Dinah for many years, and I have yet to dine with her. Or give her a flower."

"Perhaps I am much more likeable."

"That couldn't possibly be it."

"Regardless, I had a pleasant evening, but I have no intention of ever dining with Miss Dinah again."

"Why is that?"

"I need to focus on the case, and I don't have time for distractions."

"Have you come any closer to finding Evie?" Haddington asked.

"No, but I do believe she is connected with Rutledge's case somehow."

"Why do you suspect that is the case?"

"I don't rightly know, but I will root out the truth soon enough."

Haddington tipped his head. "I need to go, but if you need any help, all you need to do is ask."

"That is unlikely."

"I know you prefer working alone, but there are advantages to having a partner," Haddington said lightly.

"I haven't discovered any."

Haddington chuckled. "You never change, Hawthorne," he said as he started walking down the street.

Nathaniel approached his main door and stepped inside. The dark townhouse was quiet as he made his way to his study in the rear. Unfortunately, it wasn't empty. His father was sitting in front of the fireplace, a drink in his hand.

"Where have you been, son?" his father demanded.

"Out."

"You left before dawn and are only now returning," his father said. "Why?"

"I had business I needed to attend to."

His father took a sip of his drink, then asked, "Who is she?"

"Pardon?"

"I must assume that you were visiting your mistress."

Nathaniel walked over to the drink cart and picked up the decanter. "I was doing no such thing," he stated. "I have no mistress."

"Then what are you about?" his father asked. "Your appearance is hardly befitting a man of your station. That clothing should be thrown out at once."

Nathaniel poured himself a drink, then lowered the

decanter and picked up his glass. "I am quite fond of these clothes."

"Mr. Bolton informed me that you missed a meeting with him today."

"I hadn't realized that I had a meeting with him," Nathaniel said, walking over to the settee. "I will send word about rescheduling."

His father shifted in his seat to face him. "You have a duty to this family, son," he said sternly, "yet you disappear at all hours of the day, and sneak home after everyone is in bed."

"I did not sneak home. If you must know, I had dinner with Miss Dinah Ashmore and her aunt this evening."

"In those clothes?"

"They didn't seem to mind."

"Miss Dinah Ashmore would be a fine choice for a wife, but I have heard that her older sister is quite the bluestocking."

"I am not searching for a bride."

"That is unfortunate. You need to produce an heir."

"I know my duty."

His father huffed. "Then prove it."

"I am only thirty," Nathaniel said with his glass to his lips. "I have many years ahead of me to search for a bride."

"By your age, I had already sired two sons," his father shared.

"It was a different time."

"Yes, it was," his father agreed. "It was a much simpler time, and we honored our parents."

"Father—"

His father held his hand up in front of him. "I know I can't tell you how to live, but I am worried about you. I fear that you are involved in something that could damage this family's reputation."

"I assure you that is not the case."

"If I had my wish, you would remain at home and manage our properties and investments."

"I do that."

"Until you disappear for days on end, only to return with no explanation as to where you have been." His father shook his head. "And Hugh is no better. He staggers in during the early morning hours after spending the evening at a gambling hall."

"Hugh will come around."

"I'm not sure that is true."

Nathaniel took a sip of his drink. "He wants to prove his worth."

"By gambling?" his father asked in disbelief. "That is not the way to go about it."

"I agree, but Hugh has always had a mind of his own."

"A vexing mind," his father muttered. "I worry that no woman will want him, given his reputation."

"It only takes one woman who is willing to take a chance on him."

"I just want you and Hugh to be happy," his father said, "just as I am happy with your mother. There is great satisfaction with marrying well."

"I do not know if I wish to marry."

His father frowned. "Do not let your mother catch you saying that," he warned. "She would be devastated."

"My life is not conducive with having a wife."

"You may say that now, but when you find the right young woman, nothing else will matter," his father counseled. "You will fight to keep her in your life."

"Then I haven't met the right woman yet."

His father set his empty glass on a table and rose. "Life is much easier when you have a helpmate by your side."

"I will take that into consideration."

"No, you won't," his father said. "You will continue doing

things your own way, in your own time. It is quite maddening."

"I can assure you that there is a method to my madness."

"I truly hope so, because your actions are going to send me into an early grave." His father walked over to the door and stopped. "It is time that you accept your responsibility to this family."

After his father left, Nathaniel leaned his head back against the settee, casting his eyes towards the ceiling. He hated lying to his family, but he had no choice. He couldn't very well tell them the truth about who he was.

He had always known that his position as an agent was a lonely one, but his days were numbered. Once his father died and Nathaniel inherited his title, he would be forced to retire from being an agent. So, he intended to work as long as he could until then.

Nathaniel knew he was a grand disappointment to his parents in the meantime, but it didn't alter his course. His duty was to the Crown. Nothing else mattered.

Chapter Nine

The sun was just about to break over the horizon as Nathaniel walked towards Abrams' shop. He was frustrated by the lack of progress that he had made on this case, and he knew he needed to find a break in the case, and quickly.

He approached the main door of the plumassier shop and knocked. It was only a moment before Mr. Abrams opened the door and ushered him inside.

"Morning," Mr. Abrams greeted him. "Why don't you start sweeping the back room?"

"It would be my pleasure."

Mr. Abrams retrieved the broom that was leaning against the wall and extended it towards him. "Once you are finished, you can help me start preparing the orders that need to be delivered today."

Nathaniel accepted the broom and headed into the back room. He started sweeping the floor as his eyes roamed the rectangular room. Nothing appeared out of order, but there had to be something here that would aid in his investigation.

His eyes landed on the desk in the corner, and he saw a pile of papers stacked in the center of the desk. He wondered if there was anything of interest. With a quick glance at the door, he hurried over to the desk and rifled through the papers, but he found nothing that piqued his interest.

As he stepped back, he noticed a paper that had fallen under the desk. He reached down and picked it up. It was another advertisement for the rally at Winstead Square. Why was Abrams interested in the rally?

He set the paper on the desk and continued searching. He quietly pulled out the drawers, but nothing aroused his suspicion. Blast it! There had to be something here that would tie Abrams to the Red Ravens.

The sound of Abrams' booted steps could be heard approaching, and Nathaniel quickly picked up the broom. He stepped away from the desk and continued sweeping.

"You finished?" Abrams asked as he stepped into the back room.

"Not yet."

Abrams stepped over to the desk and picked up the advertisement. He held it up. "Are you attending the rally?"

"I am."

"Very good," Abrams said. "The only way we can enact change is to prove to the powers that be that we deserve more."

"More?"

Abrams put the paper back on the desk. "The government should be working for us, not against us."

"Why do you assume they are working against us?"

"They put laws in place that help them get richer, while we get poorer," Abrams asserted. "It is time for the people to rise up and be heard."

"How can we do that?" Nathaniel asked. "The moment the Crown gets a whiff of rebellion, they sniff it out and stop it."

"They are not as clever as they want you to believe."

"In what regard?"

"Constables and justices of the peace are worthless and

can easily be swayed to look the other way by a few coins," Abrams said. "Everyone has a price."

Nathaniel opened the back door and swept the dirt out into the alley. "I would agree with that sentiment."

Abrams leaned back against his desk. "What is your price?"

"Pardon?"

"What are you willing to do for a nice payday?"

"It depends on how much we are talking about."

"Twenty pounds."

Nathaniel let his eyes grow wide. "I would do just about anything for twenty pounds," he said. "That's more money than I have ever seen before."

"Would you kill someone for it?" Abrams asked.

He took a moment to pretend to consider Abrams' words. "It depends on who that person was," he said.

"What if I told you that it was a man who is intent on repressing us?"

Nathaniel huffed lightly. "More so than we have already been repressed?"

"Precisely," Abrams responded.

Nathaniel rested the broom against the side of the wall. "I don't want to do anything illegal," he said. "I may not have much, but at least I have my freedom."

"Does anyone have freedom in England?" Abrams argued. "We are neglected by the government, and they wonder why there is such discontent amongst us."

"They're all fools."

"That they are," Abrams agreed. "That's why we need to ensure someone is appointed who has our best interest at heart."

"We are represented by the House of Commons."

"Are we?" Abrams questioned. "The House of Lords can veto any bill approved by the House of Commons. Furthermore, we both know that the House of Common consists of friends of the aristocracy."

"This is all true, but we can't do anything to change that fact."

"Yes, we can."

"How?"

Abrams stepped closer to him. "We need a prime minister who is sympathetic to the people," he said, "someone who cares for our voices."

"That will never happen. Lord Liverpool is a Tory, and they only care about the divine rights of our King and church," Nathaniel pointed out.

"Not all Tories are as conservative as they want you to believe," Abrams remarked. "Some are just playing the fine line of teetering between a Tory and a Whig."

"How can that be true? Whigs believe in the rights of the common man. It is contrary to their fundamental beliefs."

"Tories would care if it was in their best interest."

"I'm afraid I don't understand."

"When Perceval was assassinated, the prince regent struggled four times to appoint his successor, but none of those men were able to form ministries," Abrams shared. "Lord Liverpool was the prince regent's fifth choice."

"I am sure that there was some hesitancy on their parts because Perceval had just been assassinated."

"Exactly," Abrams said. "What if Liverpool was killed? How many people would pass on the post before someone accepted the office?"

"I would imagine many lords would, for fear of their safety."

Abrams nodded approvingly. "Which is why it would be in our best interest if Liverpool died."

Nathaniel let a believable amount of shock and concern cross his face. "Why?"

"Liverpool only cares about himself," Abrams said. "He has made a career out of suppressing the people."

"That isn't uncommon in the House of Lords," Nathaniel argued. "Besides, the prince regent would only appoint another Tory, one that has a governing majority."

"That may not be entirely true. The prince regent used to be a Whig in his earlier days, and we believe he might see the merits of a Whig as prime minister.""

"We?"

"A few other like-minded people, ones who truly care about the state of the government," Abrams said. "Are you one of those people?"

Nathaniel bobbed his head. "I am."

"These are troubling times, but it only takes a few good men to stand up to the tyranny and enact change," Abrams remarked.

"What can I do?"

Abrams considered him for a moment before saying, "Join us tomorrow at the Rotten Rabbit. We'll be meeting there at dark."

"I'll be there."

A hardened gleam came into Abrams' eye. "I should warn you that we do not take kindly to people betraying us."

"I understand."

"Good, because I would hate to have a reason to kill you."

"As would I," Nathaniel responded.

Abrams clasped his hands together. "Now, let's get back to work and prepare the orders for delivery."

Nathaniel followed Abrams into the main part of the shop. He had enough information to have Abrams arrested, but that wouldn't be beneficial to his investigation. He needed to infiltrate the Red Ravens and discover their whole plan.

Dinah laid on a blanket and stared up into the sky. Her aunt would chide her for not wearing a bonnet, but the sun felt delightful on her face. No matter how hard she tried to distract herself, though, her thoughts kept returning to Evie.

Why had her sister left her? What could have compelled her to do such a thing? Was Evie's life so awful that she felt like she had no choice but to leave it? Dinah didn't have any answers, and it frustrated her.

Furthermore, it infuriated her that she couldn't do a thing to get her sister home. She just had to sit and wait, hoping Mr. Collier was doing his due diligence in finding her. Dinah wasn't sure she could trust him. He had secrets; she could see it in his eyes. He would never confide in her, though. She was sure of that.

Mr. Collier was still far better than the constable. At least he seemed somewhat competent at his job. She wondered if he had made any more progress with Mr. Abrams.

The sound of booted footsteps came from behind her, and she sat up to watch the man in question approach.

He stopped next to the blanket. "I do not wish to intrude," Mr. Collier said. "Would you like me to come back at a later time?"

Dinah rose and smoothed out her pale pink gown. "That won't be necessary."

"You seemed troubled," Mr. Collier observed.

"I was just thinking about my sister," she said. "Have you made any progress?"

"I'm afraid not. I have contacts all over London looking for your sister, but to no avail."

Dinah reached down and picked up the blanket. "Why do you suppose my sister would wish to disappear?"

"We don't know that for certain," Mr. Collier replied. "You mustn't lose hope that we will find her."

"I'm holding out hope that my sister will be at that rally tomorrow."

Mr. Collier glanced over his shoulder at her townhouse. "Have you asked permission from your aunt to attend?"

"Heavens, no," she responded with a shake of her head. "I intend to sneak out the servant's entrance and meet you."

"You do understand that your reputation is at stake, because we will have to share a hackney to the rally," he said. "If anyone saw you—"

She spoke over him. "I understand what is at stake."

"Yet you still plan to attend?"

"I do," Dinah said. "I want to know why my sister was so secretive about this rally."

Mr. Collier wiped a hand over his mouth. "I do worry that you may be wasting your time."

"It is my time to waste."

"Why don't I just attend—"

Dinah cut him off. "I am going, and that is final."

Mr. Collier scowled. "Have you always been this stubborn?"

"Yes."

"If the rally gives even the slightest indication that it may turn violent, we will leave at once," Mr. Collier said firmly.

"I understand." Especially considering that he'd already told her this yesterday.

Mr. Collier heaved a frustrated sigh. "Meet me outside your townhouse at noon."

"Thank you."

"Don't thank me yet," Mr. Collier said. "Your sister might not even be there."

"I am aware."

"I know attending a rally may seem exciting, but it can be rather dull."

"In what way?"

"The orator will speak to the crowd, sometimes going on for hours upon hours about politics," Mr. Collier shared. "Most people lose interest after a while."

"It sounds exciting."

"Then I must have said it wrong," Mr. Collier joked, tugging down on his brown waistcoat.

Dinah tightened her hold on the blanket in her arms. "If not for finding my sister, I would have no desire to attend a rally. I have never been as adventurous as she is."

"Will you tell me more about your sister?"

"Evie is…" Her voice trailed off as she attempted to find the right word. "Courageous. She isn't afraid of anything."

"It may appear so, but everyone has something, or someone, that they are afraid of losing."

Dinah eyed him curiously. "What are you afraid of losing?"

"It's different for me."

"How so?"

"I understand the dangers of my job, and I know that I am living on borrowed time," Mr. Collier said. "My affairs are in order."

"That sounds like a depressing way to live."

"No, it is the only way to live," Mr. Collier responded. "Being alive is a gift, at least for me."

"I hadn't realized being a Bow Street Runner was so dangerous."

"Any profession is dangerous, given the right circumstances."

Dinah turned towards the townhouse and spied Aunt Nancy watching her from the window.

"It would appear that my aunt is watching us," she informed him.

Mr. Collier followed her gaze. "I'm not surprised."

"I do apologize for her interrogation last night."

Mr. Collier smiled. "It was a far cry from an interrogation."

"I don't know what came over her, but she normally isn't so direct with our guests."

"I didn't take any offense," Mr. Collier said. "Frankly, I find it admirable that Mrs. Carter is so protective of you."

"That she is, almost to a fault."

"It is a good thing when you are surrounded by people who love you."

"I agree."

Mr. Collier stepped closer and held his hand out. "May I take the blanket and escort you back to the townhouse?"

"You may," she replied, extending him the blanket.

As she took his arm, Dinah asked, "Did you make any more progress with Mr. Abrams?"

"I did."

Dinah waited for him to explain, but when he failed to do so, she pressed, "Can you expand on that?"

"I see no reason to."

"Why not?"

Mr. Collier glanced over at her. "I can only give you information that you absolutely have to know," he said. "It is much safer for you that way."

Dinah let out a slight huff. "You are quite infuriating, Mr. Collier."

"I have been called worse."

"I bet," she muttered.

Mr. Collier stopped and turned to face her. "I know you must think me a boor, but I am trying to protect you."

"I don't need your protection."

"I think you do."

"My only concern is finding my sister," Dinah stated. "Nothing else matters."

Mr. Collier frowned. "That is the problem. When you are too close to the situation, you can make poor decisions that have dire consequences."

"I already told you that I refuse to sit back and do nothing," Dinah said, tilting her chin.

"You did, but I am hoping you will come to your senses

before you get hurt." Mr. Collier perused her clothing. "I do hope you will wear something to the rally that will attract less attention."

"My lady's maid is letting me borrow one of her gowns. She didn't think I should wear men's clothing."

"She's right," Mr. Collier said. "No good would come of it if someone recognized you dressed that way. Your reputation would be tarnished."

"I am aware of the risks."

"Are you?"

"I am."

Mr. Collier shook his head. "You say that now, but it could change when you are ostracized by the *ton*."

"It is a chance worth taking," she replied. "Tell me, Mr. Collier, what does a Bow Street Runner know about the *ton*?"

"I know enough."

"The *ton* doesn't frighten me."

"It should."

"What truly frightens me is living my life without my sister," Dinah admitted.

Mr. Collier held her gaze. "I will do everything in my power to ensure that won't happen." Despite the sincerity in his voice, she was unsure if he would be able to deliver on that promise. After all, what did she really know about the man?

"Thank you," she said.

They stood for a moment, staring at one another, neither of them willing to look away first. Dinah felt the warmth of color invading her cheeks and wondered if Mr. Collier could see her discomfort.

She had barely finished her thought when Mr. Collier asked, "Shall we proceed to the townhouse?"

"Yes," she murmured.

As they resumed walking, Dinah chided herself on feeling the least bit uncomfortable around Mr. Collier. He was only here because she had hired him to find her sister, and nothing more.

It would be foolish to let her attraction to him, or her own feelings of loneliness, so weaken her that her feelings would continue to grow for Mr. Collier. It would be best if she could squash them now before they deepened. If not, she would leave herself open to the pain that would no doubt arise when he departed abruptly from her life.

Chapter Ten

Dressed in a grey jacket, Nathaniel descended the stairs of his townhouse just as his brother staggered into the entry hall.

Nathaniel took in his brother's wrinkled clothing. "I see that some things never change."

"I could say the same thing about you, brother," Hugh replied with an almost indecipherable slur.

"You're drunk."

"Says who?" Hugh asked defiantly.

Nathaniel put his hand on his brother's sleeve and leaned in. "Go sleep it off, Hugh," he said. "You wouldn't want Mother to see you like this."

"Does it matter?" Hugh asked, throwing his hands up. "It would just confirm what she already knows."

"Which is?"

"I am just a disappointment to them."

Nathaniel removed his hand and lowered it to his side. "I daresay you are quite good at theatrics."

"I am no such thing."

"We keep having this same conversation, and yet, you still haven't made any changes in your life."

"What's the point?"

Nathaniel lifted his brow. "Do you not wish to wed?"

"Heavens, no," Hugh rushed to reply. "The last thing I want is a wife."

"Why is that?"

"I don't wish to have any woman nag me relentlessly."

"Not all women do that."

Hugh walked over to the stairs and slapped his hand on the iron banister. "I do not wish to take my chances. I would rather be alone."

"That is what I am worried about."

"Why?" Hugh asked. "Unlike you, I answer to no one."

His mother's voice came from behind them. "Good morning," she greeted. "I see that both of my sons are up and ready to embrace the day."

"Not quite," Hugh muttered. "I'm afraid I was just off to bed."

"Are you sure you won't join me for breakfast?" she asked.

Hugh grimaced. "I ate at the gambling hall."

"I see. Well, I wanted to save the good news for over breakfast, but I shall tell you now."

"What good news is that, Mother?" Nathaniel asked.

"You remember my dear friend, Lady Wycombe?" she started.

Nathaniel shook his head. "I don't."

"You have a lot of dear friends," Hugh remarked.

Their mother waved her hand dismissively. "Lady Wycombe is hosting a ball for her daughter in six days, and I already sent word that we will all be in attendance."

"No," Hugh said. "Absolutely not."

She gave him a sad look. "You must attend."

"Why?" Hugh asked.

"We wouldn't want to offend Lady Wycombe now, would we?"

Hugh removed his hand from the banister. "I'm afraid I

don't even know who this Lady Wycombe is," he said, "so you must excuse me if I don't attend."

Pleading eyes turned towards Nathaniel. "Please tell me that you will attend with us."

Nathaniel frowned, knowing he couldn't refuse her simple request. "I suppose I can move a few things around."

"Wonderful," their mother said. "At least one of my sons will be attending."

As she walked towards the dining room, Hugh grumbled, "The golden child has come through again."

"You could join us," Nathaniel said.

"For what purpose?"

"To have fun."

"I will have to pass."

Nathaniel walked over to the door. "A word of advice," he started, "if you want things to change, you have to look inward first."

"Are you a philosopher now?"

"No, but I am worried about you," Nathaniel said as he accepted his top hat from the butler. He set it on his head and exited the townhouse.

As he started walking down the pavement, he heard his name being shouted from the other side of the street. "Hawthorne!"

Nathaniel turned and saw Haddington. He stopped and waited until Haddington crossed the street, expertly dodging coaches.

"You're up early," Nathaniel commented as Haddington approached him.

Haddington smirked. "I haven't gone to bed yet."

"Whyever not?"

"My assignment keeps me up till the early morning hours," Haddington revealed. "It has wreaked havoc on my sleeping schedule."

"I think you will survive."

Haddington's smile slipped. "I wanted you to know that none of my informants know anything about a missing lady."

"Drat."

"They have scoured the rookeries, and I even had my contacts stroll the alleys by the rivers," Haddington said. "We both know it isn't uncommon to buy a woman there."

"We do."

"I know you didn't ask for my help on this case, but I am friends with Miss Ashmore and her sister," Haddington said. "I couldn't stand by and not do anything."

"I don't fault you for that," Nathaniel remarked. "Miss Ashmore is somehow connected to my case, but I haven't figured out how yet."

"Have you found a lead on Rutledge?"

Nathaniel winced. "No," he admitted. "I have yet to find a clue on his whereabouts."

"Merritt won't be pleased with your lack of progress."

"No, he won't," Nathaniel agreed, "but I am hoping this rally provides me with some answers."

"Would you care for me to join you?"

"I could use some support," Nathaniel said. "Miss Dinah is accompanying me."

Haddington stared at him in disbelief. "You are taking Miss Dinah to a rally?"

"I am."

"Are you mad?" Haddington demanded.

"No."

Haddington looked thunderous. "Pray tell, how are you traveling to Winstead Square?"

"A hackney."

"You are going to ride in a hackney with Miss Dinah?" Haddington asked. "A lady does not ride in a hackney or alone with a gentleman who is not her husband."

"I couldn't very well take her in one of my coaches."

Haddington muttered a curse word under his breath. "You

mustn't take her at all," he urged. "Just think of the damage that could come to her reputation if anyone saw her."

"I am well aware, but Miss Dinah is adamant about going. I have no doubt she would attend, with or without me."

"I will accompany you for propriety's sake."

"Do you truly think that would make a difference?"

"I do," Haddington said firmly.

"You will receive no complaints from me," Nathaniel responded as he resumed walking down the pavement. "How is it that you are so acquainted with Miss Dinah and her sister?"

"We grew up on neighboring country estates," Haddington said. "Evie and I were rather close when we were younger."

"But not anymore?"

"Sadly, Evie and I grew apart after I went to Eton," Haddington revealed. "I always thought we would grow up, get married, and have a horde of children running around."

Nathaniel glanced over at him. "I couldn't imagine that."

Haddington gave him a sad smile. "Apparently, neither could Evie."

"Have you attempted to court her?"

"No," Haddington said with a shake of his head. "Evie has not given me any indication that she would welcome my advances."

"Women are a fickle lot."

"That they are, but Evie has a strong head on her shoulders," Haddington revealed. "She is clever and quick witted."

"Much like her sister."

"I won't disagree with you there," Haddington said. "Stubbornness also runs in that family."

"I am well aware."

Haddington chuckled. "When Evie was younger, she begged her parents for a dog, but they refused her," he shared. "So, she had a groom carve her a dog from a piece of wood and put a string around it, then dragged it all over the village, pretending it was her pet."

"What an odd thing to do."

"She even named it."

"She did?"

Haddington nodded solemnly. "She called it Wood Dog."

"Wood Dog?" he repeated. "That isn't very clever."

"She was rather young still."

"Did she ever get a dog?" Nathaniel asked.

Haddington grinned. "In a way," he replied. "Her father acquired hunting dogs, and that seemed to appease her. She used to sneak treats to them in their cages. It infuriated Lord Gladstone."

"I can imagine, since hunting dogs are bred and trained for a specific purpose."

"That is precisely what Lord Gladstone would tell Evie when he caught her," Haddington said, "but that didn't stop her. Nothing can stop Evie when she sets her mind on something. It is one of the things that I admire most about her."

"Do you think Evie disappeared of her own accord?" Nathaniel asked.

Haddington sobered. "I don't know, but Evie always has a reason behind everything."

"That is what worries me," Nathaniel said as he put his hand up to signal a hackney.

Dinah anxiously watched the long clock in her bedchamber as she waited for the appointed meeting time. She smoothed down the plain dress she had borrowed from Julia. Her hair was pulled back into a tight chignon covered by an unassuming bonnet.

She glanced at her reflection in the mirror and wondered

if Mr. Collier would be impressed with her transformation. She frowned and chided herself. Why did it matter if he was? His opinion should mean nothing to her.

The door opened and Julia stepped in, closing the door behind her. "Your aunt just left to call on Lady Barrington."

"Wonderful."

"I thought so, as well," Julia said. "That should buy you a couple of hours."

"Maybe longer. We both know how my aunt loves to gossip with Lady Barrington."

The long clock chimed, alerting them of the time. A thrill coursed through Dinah, excitement mixed with apprehension.

Julia's brow was furrowed. "Are you sure I can't talk you out of this?"

"I'm afraid not."

"Then I wish you luck."

"Thank you," Dinah said as she walked towards the door. "I will be fine." She hoped she sounded more confident than she felt.

"Do you have your muff pistol?"

Dinah held up the reticule around her wrist. "I do."

Julia cocked her head. "May I ask you a question?"

"You may."

"Why are you putting your trust in a man you hardly know?" Julia asked.

"I'm not."

Julia frowned. "You are attending a rally with Mr. Collier, someone you know nothing about."

"He is a Bow Street Runner."

"Not all Bow Street Runners are honorable."

"Mr. Collier is."

"How can you be so sure?"

Dinah was silent a moment. "I can't explain it, but I do trust Mr. Collier." Julie didn't have to know about her doubts.

"That is a foolish thing to do," Julia said. "You are risking your reputation by attending this rally with him."

"I have to go."

"What if Evie isn't there?"

Dinah shrugged. "I don't rightly know. I haven't thought beyond that."

Julia sighed and opened the door. "You'd better go before Mr. Collier comes to his senses and leaves you behind."

Dinah hurried down the servant's stairs, ignoring the questioning glances she received as she passed by.

Mrs. Lorraine was stirring something in the pot in the kitchen. The short, round cook turned around to face her and gave her an exasperated look.

"Not you, too," Mrs. Lorraine said.

"Pardon?"

Mrs. Lorraine wiped her hands on the white apron she was wearing. "Where are you going?"

"A rally in Winstead Square."

Mrs. Lorraine pressed her lips together. "I assume Mrs. Carter doesn't know."

"She does not."

"I hadn't realized that you were going to follow in your sister's footsteps," Mrs. Lorraine said. "I can't say that I'm surprised."

"You aren't?"

"No, you and your sister have always done things together." Mrs. Lorraine tipped her head towards the door. "Go on, then. I will ensure that door remains unlocked."

"Thank you, Mrs. Lorraine."

Dinah quickly exited the servant's entrance and stood by the road. Her eyes roamed the busy street until she noticed a black hackney parked further up the street.

She cautiously approached it, hoping that this was the hackney she was waiting for. The door opened, and Mr. Collier stepped out, dressed in a worn grey jacket.

"You're late," Mr. Collier said.

"I hope that isn't an issue."

"We almost left you."

"We?" she asked.

A familiar voice came from inside the coach. "I decided to join in on the festivities," Reginald said, his voice entirely too cheerful.

Mr. Collier put his hand out to assist her into the hackney. "We need to get you off the street," he advised.

She slipped her hand into his and stepped inside. She sat across from Reginald and attempted to ignore the pungent smell within the hackney.

Mr. Collier entered and sat next to Reginald. The hackney jerked forward, and Dinah glanced between the two men.

"May I ask how you two are acquainted?" she asked as she shifted on the uncomfortable bench.

"That is a good question," Reginald replied slowly, as if he was trying to buy some time. "After all, it is not every day that someone from Society is friends with a Bow Street Runner."

"No, it isn't," Dinah agreed.

Mr. Collier spoke up. "Lord Haddington hired me when he suspected that one of his servants was stealing from him."

"That's awful," Dinah said. "Was the case resolved?"

"It was, to everyone's satisfaction," Mr. Collier confirmed, "and Lord Haddington and I discovered that we share a love of boxing."

Dinah furrowed her brow. "Boxing?" she asked, turning her attention to Reginald. "I thought you detested the sport."

"Not anymore, apparently," Reginald said curtly. "Where did you get the dress?"

"It's my lady's maid's," Dinah replied, surprised by the abrupt change of topic.

"And the bonnet?" Reginald asked.

Dinah reached up and fingered the strings of the bonnet. "It's my lady's maid's, as well."

Mr. Collier nodded approvingly as he gave her a sweeping glance. "You did well," he said. "With any luck, no one will pay you any heed."

"I do hope that is the case," Dinah replied.

The hackney rolled to a stop, and Dinah glanced out the window to see a large crowd gathered in Winstead Square.

The men exited, and Reginald extended his hand back to assist her out of the coach. She noticed that Mr. Collier's alert eyes were fixed firmly on the growing crowd.

Mr. Collier turned back around to face her, his face grim. "This was a bad idea, you coming."

"Well, I'm here now," Dinah replied. "We should make the most of the situation."

Mr. Collier extended his arm towards her. "You will stay between Haddington and me the entire time."

"I can agree to that," Dinah said, feeling oddly safe being so close to Mr. Collier.

Reginald pointed towards the stage erected in the front of the square. "We should try to make our way up front."

"That might be an impossible feat," Mr. Collier said. "There are too many people here, and they all seem to be clambering to do the same."

"We have to try, assuming we want to hear the speaker," Reginald remarked.

As they slowly made their way towards the front of the square, Dinah couldn't help but notice the men and women in the crowd around her. Their faces were pale and drawn, and their clothes were dirty and crumpled. No one seemed to give her any heed, and she remained close to Mr. Collier and Reginald.

Reginald stopped near the front of the square and turned to face them. "This should be good," he said.

A burly man pushed past her, not bothering to apologize. Dinah found herself leaning closer to Mr. Collier, drawing strength from him.

"You're safe with me," Mr. Collier assured her. "Just do everything I tell you to, when I tell you to do it."

"I will."

Mr. Collier met her gaze. "Do you see your sister?"

Dinah rose onto her tiptoes and scanned the crowd. "I don't," she said dejectedly.

"Just keep a look out," Mr. Collier advised.

"I will." Her eyes strayed towards the stage, and she saw Lord Barnwell sitting there next to a man she wasn't familiar with. "Who is that sitting next to Lord Barnwell?"

"It must be the orator, John Tilbury," Mr. Collier replied.

"What is the purpose of this rally?"

"I'm not sure," Mr. Collier responded. "The handbills were rather vague, but I have a feeling we're about to find out."

Mr. Tilbury rose from his seat next to Lord Barnwell and addressed the crowd. "Thank you to all of you for attending this rally," he said. "I hope that I don't need to remind you that we aim to keep this nonviolent. We do not want to give the constable any reason to disperse us."

Mr. Tilbury gestured towards Lord Barnwell. "I would like to thank Lord Barnwell for his attendance, giving this rally some credence." Mr. Tilbury began pacing the stage as he spoke. "We are at war with Napoleon, and we are at war as a country. No one is happy with the way that the Tories are handling the government. Yet they still remain in power. How is that possible? Does the power not belong to the people?"

"Hear, hear," a few men in the crowd murmured.

Mr. Tilbury stopped pacing and looked intently into the crowd. "We are not asking for much," he continued. "We just want the prime minister to sympathize with our plight. He lives in his spacious townhouse while we can scarcely afford the rising costs of bread and other basic necessities.

"Lord Barnwell sympathizes with us, as do the other

Whigs," Mr. Tilbury shouted. "They have not abandoned us like the Tories have."

A movement in the crowd caught Dinah's attention, and she turned her head towards it. She couldn't quite get a good look at the person, as they had a brown cape pulled over their head, but she noticed that their hand was moving slowly down the length of their brown cloak. The hand disappeared for a moment and then it reappeared with a pistol.

Dinah was about to turn to warn Mr. Collier when the hood slipped slightly, revealing her sister.

Evie.

Why had her sister brought a pistol to the rally?

Dinah watched in horror as Evie raised the pistol up, taking aim at the stage.

"Evie!" Dinah shouted.

Her sister turned her head as she fired, her eyes wide.

As the sound of the shot rang through the square, shrieks filled the air and people started pushing and shoving, trying to escape the crowd and the unseen danger. Mr. Collier grabbed her arm. "We have to get out of here, now!"

"No!" Dinah shouted, jerking her arm back.

"What?"

Dinah shifted to face Mr. Collier. "My sister is here!"

"Where?" he asked, his eyes scanning the crowd.

Dinah turned towards where she'd last seen her sister, but saw she wasn't there anymore. "Evie was right there," she pointed, frantically looking around. Lord Barnwell was being ushered off the stage, holding his bloody arm with his other hand, and the rest of the square was utter chaos.

"It isn't safe for you here," Mr. Collier declared. "We need to leave."

"But—"

"I agree with Collier," Reginald asserted. "If we remain here, we might get trampled."

He had barely uttered his words when someone plowed his

shoulder into the side of her, knocking her backwards. Mr. Collier grabbed her before she fell to the ground and kept a tight hold on her. "Are you going to come willingly, or do I have to throw you over my shoulder?"

"I'll go."

He grabbed her arm and led her through the panicked crowd. Dinah tried to look for Evie, but she could barely move fast enough to keep up with Mr. Collier's swift pace.

Mr. Collier loosened his hold on her arm as they broke through the crowd, but he didn't stop until they arrived at a hackney. "Get inside," he ordered as he opened the door wide.

She obeyed, and Reginald and Mr. Collier sat across from her, their eyes ablaze.

Mr. Collier spoke first. "Did you truly see your sister?"

"I did."

"Where?"

"She was there, wearing a brown cloak, and…" Her voice stuck in her throat. She couldn't admit to a Bow Street Runner that Evie had attempted to kill Lord Barnwell. She'd be arrested and then sent to the gallows. No, Dinah couldn't reveal the truth. She had to protect her sister.

"And?" Mr. Collier prodded.

Dinah brought a hand up to her head. "I saw her there, in the crowd."

"Are you sure?" Mr. Collier asked. "After all, there were a lot of people."

"I know my sister, sir," Dinah declared firmly.

Reginald put his hand up. "We don't dispute that," he said, turning his attention towards Mr. Collier. "Do we?"

"No," Mr. Collier grumbled as the coach started rolling down the street. "I knew you attending a rally was madness. You could have been seriously injured."

"But I wasn't," Dinah insisted.

"Thank heavens for that," Reginald said. "Did Evie see you?"

"Yes."

"Do you believe she was there of her own free will?" Reginald questioned.

Dinah nodded slowly as she reluctantly admitted, "I do."

Reginald let out a deep, heartfelt sigh. "What is Evie about?"

"I don't know," Dinah muttered as she turned her attention towards the cracked window. She had no desire to continue this conversation. Her heart was breaking. Not only had her sister left her, but she almost killed someone.

One thing had been made abundantly clear: she didn't know her sister at all.

Chapter Eleven

Dinah held back tears and attempted to ignore the concerned looks Reginald and Mr. Collier were tossing her way. She knew they meant well, but she didn't want their pity. She just wanted to be home.

Luckily, they'd finally arrived there. Reginald bid Dinah farewell, and Mr. Collier exited and extended his hand back towards her. Dinah placed her hand in his and stepped down. "Thank you," she murmured as she slipped her hand out of his.

"Are you all right, Miss Dinah?" Mr. Collier asked.

"I will be."

"There is no shame in admitting that you aren't."

"You don't need to fret about me, Mr. Collier," she said firmly.

Mr. Collier's eyes were compassionate, but he didn't press again. "Would it be permissible if I called upon you tomorrow?"

"You may, but for what purpose?" she asked. "It's evident that my sister wasn't abducted."

"True, but that doesn't mean she isn't in some sort of trouble."

Dinah stiffened. "Why do you say that?" she asked hesitantly.

"It's an impression I have."

Dinah took a step back. "I should be going."

"Of course." Mr. Collier bowed his head. "Good day, Miss Dinah."

"Good day, Mr. Collier," she responded before turning towards the servant's entrance. She opened the door and stepped inside the kitchen.

Mrs. Lorraine glanced up from kneading bread. "You're back," she said, clearly relieved. "I've been worrying about you."

"There was no need," Dinah replied. "I was perfectly safe."

Mrs. Lorraine didn't appear convinced. "Would you care for a bath?" she asked.

"That would be heavenly."

"Then I shall see to warming the water for you," Mrs. Lorraine said. "I'll also send up those biscuits you love so much."

"Thank you," Dinah responded as she walked towards the stairs.

Dinah made her way to her bedchamber, fighting tears the whole way. How could her sister do this to her? Evie had left as if she meant nothing to her.

She had just reached for her door's handle when Aunt Nancy's voice reached her from further down the hall. "Dinah," she said sternly, "where have you been?"

Dinah turned to face her aunt as she swiped at a rogue tear. "Evie left us," she murmured. "She left us."

Aunt Nancy came to stand in front of her, searching her face. "It would be best if we had this conversation in private," she stated as she opened the door.

Dinah followed her aunt into the room and closed the door behind her.

Aunt Nancy walked over to the settee at the base of the bed and said, "Come have a seat and explain to me what has happened."

Dinah walked over to the settee and sat down next to her aunt. "I searched Evie's room and found a handbill for a rally in Winstead Square today. I thought it would be a good place to search for her."

"I see," her aunt said. "I must assume that is where you were today, dressed like that."

"It was."

Aunt Nancy pursed her lips. "Did you go by yourself?"

"No, Mr. Collier and Lord Haddington escorted me."

"I shall have a word with Reginald, then."

"Please don't be angry with him—with either of them," Dinah encouraged. "I was adamant about attending, despite Mr. Collier trying to talk me out of it."

"A rally is no place for a lady. What if you had been seen?"

"That's why I wore this dress," Dinah explained. "I borrowed it from Julia, and I can assure you that no one gave me any heed."

"Let's hope that proves to be true."

"It is true," Dinah asserted. "Furthermore, Mr. Collier and Reginald ensured that I remained safe."

"Thank heavens for that."

Dinah untied the ribbon from her bonnet. "I saw Evie."

Her aunt's brows flew up. "You did?"

"I did," she replied. "She was a short distance away from me in the crowd, wearing a brown cloak."

"Did you speak to her?"

"I called out to her, but only after I saw her remove a pistol from her cloak. She aimed at Lord Barnwell, and that's when I shouted her name."

"What happened next?"

"Evie met my gaze, and I could see that she was surprised

to see me," Dinah shared. "Frankly, it happened so quickly, I feared that I had imagined it at first."

"Did she kill Lord Barnwell?" Aunt Nancy whispered with a hand over her mouth.

"She didn't," Dinah replied. "She only wounded him."

"Why would Evie try to kill Lord Barnwell?"

"I don't know."

"This doesn't make any sense."

Dinah felt the tears forming in her eyes again. "I agree," she replied. "I keep telling myself the same thing."

"There must be a mistake."

"I'm afraid not," Dinah said. "I know what I saw."

"Did anyone else witness Evie's actions?"

"I'm not sure."

Aunt Nancy rose and walked over to the window. "If anyone saw her, she is ruined," she hesitated a moment before finishing the thought, "we are ruined."

"I am well aware of the repercussions."

"Did you see where Evie went?"

"After the shot was fired, the square turned chaotic, and Mr. Collier escorted me to an awaiting hackney."

Her aunt gave her a disbelieving look. "You rode in a hackney?"

"I did."

"What possessed you to do such a thing?"

"I wanted to find Evie."

"And look what good it did," Aunt Nancy said, tossing up her arms. "You witnessed her trying to kill Lord Barnwell!"

"If I hadn't interceded, she would have killed him, I'm sure of it."

Her aunt shook her head dejectedly. "I'm sorry," she said. "I'm afraid my emotions are getting the best of me. I have no right to yell at you."

"I can understand why you did."

Her aunt walked back over to the settee and sat down. "I don't know how to fix this," she remarked softly.

"Neither do I."

"We must keep this between us," her aunt asserted. "With any luck, Evie will come to her senses soon and come home."

"I hope so."

"I don't know what is going through your sister's head right now, but I am worried about her."

Dinah swiped at the tears that were now falling unchecked down her cheeks. "As am I," she said. "I thought I knew Evie, but I have come to realize I know very little about her."

"One thing that will always remain constant is how much she loves you."

"If that's the case, then why did she leave me?"

Aunt Nancy sighed. "I can't answer that, but at least we know she meant to disappear."

"It would have been much simpler if she had eloped to Gretna Green."

"That it would have," her aunt agreed with a hint of a smile on her lips.

A knock came at the door, interrupting their conversation.

"Come in," Dinah ordered.

Julia stepped into the room and announced, "The water for your bath is ready, Miss."

Her aunt rose. "That is my cue to leave," she said. "Enjoy your soak."

"How in the blazes did this happen?" Merritt demanded. "Do you understand the repercussions if Lord Barnwell had been killed?"

"I do," Nathaniel replied.

"Your actions say otherwise," Merritt said dryly. "You took Miss Dinah along to the rally instead of doing your job."

"That has nothing to do with this."

Merritt narrowed his eyes. "Did you see who fired at Lord Barnwell?"

"No."

Turning his attention towards Haddington, Merritt asked, "How about you?"

Haddington shook his head. "I didn't, either."

"Why was that?" Merritt asked pointedly. "Perhaps it was because you were both distracted by Miss Dinah."

"I admit that I was concerned for her welfare—" Nathaniel started.

"Yet you took her anyway," Merritt finished.

"She was persistent."

"You have to do better than that, Hawthorne," Merritt stated.

Nathaniel shifted in his seat. "It is evident that Miss Dinah's older sister, Evie, is somehow connected to this investigation."

"Did Miss Ashmore attend the rally?" Merritt asked.

"Miss Dinah claimed she saw her briefly before the shot was fired, but she disappeared back into the crowd," Nathaniel replied.

"It would appear that Miss Ashmore did not wish to be seen."

"That is my thought, as well."

Merritt leaned back in his chair and considered him for a moment. "Why entertain Miss Dinah at all?" he asked.

"I believe she has further insight in the case that she might not be aware of."

"Such as?"

"Miss Dinah knows her sister better than anyone," Nathaniel said. "With any luck, she may be able to help me track down Miss Ashmore."

"That is a big 'if'. What will happen when you find Miss Ashmore?"

"I will question her about Rutledge and their shared connection to the rally."

"And if she knows nothing?"

"It can't be a coincidence that her name appeared on that paper in his room."

Merritt frowned. "I want you to proceed with caution when you find Miss Ashmore," he said. "Her father, Lord Gladstone, was a friend of mine, and I will not tolerate any unnecessary force against her."

"I have no intention of torturing her, if that is your concern."

"Good," Merritt responded. "Miss Ashmore is still a lady and should be treated accordingly."

Nathaniel cocked his head. "I've never known you to go soft on anyone before."

"It is different with Miss Ashmore."

"In what regard?"

Rather than answer his question, Merritt reached for a piece of paper and asked, "Have you made any progress with Abrams and the Red Ravens?"

"I've been invited to a meeting tonight."

"That's promising," Merritt said. "Do try to avoid getting yourself killed."

"Thank you for the vote of confidence."

Merritt picked up a quill and signed his name to the paper in his hand. "Once we discover the full extent of their plan, we can arrest them and deport the miserable lot."

"I fear they are aiming to kill the prime minister."

Merritt put the quill back in the inkpot. "That is a serious allegation. What proof do you have of that?"

"Nothing written, but Abrams has waxed poetic about the man."

"It is illegal to run one's mouth, especially if there is a potential threat on the prime minister's life."

Haddington spoke up. "Should we be keeping an eye on Lord Liverpool?"

Merritt nodded. "I will assign an agent to guard him—discreetly, of course," he said. "I refuse to lose another prime minister on our watch."

"No one could have foreseen Spencer Perceval's death. His murderer acted alone, after all," Haddington remarked.

"He had to have spoken to someone about his intent," Merritt said. "It was a failure on our part not to have uncovered the plot before it was too late, and we were fortunate that his death didn't cause an uprising."

Merritt waved his hand in front of him. "You are both dismissed," he said, "unless there is something else you would like to report."

Nathaniel rose. "I'll send word after the meeting tonight."

"See that you do," Merritt said gruffly. "I don't have time for incompetence."

After they left Merritt's office, Nathaniel glanced over at Haddington. "Did you find it odd that Merritt was rather protective of Miss Ashmore?"

"I do," Haddington replied. "Lady or not, he is always determined to root out the answers, by any means necessary."

"Agreed."

They exited the building and started down the street. "If Miss Ashmore was at the rally, that means she disappeared for a reason," Nathaniel said.

"What would that be?" Haddington asked.

"You know her better than me. Why would she just desert her sumptuous townhouse and attend a rally in Winstead Square by herself days later?"

"How do you know she was by herself?"

"Good point. I didn't actually see her," he said. "I do believe Miss Dinah knows more than she is letting on."

"Why do you say that?"

Nathaniel glanced over at him. "She became distant when we asked about seeing her sister," he shared. "It's like she was holding back about something."

"It was a painful subject."

"True, but there was more to it."

Haddington gave him an amused look. "Maybe you are just looking for reasons to call on Dinah?"

Nathaniel felt his jaw clench. "Why would I do such a thing?"

"You seemed very attentive to her today."

"There is nothing going on between Miss Dinah and myself," Nathaniel asserted. "I am just using her for information."

Haddington put his hands up in surrender. "Forget I said anything."

"I will, because it was quite ludicrous," Nathaniel said. "Miss Dinah is innocent in all this, and if you must know, I find her to be quite maddening."

"I do think you protest too much," Haddington joked.

"Regardless, I have no desire to wed."

"I never said anything about marriage."

Nathaniel stopped on the street and put his hand up to hail a hackney. "This conversation is over. I do not wish to continue speaking about Miss Dinah."

Haddington chuckled. "You are the one who keeps mentioning her."

A black hackney stopped in front of Nathaniel and he shouted up the address of his townhouse. He turned back to Haddington and said, "If you will excuse me, I have a meeting I need to prepare for tonight."

"I wish you luck," Haddington remarked before continuing down the street.

Nathaniel stepped into the hackney and closed the door. What a ridiculous notion, that he looked for reasons to call on

Miss Dinah. Haddington had it all wrong. Miss Dinah meant nothing to him.

Her image came to mind, and he thought about the dimple that appeared on the right side of her mouth when she smiled. She was a beautiful young woman, but that didn't mean he was interested in pursuing her. He was content with how his life was going, and he didn't want to complicate it by taking a wife, no matter how appealing a life with Miss Dinah sounded.

Chapter Twelve

Nathaniel walked down the narrow street towards the Rotten Rabbit, skirting piles of manure. The tavern was in a shabby part of town, where the dilapidated buildings were darkened, many falling in on themselves. He took notice of the men loitering near doorways, and he knew he needed to be prepared for a fight. This was not a place to let his guard down, for any reason.

To appear that he was down on his luck, he was dressed in a worn brown jacket, a blue waistcoat, and trousers. His boots had holes along the top and the soles, making walking on the cobblestone deucedly uncomfortable.

As he approached the Rotten Rabbit, a man staggered out of the establishment and barged right into him.

"Watch where you're going," the man growled drunkenly.

Not wanting to start a fight, Nathaniel took a step back and let the man pass by. He watched as the man walked a few feet, then leaned over and emptied the contents of his stomach on the road. Once he was done, he wiped his mouth with the back of his hand and continued walking down the street.

Nathaniel headed into the tavern and saw the square hall

was filled with boisterous patrons. Serving wenches were walking around the tables with drinks in their hands. As he scanned the hall, Nathaniel was surprised to see Haddington at one of the tables, surrounded by a rough-looking group of men.

Haddington met his gaze and raised his tankard slightly towards him before turning back to his companions.

An older, dark-haired serving wench approached him. "Don't be shy," she said cheerily. "Pull up a chair, and I'll get you something to drink."

"I'm meeting someone here."

"And who might that be?"

"Abrams."

The serving wench pointed towards a door at the far end. "His group meets in the back."

He pulled out a coin and extended it towards the woman. "Thank you."

The woman accepted the coin and slipped it into the pocket of her gown. She stepped closer and lowered her voice. "If I were you, I wouldn't go back there."

"Why not?"

"You seem like a decent bloke, and Abrams is not."

"No?"

The serving wench took a step back. "If you were smart, you would turn around and never come to this tavern again."

"I'm afraid Abrams is expecting me."

She frowned. "Then off you go," she said before spinning back around. He'd clearly been dismissed.

Nathaniel made his way around the tables to the door in the back. He opened the door and stepped inside. Everyone in the room turned towards him.

"Do come in!" Abrams encouraged, rising from his seat at one of the tables.

Nathaniel looked around the small, dimly lit room, counting ten men seated around the three round tables. A crackling fire in the hearth at the front of the room provided most of the light, with only a lone candlestick in the middle of each table. There was another door; based on the size of the tavern, Nathaniel presumed it led outside.

Abrams pulled out a chair for him. "We've been waiting for you."

"You have?"

"Yes, and I've been telling everyone all about you."

"That can't be a good thing," Nathaniel remarked as he sat down.

Abrams chuckled, putting his hands on the back of the chair. "Now that you're here, we can begin," he said. "I would introduce you, but we don't use names here. We have agreed that it's much safer for everyone involved."

"What exactly are we involved in?"

Abrams' eyes hardened. "We intend to assassinate Lord Liverpool."

The only noise that followed was the crackling of the fire in the hearth.

A tall man spoke up from another table. "That wasn't part of the plan."

"It is now," Abrams said, turning to face the man. "Do you take issue with it?"

"I do," the man replied. "We could be transported for even thinking about such things and drawn and quartered if convicted."

Abrams walked to a door that led to the alleyway and opened it. "You are free to go, then."

The man rose from the table and walked over to the door. "I hope there's no hard feelings, but I have a wife and unborn babe to consider first."

"I understand," Abrams said.

The man left, and a brawny man with a prominent scar on his chin rose from his chair. He suspected that must be the man who had gone to Rutledge's boarding house for information.

Abrams removed a pistol from the waistband of his trousers and extended it towards the man. "Go get him."

The brawny man accepted the pistol and hurried through the door into the alleyway.

Once the door was shut, Abrams turned his attention towards the group. "Is there anyone else who takes issue with what we are planning?"

Everyone was silent, and a few shook their heads.

"Good," Abrams said, "because this is bigger than any of us." He reached into the pocket of his jacket and pulled out a piece of paper. "I have been given Lord Liverpool's schedule. We just have to determine the perfect time to kill him."

Abrams slapped the paper down on the table. "We aren't alone in this," he reassured them. "Once Lord Liverpool is dead, the people will rise up, and it will be our time to rule."

"Hear, hear," a few men called.

"Now, I know it was a surprise when someone tried to kill Lord Barnwell at the rally earlier today, and I assure you that that person will pay for their actions," Abrams asserted, "but this does not alter our course. If anything, it solidifies it."

Abrams raised his hands above his head. "Drink up, men!" he encouraged. "We are on the cusp of a new era for England!"

The men turned to their drinks and the group broke up into smaller conversations. The door opened, and the brawny man stepped back into the room. He met Abrams's gaze and nodded once, a gesture Abrams returned. The man returned to his seat and picked up his tankard, apparently unperturbed by whatever he had just done.

Abrams sat next to Nathaniel. "I saw you at the rally earlier today."

"You did?"

"I did," Abrams said. "I was even more surprised that you were accompanied by the lovely Miss Dinah Ashmore."

Nathaniel felt dread make a knot of his stomach. "You are familiar with Miss Dinah?"

"I am. She frequents my shop, as does her sister." Abrams took a sip of his drink. "Although, I almost didn't recognize her in that plain dress. It was quite unflattering to her figure. Don't you agree?"

"I have no opinion on the matter."

Abrams looked amused. "You two appeared quite close," he remarked. "How is it that a man like you has landed a woman like Miss Dinah?"

Nathaniel bristled. "I have not landed her."

"You should," Abrams said, nudging him with his shoulder.

"If you must know, I worked for her once. I was assigned to the stables, but I was let go a few months ago."

"Because of your relationship?" Abrams pressed.

"We have no relationship."

Abrams shrugged. "That's not what it looked like to me. I sure would hate for harm to befall Miss Dinah, wouldn't you?"

"I would."

"Then you will do precisely what I tell you to do," Abrams said, his voice hardening on the threat. "If not, I will kill you and Miss Dinah."

Nathaniel met Abrams' gaze. "What would you have me do?"

Abrams smirked. "I want you to kill Lord Liverpool."

The sun had risen long ago, but Dinah still sat in her bedchamber, staring out the window. She was still trying to make sense of what she saw at the rally. She didn't want to accept that everything was how it seemed. Something felt off, and she wasn't quite sure what that was.

What she did know for certainty was that her sister had tried to kill Lord Barnwell. But why? What would cause her to do such a thing?

Dinah sighed. Evie was out there somewhere, and she would do anything to speak to her. No matter what happened, she still loved her sister. That would never change.

Someone knocked on the door, and she turned at the sound. "Come in."

The door opened, and Sarah stepped in. "Mr. Collier has come to call, miss," the young maid informed her. "Are you available for callers?"

"I am."

Sarah acknowledged her words with a tip of her head. "I shall see that he waits for you in the drawing room."

"Thank you." Dinah rose and smoothed out her white gown. Aunt Nancy had insisted that she at least get out of bed and dress, even if she didn't take part in her usual pursuits. She exited her bedchamber and headed down to the main level.

Mr. Collier was gazing out the window when she arrived in the drawing room.

"Good morning," she greeted.

Mr. Collier turned to face her, and she could immediately see that something was wrong. "What's happened?" she asked.

"Nothing," Mr. Collier was quick to say, followed by a more hesitant, "yet."

"What does that mean?"

Mr. Collier glanced at the maid in the corner before asking, "May we speak somewhere privately?"

"We could take a tour of the gardens."

"That would be preferable." Mr. Collier approached and offered his arm. "Allow me to escort you."

"I appreciate that."

They walked in silence towards the rear of the townhouse, and a footman opened the door, then discreetly followed them onto the veranda.

Once they were walking along the lined path, Dinah removed her arm from Mr. Collier's and asked, "Has something happened to Evie?"

"Not that I am aware of, but that isn't why I am here."

Dinah eyed him curiously. "Why are you here, then?"

Mr. Collier's face became stony. "I came to tell you that your life may be in danger."

"Pardon?" Had she misheard him?

Mr. Collier stopped and turned to face her. "Someone saw us at the rally together, and now they are threatening to harm you if I don't do something for them."

"Which is?"

"I'm afraid I can't tell you."

"Who saw us?"

"I can't tell you that either."

Dinah frowned. "Then what *can* you tell me?"

"I'm afraid not much more than I already have."

"You haven't told me much."

"I am aware."

Dinah put a hand on her hip. "You need to do better than that," she said. "You can't expect me to take you seriously if you are not forthcoming with information."

Mr. Collier's gaze left hers for a moment. "I'm not in a position to tell you more."

"What does that mean?"

"My recommendation is that you remain at your townhouse for the time being," Mr. Collier advised. "Do not go out for any reason."

"For how long?"

"Until I sort out this mess."

Dinah shook her head. "I don't believe that is necessary. Footmen accompany me wherever I go."

Mr. Collier stood completely still and observed her. "Two footmen will not be able to protect you from these men," he said in a tone that brooked no argument. "Stay in your town-house until I tell you otherwise."

Dinah wasn't ready to concede, not without more information. "I do not think that is necessary."

"Are you in earnest?" Mr. Collier asked. "Did you not hear what I just said?"

"I did, but you have told me little else."

Mr. Collier ran a hand through his blonde hair. "These men that I am speaking of will kill you without any hesitation."

"Why are you associating with these men?"

"That is my job," Mr. Collier said.

"Perhaps it is time to find a new job," she snapped.

Mr. Collier didn't appear amused. "I don't expect you to understand what I do, but I do want you to understand the dire situation you are in."

"Is my aunt in danger, as well?"

"Yes," Mr. Collier replied. "Anyone who is close to you can be used to get to you."

Dinah let her hand fall from her hip. "Will you at least tell me why I am being threatened?"

Mr. Collier shifted in his stance, looking uncomfortable. "The person who saw us together assumed that we hold each other in high regard."

"Why would they believe that?"

"I don't know, but it was clearly a misconception."

"That it was."

Mr. Collier grew silent as he took in the scenery. "You have a lovely garden."

"Thank you," Dinah said. "It was my mother's creation, but the work wasn't completed until after her death."

"That is most unfortunate."

"It is." Dinah pointed towards an iron bench in the back

of the gardens. "Whenever I want to be close to my mother, I go sit on that bench. I used to spend hours there, but I don't go as often anymore."

Mr. Collier looked introspective as he shared, "My grandfather used to love fly fishing. Sometimes I go to the river that he used to frequent and just stand at the water's edge. It brings back a wave of pleasant memories."

"How long ago did he pass?"

"Oh, it was many years ago," Mr. Collier said.

"That doesn't make it any easier, does it?"

"No, but the passage of time does heal the deep wounds from his loss. I have come to realize that death is a necessary part of life."

"I wasn't prepared for my parent's death," Dinah admitted.

"I should think no one is."

Dinah felt tears prick in the back of her eyes. "They were taken much too soon," she said. "I wish I could go back in time and spend even a moment with them." She paused. "I don't remember their voices anymore."

"That must be hard."

"Yes," Dinah responded as a tear escaped and ran down her cheek. She reached up to wipe it away. "On the day that my parents left for the last time, I was too busy to say goodbye."

"What were you doing?"

She let out a puff of air. "A watercolor painting on the lawn," she replied. "They were only supposed to be gone for a few days, and I couldn't be bothered to stop what I was doing."

"You couldn't have predicted what would happen."

"No, but it made me look at what was important in my life."

"What did you conclude?"

Dinah gave him a weak smile. "There are many distractions in life, and even though many of them are worthwhile, they don't truly matter. The only thing that binds us together is family."

"That is an astute observation."

"Do you not agree?"

Mr. Collier winced. "I'm afraid I am not a part of a tightly-knit family."

"You should change that."

"I don't think that's possible," Mr. Collier admitted. "My brother is a gambler, and my parents, albeit kind, aren't known for their warm dispositions."

"If you want something to change, you must first change yourself."

"I agree, but I'm afraid I don't have time to do such a thing."

"Is being a Bow Street Runner so important?" Dinah asked.

"My job keeps England safe."

"I have no doubt that you do so admirably, but you must live each day as if it could be your last."

Mr. Collier smirked. "I assure you that is not an issue."

"I just don't want you to have any regrets."

"I already have too many to count."

Dinah reached out and placed a hand on his sleeve. "You are not alone in that."

"But I am," Mr. Collier said. "My position is such that it is better to be alone."

"Better for whom?"

"For everyone."

"But not for you."

Mr. Collier glanced down at her hand, and she quickly withdrew it. "I have little time to think of myself."

"Then we must change that."

His eyes shot back up to hers. "There is no 'we'," he asserted.

Feeling the warmth in her cheeks at the sheer brazenness of her comment, she rushed out, "I apologize for insinuating—"

Mr. Collier held up his hand, stilling her words. "I think I know what you meant, but, quite frankly, it is much too dangerous to even be associated with me."

"Surely it cannot be as dangerous as you claim."

"Your life is in danger because of me," he reminded her. "There is a reason why I am alone."

Dinah could hear the heartache in his voice and involuntarily stepped closer. "No one is truly alone," she said, tilting her head so she could look up at him. "You just have to know where to look for someone to bolster you up."

"It isn't that simple," he replied as his eyes searched hers. "I have too many secrets."

"Everyone has secrets."

"Not like mine."

Dinah bobbed her head. "You may be right, but that doesn't mean you have to walk your path alone."

"It is much safer if I endure this journey alone," Mr. Collier said, his voice soft but firm. "You must believe this to be true."

"I believe it is what *you* believe."

Mr. Collier's face softened as he watched her, and she thought she had finally gotten through to him, but then he blinked and took a step back. "You are a foolish, naïve girl."

She blinked. "I beg your pardon?" What had just happened?

"I do not wish to take up any more of your time, Miss Dinah," Mr. Collier remarked dismissively. "May I escort you back inside?"

"You may, but—"

"I do not have any more time to dillydally."

Dillydally? Is that what he thought they were doing?

Dinah's back grew rigid, and her words were terse. "There

is no reason to escort me inside. If you would care to leave now, you may do so by the back gate."

"I believe I shall." Mr. Collier started walking away, but spun back around and ordered, "You will not leave your town-house for any reason."

"For how long?"

"Until I tell you that it is safe to do so."

Mr. Collier didn't bother to wait for her response. He left, and Dinah found herself standing there alone, confused. She'd thought the conversation was going well, but clearly, he did not feel the same.

Dinah let out a sigh. Against her greater judgment, her feelings were starting to deepen for the infuriating Bow Street Runner—and it seemed that those feelings would in no way be reciprocated.

Chapter Thirteen

Nathaniel stared out the window of the fetid hackney. How dare he let his guard down with Miss Dinah. He was a spy, and he didn't have time to sit around and discuss his feelings. He had much more important things to do with his time.

So why did he keep finding reasons to be with her? He felt connected to her in a way that he couldn't explain; but that was ludicrous. The less time he spent with Miss Dinah, the better. He needed to put her from his mind and remember that he was just using her for information, and nothing more.

The hackney stopped a few buildings away from headquarters. He stepped out and paid the driver.

As he walked down the pavement, he saw Talbot and Worsley at their cart, holding roses out toward people passing by.

Nathaniel stopped by the cart. "You're selling flowers now?" he asked incredulously.

"We are," Talbot replied. "Would you care to purchase some?"

"Where'd you get the roses?"

Worsley spoke up. "From some bloke that won't even notice they're missing."

"I take it the bread was not a lucrative venture," Nathaniel commented.

"Actually, it was going quite well, but we were garnering too much attention around the building," Talbot revealed. "We decided to switch courses and sell roses."

Nathaniel nodded. "That was wise. Not too many people will buy flowers in these parts."

"Agreed, especially since we are charging a pence per rose," Talbot said.

"That is outlandish!"

"Precisely, which is why no one will be foolish enough to buy them, thus keeping us from having to restock the cart," Talbot explained.

"At least your logic is somewhat sound," Nathaniel said, "but I do contend that you both are simpletons."

Talbot placed a hand on his chest. "You wound me, sir," he declared. "No roses for you."

Nathaniel gave them an amused look. "It is a good thing you two are competent agents."

"That we are," Worsley said, waving a rose in the air.

Talbot nodded. "We might even be the two best agents working for the Crown."

"I agree," Worsley declared. "Not only are we two fine looking gentlemen, but we guard this building with exactness and honor."

"Well said, Worsley," Talbot said.

Nathaniel chuckled. "Heaven help us if either of you are ever called into the field."

Talbot feigned outrage. "You are just jealous of our divinely appointed skills."

"I don't think that is it," Nathaniel remarked.

"It's true," Talbot continued. "Not only can we guard this building, but we can run a business while doing so."

"How much have you earned?" Nathaniel asked.

"We haven't made any money, but we are looking to take on investors," Talbot said. "Are you interested?"

Nathaniel shook his head. "I think it would be a foolish investment for me."

"That is a shame," Talbot responded. "You are missing out on an opportunity."

"As informative as this conversation is, I need to speak to Merritt," Nathaniel said, walking to the door.

Worsley held up a rose. "You could always bring Merritt a flower," he suggested. "It might put him in a better mood."

"I'll take my chances without it," Nathaniel said before he stepped inside of the building.

He tipped his head to acknowledge Mostyn and headed towards Merritt's office, knocking on the door once he reached it.

"Enter."

Merritt was sitting at his desk. "About time you showed up," the spymaster grumbled. "I have been waiting for hours for you to make a report on how the meeting went last night."

"I would have been here sooner, but I stopped and spoke to Worsley and Talbot."

Merritt huffed. "Their flower venture is even more ridiculous than the bread one."

"I agree with you," Nathaniel said.

Merritt pointed towards a chair that sat in front of his desk. "Take a seat," he encouraged. "We have much to discuss."

"That we do," Nathaniel replied as he sat across from the man.

"How'd the meeting go?"

"They intend to assassinate the prime minister, and they want me to do it."

Merritt's brow lifted. "Why would they want you, a newcomer, to do such a thing?"

"It's a fool's errand, since it would ultimately end in my

death, and they care not a whit for me, so no loss there," Nathaniel responded. "Furthermore, they threatened to kill Miss Dinah as well as myself if I didn't do it."

"Why Miss Dinah?"

"Abrams saw us at the rally together and mistakenly believed that we have formed an attachment."

"Have you?"

"No," Nathaniel said through gritted teeth. "I am just using Miss Dinah for information."

Merritt didn't quite look convinced but thankfully let the matter drop. "Now that you've discovered their intent, should we arrest them and be done with this?"

"Not yet. I still haven't discovered the full extent of their plan."

"We could easily arrest Abrams and force him to talk," Merritt said.

"Right now, Abrams believes he has the upper hand with me, and I want to use that to my advantage."

"Fine, but this isn't the only radical group that has nefarious intent. We don't have enough agents to handle all of the potential threats, and I need you to wrap this up quickly so I can assign you to another case."

"I understand, sir."

"Did Abrams explain why they want Lord Barnwell dead?"

"They don't," Nathaniel replied. "They're supportive of Lord Barnwell."

"Then who tried to kill him?"

"I don't know."

Merritt leaned back in his chair. "I spoke to the magistrate, and he informed me that a brown cloak was recovered from Winstead Square."

Nathaniel paused. "Did you say, a brown cloak?"

"Yes. The magistrate believes that whoever tried to kill

Lord Barnwell escaped into the crowd by removing the cloak."

"That would be logical," he acknowledged. "Miss Dinah mentioned that she saw her sister wearing a brown cloak. Surely, it can't be a coincidence."

"I don't believe in coincidences."

"Neither do I," Nathaniel said. "Why would Miss Ashmore want to kill Lord Barnwell?"

"I can't answer that, but you need to go back and question Miss Dinah. It would appear that she is keeping something from you."

"I don't like being lied to."

Merritt smirked. "Says the spy."

"I do see the irony in my statement."

The amusement vanished as Merritt asked, "Have you made any progress in finding Rutledge?"

"I haven't, but I do believe that Miss Ashmore is the key to finding him."

"Then you must find Miss Ashmore."

"That's easier said than done," Nathaniel said.

"Miss Ashmore is a genteel woman. How could she just disappear?"

"I have been asking that same question."

"Perhaps she had help," Merritt suggested.

"That may explain how she disappeared without a trace, but who would help her?" Nathaniel asked, retreating to his own thoughts.

Merritt gave him an expectant look. "Do you expect me to answer that question, agent?"

"No."

"Good," he said. "Go solve this case and report back to me."

Nathaniel rose. "Will do."

Dinah sat on the bench in the back of the gardens and wiped away her tears. All she wanted was to not feel so alone. She was fortunate enough to have her aunt in her life, but the ache in her heart at the departure of her sister and absence of her parents threatened to consume her.

Why did Evie have to leave her? What had she done to deserve such treatment? Evie had left her behind, just as her parents did. Dinah knew she wasn't being rational, but she was so tired of pretending that all was well. She couldn't do it anymore. Her life was crashing down all around her, and she had no one to help pick up the pieces with her.

She looked heavenward. "You said you would never leave me, but you did," she murmured as tears welled up in her eyes again. "You left me, and now I have to face this world without you."

To her surprise, Mr. Collier appeared over the back fence. "Is this a bad time?"

Dinah swiped at the tears streaming down her face. "I'm afraid it is," she replied.

Mr. Collier made no attempt to move. "May I ask who you were talking to?"

"Myself."

"That was evident, but who did you hope would answer?"

Dinah lowered her gaze. "My mother," she admitted. "This is where I come to be close to her."

"I remember you saying as much earlier," Mr. Collier said, walking over to the gate. "May I enter?"

"This really isn't a good time…"

Mr. Collier came through the opening anyway. "You are a damsel in distress, and I am here to assist you."

"I am not in distress," she huffed.

He gave her a look. "You have been crying."

"So I have," she replied defiantly. "It is not uncommon for women to cry."

Mr. Collier approached and stopped a short distance from the bench. "You may be right, but this is different."

"In what way?"

"It was quiet, but I could hear the anguish in your voice, and I cannot in good conscience walk away and leave you be."

Dinah met his gaze. "Why do you care?" she asked.

"I'm not rightly sure, but I feel as if you could use someone to talk to right now," he said. "Am I incorrect in my assumption?"

The compassion in his eyes was undeniable, softening her stance slightly. Swallowing her pride, she admitted, "You are not."

Mr. Collier gestured at the seat next to her. "May I join you?"

"You may," she said, moving to create proper distance.

Once Mr. Collier sat down, he shifted on the bench to face her. "Now, what has you so upset?" he asked, his eyes not straying from her face.

"I was just thinking about my sister," she hesitated, "about how she up and left me of her own accord."

"I know that must be painful, but you don't know her reasons."

Dinah bristled. "Please do not pacify me, sir."

"I'm not trying to," Mr. Collier said. "I'm afraid I am not acquainted with your sister, so I cannot speak to her actions."

"She left me. That is all that you need to know."

Mr. Collier grew silent. "You are angry, and you have every right to be. But you mustn't let your anger consume you."

"Pardon me if I don't take advice from someone who is only a recent acquaintance."

"Then don't," he said. "Continue to wallow in your self-pity until you hardly recognize the woman you've become."

Dinah jumped up from her seat. "How dare you speak to me in such a way!"

Mr. Collier rose slowly. "You left me little choice in the matter. Frankly, it seems to me that you don't want to talk to someone, you just want to argue."

"I think you should go, Mr. Collier," she stated.

He nodded. "I think that might be for the best." He walked over to the gate, opened it, and stopped. "You are not the only one who has lost someone."

"I do not contend that."

"Evie is not gone forever, you know," Mr. Collier said, his voice steady. "I will find her, but I need your help."

"I don't believe she wants to be found."

"That hasn't stopped me before." Mr. Collier closed the gate and turned back around. "It almost seems as if you don't want me to find her anymore."

"I don't," Dinah said. "You are dismissed."

Mr. Collier leaned back against the gate. "Is this because Miss Ashmore tried to shoot Lord Barnwell?"

Dinah's mouth dropped. "How did you know about that?"

"I didn't, until now. I mean, I had my suspicions, but you just confirmed them." He crossed his arms over his broad chest. "What did you see at the rally?"

Dinah pursed her lips together. "I saw nothing."

"I respect that you are trying to protect your sister, but something bigger is going on here," Mr. Collier said.

"And what would that be?" Dinah asked.

"I'm afraid I can't answer that."

"Can't, or won't?"

"I don't see much of a difference between the two."

"Yet you expect me to confide in you?"

Mr. Collier pushed off from the gate. "You need to trust me."

"I've told you before, trust needs to be earned."

He walked forward and stopped in front of her. "There are men that won't be satisfied until your sister is dead."

Her face paled. "Which men?"

"The same dangerous men who threatened you," Mr. Collier explained. "Your sister crossed these men when she pulled that stunt in Winstead Square."

"It was no stunt," Dinah said. "She meant to kill Lord Barnwell."

"How do you know?"

"I saw it in her eyes, but she missed when I called out her name."

Mr. Collier nodded. "You did the right thing."

Dinah bit her lower lip. "I suppose you will want to arrest her once you find her."

"I am actually more interested in speaking to her than arresting her."

"But aren't Bow Street Runners responsible for upholding the law?"

"I am more progressive in my thinking than others in my profession."

"What does that mean?"

Mr. Collier's lips quirked. "I don't always follow the rules."

Dinah studied him for a moment. "You are a complex man."

"I have been called far worse."

"I can assure you that was no insult."

Mr. Collier's eyes roamed her face. "Why is it that you are not married?" he asked. "You are a handsome young woman."

Dinah blinked at the abrupt change of conversation. "Evie isn't married yet," she said.

"Is that the only reason?"

Dinah shook her head. "No one has shown me favor."

"I don't believe that," Mr. Collier scoffed. "You could easily have a line of suitors, if you so desired."

"You flatter me, sir."

"So, what is the real reason?"

Dinah held his gaze. "You'll think me terribly silly."

"I can assure you that I will not."

"If you must know, I want a love match." She tilted her chin, challenging him to criticize her choice.

Mr. Collier nodded. "You deserve that."

"Are you in earnest?"

Mr. Collier grinned. "I don't know why you sound so surprised. It's not as if we are at odds with one another."

"I'm not sure about that at times."

He took a step closer, and she had to tilt her head to see him grin. "Most of it's just good fun, and I only tease those I care about."

"You care about me?" she asked, taken aback.

Mr. Collier visibly stiffened, making her wonder if he had intended to say those words out loud. "I do," he hesitated, "but only as a friend."

"You don't need to be embarrassed. I feel the same way."

He cleared his throat. "That's good," he said, taking a step back. "Now that we've established that, we need to discuss how to find your sister before someone else does."

"I don't know how. I already searched her room, and I only found that advertisement for the rally."

"May I search your sister's room?"

"How do you propose to do that?" Dinah asked. "I know my aunt, and she would never agree to it."

Mr. Collier glanced over her shoulder at the townhouse. "I'll climb up," he replied. "Just tell me which window is hers."

Dinah furrowed her brows. "You're going to climb up the side of the townhouse?"

"That is my intention."

"How do you intend to do such a thing?"

Mr. Collier looked amused by her question. "This won't be the first townhouse I've been forced to climb."

Dinah turned and pointed at Evie's window with a sigh. "It's the third window from the left on the second level."

Mr. Collier followed her gaze. "That should be easy enough, assuming that you leave the window unlocked for me this evening."

"I'll see to it," she replied, bringing her gaze back to meet his.

"Thank you. I prefer it when we work together, not against one another."

"As do I."

Mr. Collier kept watching her, and she felt a warm blush rise to her cheeks. She was so flustered that she failed to hear someone approach from behind her.

"Dinah," Aunt Nancy said, pausing when Dinah visibly startled, "it is time to dress for dinner."

Mr. Collier bowed. "It is a pleasure to see you again, Mrs. Carter."

"Likewise, Mr. Collier," her aunt responded. "Perhaps next time you will make use of our main door."

"I shall." Mr. Collier turned back to Dinah, his expression inscrutable. "Good evening, Miss Dinah."

Dinah watched as Mr. Collier departed from the gardens, disappearing from her view.

"I would be cautious of that man," her aunt warned.

"For what purpose?"

"He is a Bow Street Runner, and therefore is entirely beneath your notice."

Moving to stand next to her aunt, Dinah said, "He is just doing his job."

Her aunt gave her a pointed look. "You are aware that if he finds Evie, he will lock her up for what she did."

"I don't believe that to be the case. He knows what Evie did, and he only wants to speak to her."

"Some men will say anything to achieve their purposes."

"Mr. Collier isn't like that," Dinah asserted.

"Do not be so easily fooled by a wolf in sheep's clothing."

"He is no wolf."

Her aunt didn't appear convinced.

Dinah looped her arm through her aunt's. "I know what I am doing. You must trust me."

"I do trust you," Aunt Nancy said. "It's Mr. Collier I don't trust."

They started walking towards the townhouse, and Dinah hoped that her aunt was wrong and that her faith in Mr. Collier wasn't misplaced.

Chapter Fourteen

The moon was high in the sky as Nathaniel walked down the pavement towards Miss Dinah's townhouse. A line of white mist hung over the cobblestones, and his booted footsteps were the only sound that could be heard on the empty streets.

Despite his thin brown suit doing little to keep out the elements, he was grateful for a cool evening. It gave him time to collect his thoughts, but he found he couldn't stop thinking about Miss Dinah. He'd developed troublesome feelings for her, which he could in no way act upon. He had lied to her, deceived her, and used her for information.

It would be best for him, and Miss Dinah, if he disappeared once this assignment was over. With any luck, their paths would never cross in polite Society, and she would never learn the extent of his deceit.

So why did the thought of pursuing her sound so appealing?

Nathaniel let out a groan. He should be focused on the case, but his thoughts repeatedly returned to Miss Dinah, no matter how hard he tried to banish them. What a mess he'd created for himself. This is how agents get themselves killed, he thought, they get distracted. And Miss Dinah was undeniably a distraction.

Regardless, she thought of him as a lowly Bow Street Runner. Yet she never treated him as inferior to her; quite the contrary, in fact. She had invited him to dine with her and had spoken to him as an equal. She truly was a remarkable young woman.

Blast it! He needed his mind to dwell on something that wasn't Miss Dinah. He could think about his lout of a brother or how his father wanted him to marry.

The sound of a man coughing in the distance drew his attention. Nathaniel reached for the pistol tucked in the waistband of his trousers and brought it down to his side. He wanted to have his weapon handy in case a fight was brought to him.

It wasn't much longer before he arrived at the back gate of Miss Dinah's townhouse, and he tucked the pistol back into his waistband. As quietly as he could, he unlatched the back gate and slipped inside of the gardens. He hurried down the gravel path and came to a stop in the shadows of the townhouse.

Once he was positive that he hadn't been seen, he stepped over to where Miss Ashmore's window was situated above him. He took a moment to determine his course before he placed his hands in the grooves of the bricks and pulled himself up. His boots found places along the bricks that were jutting out, and he nimbly made his way up to the second level.

It didn't take long before he arrived at the window, and he used one hand to slide the window open. A smile tugged at his lips knowing that Miss Dinah had done what she had promised to do.

He pulled himself through the window, and the smile vanished when he saw Miss Dinah sitting on the bed, wearing a simple muslin dress.

"What are you doing here?" he asked in a hushed voice.

"I couldn't very well have you search my sister's room without me being present," she replied, matching his volume.

He wiped the dirt off his trousers. "You will only slow down my search."

"You won't even notice me."

"I doubt that," he muttered.

Miss Dinah rose from the bed and walked closer to him. "I doubt you will find anything. I already did a thorough search of her room."

"Sometimes the most obvious places go undetected."

"Such as?"

Nathaniel ignored her question, his eyes roaming the bedchamber. His eyes landed on the hearth, and, remembering Rutledge's apartment, figured it was a good place to start.

He approached the fireplace, Miss Dinah on his heels. "I already searched there."

"Did you now?" he asked indifferently. He ran his hands along the outside bricks, looking for anything out of the ordinary. When nothing presented itself, he crouched down and ran his hands along the interior. He was just about to give up when he felt a loose brick.

Nathaniel removed the brick and quietly put it down on the floor, then reached up and felt in the opening. He pulled out a bundle of cloth and brought it in front of him.

He unwrapped the cloth, and Miss Dinah gasped. "That's my mother's." She reached for the gold locket and held it up in front of her. "Evie started wearing it shortly after my parents died. She never took it off."

"Then why is it hidden in the fireplace?"

"I can't answer that," Miss Dinah said, her eyes remaining on the locket. "She loved this locket, and I can't believe that she left it behind."

"She may have had little choice in the matter."

"What do you mean?"

"If she was attempting to go unnoticed on the streets of London, a gold locket would draw attention," Nathaniel explained. "She would want to appear as down on her luck as possible."

"How would my sister even know that?"

"Have you considered she may have had help?"

A line between Miss Dinah's brow appeared. "Who would have helped her?"

"I don't know, but it would explain how she was able to disappear so easily," Nathaniel said, "and how she is able to remain hidden."

"None of this makes any sense. Evie is a bluestocking, not a sneak." Miss Dinah gestured towards books on the table near the bed. "Evie loves nothing more than curling up by the fireplace and reading."

His eyes landed on the books. "Have you searched the books yet?"

"No, I haven't."

Nathaniel approached the table and picked up the first book. He opened it up and rifled through the pages.

Miss Dinah came to stand next to him. "What do you hope to find?"

"Anything to aid in the search," Nathaniel replied.

Miss Dinah picked up a book and followed his lead. After a few books, she stopped and said, "I found something." She pulled out a piece of paper and handed it to him.

Nathaniel could see something scribbled on the paper, but there wasn't enough light to read it. He walked over to the window and held it up towards the moon. "The Bradford," he read.

"What's the Bradford?" Miss Dinah asked from behind him.

Nathaniel turned around to face her. "It could mean many

things, but there is a boarding house on Trinity Street with that name. I intend to start there."

"A boarding house?" Miss Dinah asked. "Why would my sister wish to stay there?"

Nathaniel shrugged one shoulder. "Who knows, but I intend to find out."

"May I go with you?" she asked hopefully.

"Absolutely not," he said. "You have done enough." His words came out harsher than he'd intended, but he didn't want to be cajoled, not after what happened at the rally.

"I have hardly done anything."

Nathaniel tucked the paper into the pocket of his waistcoat. "I know this is hard, but you must strive to be patient."

Miss Dinah's eyes dimmed. "I'm afraid that patience is not one of my virtues."

"It doesn't come naturally to me, either," Nathaniel said.

"I just want my sister to come home, where she belongs," she said, seeming to wilt visibly before him.

Nathaniel reached out and put a hand on her sleeve. "You have to be strong. Can you do that?"

Miss Dinah's shoulders slumped. "I've been pretending to be strong for so long now that I don't think I can anymore. I'm afraid it's too much for me to bear."

He pulled her into his arms. He couldn't help it. She stiffened for a moment before relaxing against him and resting her head against his chest. He marveled at the way his arms fit so perfectly around her, as if she had always belonged there.

He rested his chin on top of her head. "You are strong enough to face it even if it doesn't feel like it right now."

"How could you possibly know that?" she asked against his chest.

"I am an excellent judge of character," he replied. "In my profession, my life depends on being able to discern who I can trust."

"You trust me?" she asked, tilting her head to look up at him.

"I would be a fool not to, and I don't trust very easily," he admitted. "It does help that you wear your emotions on your sleeve."

"I have always been a terrible liar."

"That isn't a bad thing."

Miss Dinah held his gaze as she shared, "My aunt believes I should be cautious around you."

"I understand her concern, but do you think you need to be cautious around me?"

"I don't," Miss Dinah replied. "I trust you."

Nathaniel took a silent breath, hoping she couldn't feel the burning in his chest that had appeared out of nowhere. How could he not fall for this young woman?

But it was all built on a lie. She only knew Mr. Collier, the Bow Street Runner. She had no idea he was Nathaniel Calvert, the Earl of Hawthorne.

He dropped his arms and took a step back. "I think it would be best if I depart. If anyone were to discover us together, you would be ruined," he said, "and I have tarried long enough."

Miss Dinah ducked her head. "When will I see you again?"

"I will come by tomorrow after I stop at the Bradford," he replied. "Until then, I do not want you to leave your townhouse for any reason."

"I understand."

"I'm relieved to hear that." Nathaniel put his hand on the windowsill. "Now, go get some rest, and try not to fret about your sister."

"That doesn't seem possible."

"I am well aware, but worrying incessantly about her isn't going to bring her home any faster," he advised.

"True, but it will make me feel better."

He smiled. "Good night, Miss Dinah."

"Good night, Mr. Collier," she replied, her eyes dropping from his eyes to his lips.

Nathaniel knew he needed to leave then or else risk doing something he would regret come morning. Without saying another word, he lowered himself out the window and climbed down the brick wall.

The morning sun streaming into the dining room windows was a direct counterpoint to his father's disgruntled voice in the doorway. "I see you have finally decided to grace us with your presence."

Nathaniel lowered the newssheets and replied, "Good morning, Father."

His father walked further into the room. "Where have you been these past few days?"

"I've been busy."

"Do I dare ask what you have been busy with?"

"The usual pursuits." He folded the paper and set it next to his plate on the table.

His father shook his head. "You have a duty to this family, son. It is time to stop gallivanting and accept your responsibilities."

"I am well aware of what is expected of me."

"I'm not entirely sure that is true," his father replied. "Have you even bothered to review the documents that Mr. Bolton left for you?"

"I did so when I returned home last night."

"What time was that?"

"It was rather late."

His father perused the length of him. "I suspect that you

need a new tailor. Your clothes are all starting to look rather ragged, and I daresay that it is not a good look."

"Duly noted."

His father looked like he had more to say on the matter, but instead he said, "I am needed at the House of Lords today. Do try to get some work done."

"I will."

"And if you see your mother, do try to be especially kind to her," his father advised as he left. "Someone had the nerve to cut all of her roses from the garden, and she is quite upset."

"That is terrible," he muttered. He had a sneaking suspicion of who the culprits were.

Nathaniel pushed back his chair and rose. He headed towards the main door and saw Balfour in the entry hall.

"I am going out," Nathaniel announced.

"Yes, my lord," Balfour replied. "Would you care for your coach to be pulled around front?"

"That won't be necessary. I'll take a hackney."

Balfour tipped his head in response, now used to Nathaniel's odd ways, and opened the main door. Nathaniel stepped outside and walked along the sidewalk until he saw a hackney in the distance. He signaled the driver and was pleased when the conveyance came to a stop in front of him.

"Where to?" the driver asked.

"The Bradford on Trinity Street," he replied. "Are you familiar with it?"

The driver shook his head. "No, but I know where Trinity Street is."

"That's good enough."

Nathaniel opened the door and stepped in the hackney. The hackney merged into traffic, and he opened the broken window, allowing fresh air to circulate in the foul-smelling coach.

It wasn't long before the hackney came to a stop on

Trinity Street. He exited the coach, paid the driver, and walked the short distance towards the boarding house.

A sign denoting the Bradford hung above the door of a three-level brown brick building. He opened the door and stepped into the entry hall, hoping that he would find someone who might be able to answer a few questions.

A woman's voice came from behind him. "May I help you?"

Nathaniel turned around to face an older woman with white hair. It would seem luck was on his side this morning. "Yes, I am looking for someone."

Her expression grew guarded. "And who is that, exactly?"

"My sister," he lied. "She left home, and we haven't been able to locate her."

"Well, she wouldn't be here, because we do not rent to single people," she declared indignantly.

"She may have been traveling with someone."

The woman looked aghast. "We are a respectable establishment, sir," she said firmly. "We do not let our rooms out to unmarried couples."

"I understand." Nathaniel reached into his waistcoat pocket and pulled out a coin. "My sister would have arrived over a week ago, and she has brown hair and green eyes."

The woman accepted the money and slipped it into the pocket of her gown. She stepped closer and lowered her voice. "There was a young woman that matches your description, but she arrived with her father."

"Are they still here?"

"They are," the woman confirmed.

"Will you take me to their room?" he asked, attempting to keep the eagerness out of his tone.

The woman remained rooted in her spot. "That will cost you."

Nathaniel pulled out another coin. "Will this be sufficient?"

The woman snatched it from his hand. "Let's be quick," she said. "If this isn't your sister, then you will be on your way."

"Yes, ma'am."

"And you'd best not make a scene," the woman urged as she started walking down the hall. "It isn't good for business."

She stopped in front of a door and knocked. "Who's there?" a man's gruff voice replied.

"It is just me, Mrs. Stanley," the woman said. "I was hoping for a moment of your time."

"Give me a moment," the man replied, followed by a loud groan.

Mrs. Stanley gave him an expectant look. "You better be right about this."

The door was opened just a crack, but it was enough that Nathaniel immediately recognized the person.

"Rutledge?"

The man opened the door wide, holding his right side. "Hawthorne?"

"I shall leave you to it, then," the woman said before she walked off.

"Come in before anyone sees you," Rutledge urged.

Nathaniel stepped inside of the room, and Rutledge glanced out in the hall before he closed the door. The agent was dressed in a terribly wrinkled white shirt, dark trousers, and black boots. His silver hair was disheveled, and there was dried blood on his fingers.

"How did you find me?" Rutledge asked, closing the door.

"I found a slip of paper with 'the Bradford' written on it in Miss Ashmore's room."

Rutledge walked over to the bed in the corner and sat down, his face grimacing with pain. "Why were you searching her room?"

Rather than answer his question, he said, "You are injured."

"I am."

"Have you consulted with a doctor?"

"I don't have time for quacks."

"Not all doctors are quacks."

"The ones that I can afford are."

"Then I'll send for my doctor."

Rutledge shook his head. "There is no need. Evie is taking care of me."

"Evie?" he asked. "Miss Ashmore is with you?"

"Not at the moment," Rutledge said. "She went out to get some bread."

Nathaniel walked over to the writing desk and pulled out the chair. "I've been looking for Miss Ashmore."

Rutledge grunted. "You're not the only one."

"Yet you let her leave unescorted?"

Rutledge shot him an amused look. "Evie is not one to follow directions. Besides, I am in no position to help, should the situation arise."

"What happened to you?" Nathaniel asked.

The sound of the door being unlocked drew his attention. The door opened, and he immediately recognized Miss Ashmore from the portrait that Miss Dinah had shown him, despite being dressed in a torn and dirtied gown. Her brown hair was pulled back into a loose chignon and her green eyes were alert, attentive.

He had barely risen from his seat when Miss Ashmore pointed a pistol at him.

"Who are you?" she demanded.

"I mean you no harm." He put his hands up in front of him to prove his point.

The pistol didn't waver in Miss Ashmore's hand. "You didn't answer my question."

"My friends call me Hawthorne."

"I am not your friend," Miss Ashmore stated.

Rutledge spoke up. "You can put your pistol down, Evie," he said. "I trust this man with my life."

Nathaniel could see the reluctance in Miss Ashmore's eyes as she lowered the pistol to her side. "Then I won't kill him," she said, "at this time."

"That is a relief," Nathaniel responded, lowering his hands.

Miss Ashmore closed the door behind her and locked it. In her other hand, she held a loaf of bread.

She approached Rutledge and extended the bread. "I know it isn't much, but I didn't dare stray farther than I had to."

"It will do," Rutledge said, accepting the bread. "Have you eaten?"

"I'm not hungry."

Rutledge broke off a piece and handed it to her. "You must eat."

Miss Ashmore frowned as she reached for it. "I suppose I can eat a little."

Nathaniel returned to his seat and met Miss Ashmore's gaze. "I have many questions to ask you, and I'm not quite sure where to begin."

"I am more interested in what your relationship is with my sister."

"We are merely friends."

Miss Ashmore's eyes narrowed slightly. "Why were you at the rally in Winstead Square with her?"

"She asked me to accompany her so she could look for you."

"That was foolishness on your part," Miss Ashmore said. "A rally is no place for a lady."

"I agree with that, yet you were there."

Miss Ashmore visibly stiffened. "What I do is none of your concern."

"It became my concern when you tried to kill Lord Barnwell."

Rutledge let out an exasperated groan. "Tell me that isn't true, Evie," he said. "We discussed this."

With a stubborn tilt of her chin, Miss Ashmore declared, "Lord Barnwell must die."

Chapter Fifteen

Nathaniel took in the firm set of Miss Ashmore's jaw and knew she was in earnest. But what had caused her to loathe Lord Barnwell to such a degree?

"Perhaps we should start at the beginning," Nathaniel suggested, glancing between them. "How are you two even acquainted?"

Rutledge swallowed the food in his mouth. "I recruited Evie to help with this assignment."

Nathaniel's brow shot up. "Are you mad?" he asked. "Miss Ashmore is a lady."

"Thank you for noticing," Miss Ashmore muttered.

Rutledge shot her an amused look. "Evie is not like most ladies," he said, "and I knew that she would prove useful to me."

"How did this even come to pass?" Nathaniel asked.

"A few months ago, I saw Evie at a rally in Ridgemont Square," Rutledge explained. "She was dressed like a man, but I would have recognized her anywhere, since she is the very likeness of her mother. After that, I started keeping an eye out for her whenever I attended a rally, just to ensure she was safe."

"I recognized Rutledge from when he used to visit my father," Miss Ashmore interjected, "and I started noticing that he was following me. I approached him, and we struck up a conversation."

"How does a conversation lead to assisting on an investigation?" Nathaniel inquired.

"Evie is clever, more so than many of the men working at the agency, so I asked for her assistance on my case."

"Does Merritt know?"

"He does," Rutledge said. "Miss Ashmore is an agent, but only on a trial basis."

"This is madness. Spying is—" Nathaniel attempted.

Miss Ashmore interrupted. "Spying is not limited to just men."

"I never said that it was, but I am concerned that you haven't thought through the repercussions of your actions."

"I am well aware of what is at stake," Miss Ashmore insisted.

"Are you?" Nathaniel asked. "Because you are holed up in a rented room as dangerous men search for you."

"You are quite the naysayer." Miss Ashmore wiped her hands off on her dress. "It would be best if you left and pretended you never saw me."

"I'm afraid that is impossible," Nathaniel said. "I have been searching for you, and I need to ask you a few questions."

"That doesn't mean I have to answer them."

Rutledge gave her an encouraging look. "You can trust Hawthorne. He has saved my life on more than one occasion, and he is proficient at what he does."

"I don't trust easily."

"I know, but you need Hawthorne's help," Rutledge said. "I am just an injured old man, and I can't protect you like I want to."

"I can protect myself," Miss Ashmore asserted.

"Not against these men," Rutledge stated. "They are ruthless, and intent on seeing you dead."

Miss Ashmore pressed her lips together, and Nathaniel saw emotions fluttering across her delicate face like shadows. It was a resolve that wouldn't be broken down easily, and his respect for her grew because of it.

"Why don't you start with the day you disappeared?" Nathaniel prodded.

Miss Ashmore held his gaze and said, "Whatever I reveal, you must promise that you won't tell my sister."

"Why?"

"Because I did all of this to protect her."

"Your sister misses you and desperately wants you to come home," he attempted.

"It is for the best that I left, and she must not know where I am," Miss Ashmore said. "You must promise me that."

Nathaniel nodded. "I swear it."

"I shall hold you to your word." Miss Ashmore paused. "Rutledge asked me to visit J. B. Abrams' shop and keep him and all the workers busy in the front room. He wanted an opportunity to search the back room."

Nathaniel glanced at Rutledge. "Did you find anything?"

Rutledge shook his head. "I only found an advertisement to a rally in Winstead Square," he revealed. "Frankly, it was a wasted endeavor."

"What happened next?" Nathaniel asked.

Miss Ashmore took a breath before sharing, "As I exited the shop, I noticed that two men were talking in hushed tones in the alleyway. I thought nothing of it until I overheard Barnwell being mentioned."

Miss Ashmore continued. "I'm not sure if you are aware, but Lord and Lady Barnwell were friends of my parents."

"I had not realized that."

"So, you can see why my curiosity was peaked," Miss Ashmore said. "I passed the alleyway and pressed myself up against the neighboring building to hear their conversation. They were discussing how the prime minister must die."

"It was foolish for you to eavesdrop."

Miss Ashmore gave him a pointed look. "Do you intend to chastise me about everything that I reveal?"

"That will be the last time, I promise."

"Thank heavens," Miss Ashmore said dryly. "I knew I needed to inform Rutledge of what I had just overheard, but when I turned to leave, my boots ground on some loose cobblestone, drawing attention to myself. I immediately started walking away, hoping that the men would lose me in the crowd, but when I looked back, they were following me."

"Why didn't you return to your coach?" Nathaniel asked.

"I was unable to," Miss Ashmore replied. "Furthermore, I didn't want to give these men a chance to learn my identity and put Dinah at risk."

"I can respect that."

"After I turned a corner, I ducked into an alleyway and hid myself behind some debris. I had a muff pistol in my reticule, but I knew I only had one shot, and there were two men," Miss Ashmore said. "The smell was terrible, but I remained hidden, hoping the men wouldn't find me."

Miss Ashmore continued. "However, I was not so lucky, and the men found me, yanking me out from my hiding spot. One of them shoved me up against the wall and pressed a pistol against my throat. He demanded to know what I overheard, and I tried to convince them I heard nothing."

With a glance at Rutledge, she said, "Rutledge stepped into the alleyway and ordered them to release me. The man turned his pistol towards Rutledge, giving me a chance to shoot him in the stomach."

"You shot a man?" Nathaniel asked.

"He left me little choice in the matter," Miss Ashmore revealed. "If I didn't kill him, I had no doubt he would kill me."

"What about the other man?"

Rutledge cleared his throat. "I thought he would give up, but instead, he took a dagger from his boot and swiped at me." He placed his hand on his side. "I removed my pistol and shot at him before he could do any more damage, but I only wounded him. He ran off, clutching his right arm."

"You didn't kill him?"

Rutledge shook his head. "No."

Nathaniel frowned. "That does pose a problem, since he can identify you and Miss Ashmore."

"Precisely," Rutledge responded. "I recognized the two men from the meetings with the Red Ravens, so I have no doubt that they reported back to Abrams about what transpired in that alleyway."

"Why didn't you send word to Merritt?" he asked.

"I'm afraid I wasn't entirely lucid for a few days, and I have yet to make a full recovery," Rutledge said. "Evie assisted me to the Bradford, and we have been here ever since." He shifted his gaze towards her. "Well, I have been here, but Evie has been coming and going."

"For what purpose?" Nathaniel asked.

Miss Ashmore shrugged one shoulder. "I had to get medicine for Rutledge's wound, and I returned home once."

"To hide your locket?"

Miss Ashmore gave him a baffled look. "How did you know that?"

"I found it behind a brick in the fireplace."

"You were in my bedchamber?" she asked.

"As I said, I have been trying to track you down," Nathaniel replied. "I also found 'the Bradford' scribbled on a paper in your book. Why did you write that?"

"Is that how you found us?" Miss Ashmore questioned.

"It was," he confirmed.

Miss Ashmore let out a soft sigh. "This isn't the first time I have stayed here."

"It's not?"

"No, the Bradford caters to people who want to be discreet."

Nathaniel chuckled. "That is not what I was told."

"I discovered that for the right price, people are willing to look the other way," Miss Ashmore said. "When we arrived on their doorstep, I feared that Rutledge might die from his wound, but he fought to survive."

"What do you intend to do now?" Nathaniel asked. "You can't keep hiding out."

"It's only until I kill Lord Barnwell," Miss Ashmore declared.

Nathaniel furrowed his brows. "Why do you hate Lord Barnwell to such a degree?"

Rutledge let out a grunt as he shifted on his bed. "That is my doing, I'm afraid," he confessed. "I discovered Barnwell is working with the Red Ravens to assassinate Lord Liverpool, and I brought Evie into my confidence."

"Can you prove any of this?" Nathaniel asked.

Rutledge shook his head. "Not yet, but I intend to once I am well enough to leave this room."

"When do you suppose that will be?"

"Days, probably." Rutledge turned his attention towards Evie. "I warned Evie not to do anything drastic while I was holed up here."

Evie interjected, "I had no choice. Lord Barnwell is attempting to start a revolution by killing the prime minister, and I knew the rally was the perfect time to shoot him."

"This is not your fight," Rutledge said.

"It is now," Evie replied. "Besides, I am more than capable of ending it."

Rutledge winced as he touched his side. "You are too headstrong. You are going to get yourself killed if you continue on without a concern for your own welfare."

"I like the path I am on," Evie remarked. "It has given me a purpose. I feel like I am finally making a difference."

"You can't go around killing people, especially a viscount," Rutledge pressed.

"If not me, then who?" Evie asked. "You aren't in a position to stop Barnwell, and I refuse to let him start a revolution. If he is dead, then the Red Ravens will disband."

"Or they will pick a new leader and continue on," Rutledge remarked.

"Then I will stop them, as well."

Rutledge gave her an exasperated look. "You have taken to spy work faster than anyone I have ever recruited before, but you can be reckless. That does not bode well for an agent. You must be mindful to use some constraint."

"I have a question," Nathaniel said to Rutledge. "I found an advertisement to the rally in Winstead Square in your room with Miss Ashmore's name scribbled on the back."

"I hoped you would find that. In case I was killed or forced into hiding, I wanted you to seek out Evie," Rutledge explained. "I wanted to ensure she would be protected."

Miss Ashmore opened her mouth to no doubt object, but Rutledge spoke first. "I know you can protect yourself, but I didn't want to leave you without a protector of some sort."

Nathaniel leaned back in his seat. "Since you went missing, Merritt asked me to investigate the Red Ravens."

"What did you discover?" Rutledge asked.

"They want me to kill Lord Liverpool."

Rutledge lifted his brow. "They are using you as the scapegoat, just as they attempted to do with me."

"They threatened to kill Miss Dinah if I don't do it," Nathaniel revealed.

Miss Ashmore gasped. "Not Dinah!"

"I'm afraid so," Nathaniel said, "but I won't let any harm befall her."

Miss Ashmore rose and walked over to the window. "I left

so I could protect her from all of this, but your association with her put her in harm's way."

"That was not my intention," Nathaniel responded.

"Then what was?" Miss Ashmore asked.

"Your sister mistook me for a Bow Street Runner and hired me to find you," Nathaniel revealed. "Unfortunately, that put her right in the middle of my investigation."

"You could have said no."

"When Miss Dinah informed me that you went missing after visiting Abrams' shop, I knew it was too much of a coincidence to ignore."

Miss Ashmore turned around and leaned back against the windowsill. "I'm afraid my sister has always been a bit impetuous."

"That she is."

"I assume that you are an agent, as well," Miss Ashmore said.

"I am," Nathaniel replied, seeing no reason to deny it.

With a shake of her head, Miss Ashmore met his gaze. "I do not condone you lying to my sister, but I do understand your reasons."

"I have great respect for Miss Dinah, I can assure you of that."

Miss Ashmore cocked her head. "I believe you," she replied. "I saw how you protected her when you left the rally."

"Is there a place you could take your sister and hide out until this matter is resolved?" Nathaniel asked.

"It is much too risky for me to come out of hiding," Miss Ashmore said.

"You can't keep hiding out here," Nathaniel pressed. "If I found you, then it is only a matter of time before someone else tracks you down."

Rutledge bobbed his head. "You're right," he said. "Where do you suppose we go?"

"You can't go home, because your room was ransacked."

"I imagined that would be the case," Rutledge responded.

Nathaniel rose from his seat. "I will go speak to Merritt, and we will find you a secure place to stay while I try to prove that Barnwell is associated with the Red Ravens."

He turned to face Miss Ashmore and ordered, "Do not leave this room. I will be back shortly with other agents to move you and Rutledge."

"I do not take orders from you," Miss Ashmore stated, crossing her arms over her chest.

"True, but we both have a vested interest in keeping your sister safe," Nathaniel said. "Besides, Miss Dinah would be devastated if anything happened to you."

Some of Miss Ashmore's defiance melted at his words. "I know."

"I'm glad we understand one another," Nathaniel remarked. "I'm meeting with Abrams and the Red Ravens this evening. With any luck, we can wrap this investigation up in a few days and send all of them to prison."

"Do not underestimate the Red Ravens," Rutledge advised. "They have been around longer than anyone has realized."

"I won't. I shall report to Merritt, and you will be hearing from me shortly."

Miss Ashmore uncrossed her arms. "Do you require any assistance?"

"I do not," he said in a tone that brooked no argument. "Your involvement ends here, Miss Ashmore."

Miss Ashmore's eyes narrowed, but she didn't say anything.

Nathaniel removed the pistol from his waistband and handed it to Rutledge. "An extra pistol may come in handy."

"Thank you."

"I will be back soon." Nathaniel turned to smile at Miss Ashmore. "Do try to avoid killing anyone."

"I will try," she replied with a ghost of a smile.

Dinah sat in the drawing room with a book, but her mind was on anything but reading. She wondered how Mr. Collier fared at the Bradford. Did she dare to hope that he found her sister at the boarding house? She truly hoped that was the case and that this horrific affair would come to an abrupt halt.

Aunt Nancy's voice broke through her musings. "Are you well, child?"

"I am," Dinah sighed.

"That was not very convincing."

Dinah lowered the book to her lap and met her aunt's gaze. "I'm just worried about Evie."

"As am I, but we must not get discouraged."

"You have been saying that since she went missing."

"It makes it no less true. We must carry on as if she were here."

"What is the point?" Dinah asked.

"Do you want the *ton* to discover that Evie has run off?" her aunt asked. "That would not only hurt her reputation, but yours, as well."

"Yes, Aunt Nancy," Dinah muttered.

Barnes stepped into the room and announced, "Mr. Burns has arrived and requested a moment of your time."

"Please send the constable in," Aunt Nancy ordered.

"Yes, ma'am."

Dinah set her book on the table as she waited for the vexing constable. She doubted he had made any progress and was thus wasting everyone's time.

Mr. Burns stepped into the room. "Good morning," he greeted. "I do hope I didn't catch you at a bad time."

"Not at all." Her aunt gestured towards a seat. "Would you care to sit down and have some tea?"

"I would," Mr. Burns replied as he went and sat down.

Dinah moved to the edge of her seat and poured a cup. As she extended it to the constable, she asked, "Have you found my sister yet?"

The constable blinked. "She hasn't come home?"

"No, she hasn't," Dinah confirmed.

Mr. Burnes took a sip of his drink. "That is most unfortunate. I was sure she would have arrived home by now."

Dinah exchanged a look with her aunt. "Will you start investigating her disappearance now?"

"The roads to Gretna Green can be rather treacherous this time of year," Mr. Burnes said. "Perhaps we give your sister a few more days before I start investigating the matter. I would hate to stir the pot, so to speak, if your sister truly is on holiday."

Dinah stared at the constable in disbelief. How could someone be so incompetent at their job?

"If you think that is best, Mr. Burns," Aunt Nancy said.

"I do," Mr. Burns replied. "There is no need to ruin anyone's reputation over this."

Dinah felt her anger rising as she reached for her own cup of tea. She would gladly give up her place in Society if it meant her sister would return home.

Mr. Burns put his teacup and saucer down. "I shall come around in a week, and we shall discuss our options then."

"Thank you," her aunt replied.

Rising, Mr. Burns smiled down at Aunt Nancy. "If I can be of any more assistance, please let me know at once."

"I shall do that, Mr. Burns."

After the constable left the drawing room, Dinah asked, "How could you be so pleasant to that simpleminded man?"

"Being rude to him would not serve any purpose."

"It would make me feel better."

"A lady does not let her emotions get the better of her," her aunt advised.

Dinah frowned. "Mr. Burns has done nothing to find Evie," she said. "It is a good thing I hired Mr. Collier."

"Has he made any progress?"

"Not that I am aware of," Dinah lied. She didn't dare admit that Mr. Collier had searched Evie's bedchamber the night before.

"You mustn't get your hopes up," her aunt said. "There is something about Mr. Collier that I can't seem to put my finger on."

"There is nothing wrong with Mr. Collier."

"He just seems so…" Aunt Nancy searched for the right word, "secretive."

"That's because he's a Bow Street Runner."

Her aunt shook her head. "Yet he has the mannerisms of a gentleman," she said. "I can almost imagine him in a ballroom."

Dinah giggled at that thought. "Mr. Collier is entirely too stiff to attend a ball. He would frighten all the young women with his demeanor."

"How much do you really know about Mr. Collier?"

"I know enough," Dinah replied.

A reflective look came to her aunt's eyes. "Before Andrew came into my life, I made the mistake of falling for another man," she revealed.

"What happened?"

"It was quite silly of me," she remarked. "His name was Garry, and I thought he truly cared about me. For a month, I thought I was living in a dream with him in my life. He showered attention on me, and he was quite handsome."

Her aunt grew silent. "When he met with my father to discuss his intentions, he discovered that my dowry was only eight thousand pounds," she said. "He declared that wasn't enough for him to take me off my father's hands and stormed out of the townhouse."

"I was devastated," her aunt continued. "I didn't believe

that Garry could be so cold and unfeeling, but he stopped acknowledging me in public. It was as if I didn't exist to him."

"How dreadful," Dinah murmured.

"I thought my heart would break, but the most serendipitous thing happened to me. I met Andrew at the next ball, and he taught me how to truly love another."

"I do miss Uncle Andrew."

"As do I." Her aunt reached for her teacup and took a sip. "Sometimes the person who is talking the loudest gets our attention, but if you are wise enough, you may discover all he is spouting is drivel."

"Are you implying that Mr. Collier only spouts drivel?"

"I don't rightly know, but you seem taken by him."

Dinah opened her mouth to object, but her aunt continued talking. "Do not insult me by denying it. I already told you my thoughts on the matter, and I do hope you will heed my words."

"I don't know what I feel for Mr. Collier, but I do know that it is unrequited."

Before her aunt could reply, Barnes stepped back into the room and met her gaze. "Mr. Collier has asked for a moment of your time. Would you care for me to show him in?"

"I would," Dinah said.

Barnes tipped his head. "Very good, miss."

Dinah took a moment to smooth out her blue dress, ignoring her aunt's critical eye.

Mr. Collier stepped into the room and bowed. "Good morning, Mrs. Carter, Miss Dinah."

Dinah smiled up at him, feeling a flutter in her stomach at the mere sight of him. "Good morning, Mr. Collier," she greeted. "Would you care for some tea?"

"No, thank you," Mr. Collier replied. "I just came to inform you that I followed a lead that linked Miss Ashmore to the Bradford, but I found no trace of your sister."

Dinah's shoulders slumped. "I must admit that I am

displeased to hear that. I had been hoping for some good news this morning."

"I do apologize for delivering bad news, and I hope I didn't distress you in any way."

Dinah forced a smile to her lips. "Nonsense," she assured him. "It is not your fault Evie wasn't at the Bradford."

Mr. Collier took a step closer, his eyes guarded. "I have not given up hope that we will find her, and neither should you," he encouraged. "I am late for another appointment, but I promised I would inform you at once of my findings."

"I do appreciate that, Mr. Collier," Dinah said.

Mr. Collier held her gaze a moment longer than was proper before turning to her aunt. "I hope you have a pleasant day, Mrs. Carter."

"Likewise, Mr. Collier."

Mr. Collier spun on his heel and departed from the room without saying another word.

Her aunt's eyes remained on the empty doorway. "That was odd."

"In what way?"

"Mr. Collier didn't tarry, as he usually does," her aunt commented.

"He was late for an appointment."

Her aunt brought her gaze back to meet hers. "I suppose that could be it," she muttered as she reached for her teacup.

"I daresay that you are reading entirely too much into Mr. Collier's hasty departure."

"You are probably right," her aunt said. "Shall we work on our embroidery?"

"I think that is a splendid idea."

As Dinah rose to retrieve her needlework, she couldn't help but wonder if her aunt was right about Mr. Collier. He did seem to leave abruptly, and he'd appeared rather tense while he spoke to her. Was he keeping something from her?

Chapter Sixteen

Nathaniel had spent the past ten years lying to everyone he cared about, but it felt different when he lied to Miss Dinah, as if he was betraying her. That was absurd; it wasn't as if he could tell her the truth of who he was or what he did. He shouldn't feel guilty for lying to her about her sister.

He had seen how her shoulders slumped at the news, but she had responded graciously.

Blast it! Miss Dinah deserved to know the truth about her sister. But he had made a promise to Miss Ashmore. For the first time, he found himself not only tired of all the lies, but ready to give them up entirely.

The hackney stopped and he exited, then shoved his hands in the pockets of his trousers and headed down the pavement. As he approached his headquarters, he saw Talbot and Worsley out front, still hawking roses, but no one was giving them any heed.

Nathaniel crossed his arms in front of the cart. "I was notified that someone trespassed on my property and stole my mother's roses."

Talbot gasped. "How terrible," he muttered. "It was probably a miscreant up to no good."

"It was definitely someone up to no good," Nathaniel said. "If either of you ever trespass on my property again, I'll shoot you."

Worsley spoke up. "We didn't think you'd notice the missing flowers."

"I didn't, but my mother is quite upset."

Talbot extended him a flower. "Then you must take her one of these roses," he insisted, "free of charge."

Nathaniel put his hand up. "I do not want the flower," he stated. "You have been warned."

"Yes, we have been properly threatened, and are quite frightened by it," Talbot said, "aren't we, Worsley?"

"Yes, I am shaking in my boots," Worsley replied.

Nathaniel looked heavenward. "You both are fools."

"We have been called much worse," Talbot said. "Just this morning, in fact."

Worsley bobbed his head. "That is true. Some people can be cruel."

With a shake of his head, Nathaniel headed towards the main door and stepped inside. He couldn't care less about the roses, but he knew his mother loved them.

He tipped his head at Mostyn as he went to step through the back door. The other agents gave him little heed as he approached Merritt's office and knocked on the closed door.

"Enter."

Nathaniel opened the door and stepped inside. Merritt was hunched over the desk as he folded a piece of paper. Nathaniel walked over to a chair that faced the desk and sat down, waiting to be acknowledged.

Merritt glanced up. "Did you find Miss Ashmore?"

"I did."

Now he had Merritt's attention. "Well, where is she?"

"I found her at the Bradford, along with Rutledge," Nathaniel revealed.

Merritt's brow shot up. "Rutledge is alive?"

"He is," Nathaniel confirmed.

"That's good, but what in the blazes was Rutledge doing with Miss Ashmore?"

Nathaniel shifted in his seat, then replied, "Miss Ashmore overheard a conversation that she wasn't supposed to hear, and Rutledge was injured when he saved her from the men who discovered her."

"How badly is he injured?"

"Enough that he hasn't been able to leave his room, but I think we need to move them to a more secure location. Rutledge and I both believe Miss Ashmore's life is in danger."

Merritt nodded. "I have no qualms about moving them and will assign an agent to guard them."

"I doubt Rutledge will agree to that."

"He doesn't have a say in the matter," Merritt said. "Did you have a chance to speak to Miss Ashmore?"

"I did, and she is adamant that Lord Barnwell must die."

"What were her reasonings?"

"The conversation she overheard was in the alley next to Abram's shop, leaving me to conclude the two men were a part of the Red Ravens. She said they mentioned Barnwell," he explained. "Furthermore, Rutledge said his investigation has led him to conclude that Barnwell is working with the Red Ravens."

"That is quite the allegation," Merritt said. "Can he prove that?"

"Not at this time."

"That still doesn't explain why Miss Ashmore tried to shoot Lord Barnwell," Merritt pressed.

With a knowing look, Nathaniel remarked, "Well, it might have something to do with her being an agent."

Merritt grew silent. "I suppose you have some questions."

"How could you allow Rutledge to recruit Miss

Ashmore?" he asked. "She is a lady of genteel birth and cannot possibly have understood the depravity of this position."

"I am well aware, but Rutledge was adamant she would be a good fit for the agency," Merritt gave him a pointed look, "just as he was right about you."

"I hope you know what you're doing, sir," Nathaniel said. "At least this explains why you asked Haddington and I to go soft on Miss Ashmore."

"I didn't dare reveal her role within the agency."

"I can respect that."

Merritt leaned forward in his chair and rested his arms on the desk. "I have high hopes for Miss Ashmore, but she will require additional training," he said. "She should have never taken it upon herself to stop Barnwell."

"I wholeheartedly agree."

"Regardless, we do need to stop Barnwell, but no magistrate would issue an arrest warrant for him unless we had proof beyond a reasonable doubt."

"I am well aware, which is why I intend to break into his study and see if I can find anything that would be noteworthy."

"Be careful," Merritt advised. "If Barnwell is truly involved with the Red Ravens, he could be very dangerous."

"You don't need to concern yourself about me. This isn't the first time I've broken into someone's home."

"If you were caught, how would you explain your presence?"

"I won't get caught."

"Be sure that you don't."

Nathaniel leaned forward in his seat. "I do not question Miss Ashmore's account of what transpired, but she seemed rather poised, despite her current circumstance."

"You expected a simpering miss?"

"No, but she exudes a confidence about her that I find

admirable," Nathaniel said. "Not only has she kept Rutledge safe, but she is also eluding the men searching for her."

"Miss Ashmore has always been a formidable young woman." Merritt smiled. "Her father once told me that he had never met a more inquisitive child. She would follow him around their home asking questions, one after another."

"It is a shame that Lord Gladstone died so tragically."

"Yes, it was," Merritt agreed. "He was a good man, and an even better agent."

Nathaniel's eyebrows lifted in surprise. "He was an agent?"

"That remains between us," Merritt said.

"Understood."

Merritt bobbed his head in approval. "Lord Gladstone was assigned to infiltrate a newly formed radical group, but he died shortly thereafter in a carriage accident."

"That seems odd."

"I thought the same thing, but we did investigate their deaths," Merritt said. "They were traveling to their country estate, but a wagon with a broken axel was in the road. By all accounts, it appeared to be a tragic accident."

"What happened to the radical group that Lord Gladstone was investigating?"

"It disbanded," Merritt replied. "We were able to arrest a few of the members, but they claimed they didn't know the names of their co-conspirators."

"That is how the Red Ravens operate, as well."

"It is awfully hard to incriminate someone if you don't know their name."

Nathaniel rose. "I have a meeting with the Red Ravens tonight," he shared. "With any luck, they will shed light on how Barnwell is involved in all of this."

"That is wishful thinking." Merritt gave him a thoughtful look. "Something doesn't add up."

"Which is?"

"If the Red Ravens are looking for Miss Ashmore, and they know you are acquainted with her sister, Dinah, then why do you suppose they have invited you to their meetings?" Merritt asked.

"I have considered that, but I'm afraid I don't have the answer."

"They might be hoping that you will lead them to Miss Ashmore."

"If that is the case, then why bring me into their confidences?" Nathaniel asked. "They did say they want me to kill the prime minister."

"Just be cautious, and remember who you can trust," Merritt advised.

Nathaniel walked over to the door. "I always do," he replied as he grasped the handle.

"I will make the arrangements to move Miss Ashmore and Rutledge to a secure location."

"Thank you."

As he opened the door, Merritt said, "This isn't a game, agent. Get the information we need for arrests and get out."

The sun had already set as Nathaniel made his way towards the Rotten Rabbit. Like Merritt, he couldn't understand why the Red Ravens had accepted him into the fold so quickly. It had been his experience that most people had an innate suspicion of each other, and it was especially true with criminals. They would turn on each other the moment it became beneficial to them.

It was true that they hadn't laid out their plan completely, but they were attempting to force him to kill the prime minister by threatening Miss Dinah. Why him? Why couldn't another member of the Red Ravens kill Lord Liverpool, one who had been around longer?

There were too many questions that remained unanswered, and that made him wary. If they just arrested the radical group now, they might never discover Barnwell's involvement.

Nathaniel glanced over his shoulder and saw a man trailing behind him, his cap pulled low on his head. He wouldn't have given it much thought, but he'd been following him for a few blocks now. He increased the length of his stride to create more distance between them and ducked swiftly into an alleyway after turning a corner.

He remained in the shadows as he waited for the man to catch up. It wasn't long before the man came strolling along the sidewalk. As he passed the alley, Nathaniel stepped out, wrapped his arm around his neck, and pulled him back into the cover of darkness.

"Why are you following me?" he growled into the man's ear.

"To see what you are about, Hawthorne."

Not a man, a woman. Nathaniel released her in surprise. "Who are you and how do you know my name?"

"You mean you already forgot me?" She turned around to face him, and he nearly groaned. Miss Ashmore.

"What are you doing here?" he demanded.

"Following you," she said simply. "I thought that was evident."

"You did a poor job of doing so."

"Perhaps this time, but you failed to notice me on other occasions."

He crossed his arms over his chest. "Why have you been following me?"

"I would like to speak plainly."

"I'd prefer it."

Miss Ashmore took a step closer and mimicked his posture. "I don't trust you, and I can't help but notice you and my sister have formed an attachment for one another."

"That is not true."

"You can deny it all you want, but I've seen you two together in the gardens."

"May I ask why you were skulking outside your townhouse?"

"That is none of your concern."

"You made it my concern when you inserted yourself into the investigation."

"I did not 'insert' myself into this investigation," Miss Ashmore stated. "You have inserted yourself into *my* investigation!"

"Merritt assigned me to it!" Nathaniel frowned. "I don't have time to escort you back right now."

"That won't be necessary."

He lifted his brow. "We are in the rookeries," he said. "This is no place for a young woman, especially one of genteel birth."

Miss Ashmore looked amused by his remark. "You don't need to coddle me. Besides, I am appropriately dressed for the occasion."

"It will only take one good look at you to know you're not a man."

"Then I won't let them take a look at me."

Nathaniel let out a frustrated sigh. "Miss Ashmore—"

"Call me Evie."

"It is entirely improper for me to do so."

She threw her hands up. "Look around you. Is there anything proper about where we are?"

"You make a good point."

Evie eyed him curiously. "Does Dinah know you are an earl?"

Nathaniel blinked. "I beg your pardon?"

"I take that as a 'no', then."

He scowled at her. "She only knows me as Mr. Collier," he muttered, running a hand through his hair. "None of this explains why you are following me through the rookeries."

"I wanted to see where you were going."

"That's foolish," Nathaniel said. "Weren't you moved from the Bradford to a safe location?"

"We were, and the agents who escorted us are still guarding the front and back doors," she smirked, "but not the alleyway next to the house."

"Those agents are there to protect you."

"I don't need protection," she said. "I've been doing just fine on my own."

Nathaniel shook his head. "What's your plan?" he asked, his curiosity piqued. "I assume you have one."

"It is more of a work in progress," she replied with amusement in her voice.

He watched her expression to gauge her reaction. "How is it that you are so composed after everything that has happened to you?"

"Did you expect me to turn into a delicate flower?"

"I don't know what I expected," he responded honestly.

"I suppose it is because I have never quite fit in," Evie admitted. "I want more out of this life than just doing what is expected of me."

Nathaniel removed a pocket watch from his waistcoat and glanced down at the time. "If I don't hurry, I'll be late for a meeting." He gave her a stern look. "Go back, Evie."

"Only if you promise to keep me abreast of the investigation," she said firmly.

"Why should I?"

Sorrow flashed across her eyes, but it was gone almost as quickly as it had come. "I want to know when it's safe for me to go home."

"I can agree to that."

Evie gave him a grateful nod as she pulled the cap lower onto her head. "Then I will retire for the evening." She spun on her heel and left.

Nathaniel let out a sigh. "Foolish, impish girl," he muttered under his breath.

He exited the alleyway. Evie was nowhere to be seen, and he hoped that she would return straight back to the house. He continued on to the Rotten Rabbit and stepped inside the boisterous tavern.

A red-haired serving wench approached him. "Don't be shy; sit anywhere you fancy."

"That won't be necessary."

Understanding donned on the wench's face. "Very well, then. I hope you aren't waiting for an invitation."

"No, ma'am," he replied as he headed towards the back room.

Nathaniel opened the door and entered the room. All the men stopped drinking and stared up at him, some with scowls on their faces.

Abrams rose from his seat. "You're late," he stated. "We were worried you got cold feet about attending our final meeting, which would have been most unfortunate for Miss Dinah."

"I know what is at stake."

Abrams pointed towards an empty chair by him. "Come have a seat. We have much to discuss."

Nathaniel approached the table and pulled out the chair. As he sat down, Abrams returned to his seat and reached for his tankard.

Abrams took a swallow, then said, "I would imagine you have questions for me."

"I do."

"Then ask them," Abrams encouraged. "I can't promise I will answer them, but at least you will get them off your chest."

"Why me?" Nathaniel asked.

Abrams smiled. "It's simple," he said, "I know who you truly are."

"What do you mean?"

"You're a Bow Street Runner," Abrams responded smugly.

Nathaniel furrowed his brow. "You think I'm a Bow Street Runner?"

"I know so," Abrams replied. "I knew the moment you walked into my shop with your red waistcoat."

"It wasn't red, it's burgundy. Regardless, if that is the case, then why did you bring me into your confidence?"

Abrams pushed his tankard away. "Because I knew you would prove useful to me."

"What is stopping me from arresting all of you?"

"If you did something so foolish, I would have no choice but to send someone to kill Miss Dinah," Abrams responded. "It may just be a flirtation, but I'm a betting man, and I bet that you wouldn't want any harm to befall the lovely lady."

"If I kill the prime minister, I will be hunted down and killed," Nathaniel said. "My life will most assuredly be over."

"But Miss Dinah will be safe."

Nathaniel leaned to the side as a serving wench placed a tankard in front of him. As he reached for it, he said, "I shall have to think on it."

"What is there to think on?" Abrams asked. "If you refuse, you will be killed, as well."

"Well, when you say it like that," Nathaniel muttered as he brought the tankard to his lips.

Abrams leaned closer. "You're not the first Bow Street Runner to try to infiltrate us, but I'm afraid their story ended much differently."

"You killed them?"

Abrams shrugged. "I had little choice in the matter," he replied. "It was either them or me."

Nathaniel put the tankard on the table. After a long

moment, he said, "If I do your bidding, you must promise that no harm will come to Miss Dinah."

A slow smile spread across Abrams' face. "I promise."

"Then I will kill the prime minister."

Chapter Seventeen

Dressed in a blue riding habit, Dinah descended the stairs of her townhouse and was pleased to see Barnes at the base of the stairs.

"Good morning," she greeted. "Will you inform the grooms that I intend to go riding this morning and wish for two of them to accompany me?"

Barnes tipped his head. "I shall see to it, miss."

Dinah stepped into the drawing room and saw her aunt sitting on a settee, working quietly on her embroidery.

"Would you care to go riding with me?" Dinah asked.

Aunt Nancy lowered the needlework to her lap. "Are you sure it is wise for you to go riding?"

"I know that Mr. Collier warned me to stay inside, but surely a ride through Hyde Park with two grooms accompanying me is acceptable. He can't possibly believe anything untoward can happen in such a busy area, surrounded by all those genteel people."

"I'm not sure that is true," her aunt said. "You said he was rather insistent on the matter."

"He is always insistent," Dinah joked.

Her aunt gave her an amused look. "He can be rather

intense, but I must wonder if that is due to the seriousness of his profession."

"Perhaps, but I do wish he would lighten up a bit."

"That is not likely to happen."

"No, I suppose not, but one can hope," Dinah said as she walked over to the door. "I will be back shortly."

"Do be careful, child."

"I have every intention to."

Dinah departed from the drawing room and headed towards the rear of the townhouse. When she reached the stables, she saw the grooms were still in the process of saddling her horse, so she sat down on the bench.

She lifted her head to look up at the morning sky and let out a sigh. It felt wonderful to be outside and feel the warmth of the sun on her face.

Mr. Collier's voice came from next to her. "What do you think you are doing?" he demanded.

"I would think it was fairly easy to deduce," she teased, bringing her gaze to meet his. "I am going riding."

"I thought I warned you not to leave your house for any reason."

"No, you ordered me to do so," Dinah said, rising. "There is a difference."

"Regardless, it is not safe for you to be outside." Mr. Collier motioned towards her townhouse. "You need to go inside at once."

"No."

Mr. Collier's brow lifted. "Pardon?"

"I said 'no'. I want to go on a ride through Hyde Park."

"Do you not care a whit for your safety?"

"Two grooms will accompany me."

He scoffed. "Do you think that will stop them from coming for you?"

"Who?"

"It doesn't matter," he remarked decisively. "You will not defy me on this."

With a posture her governess would have been proud of, Dinah took a step closer to Mr. Collier. "You have no right to dictate my actions."

"I am just trying to keep you safe."

"From what?" she asked.

"I believe I already explained that."

She shook her head. "No, you told me in the vaguest terms possible."

A groom approached her with her horse and asked, "Would you like me to assist you onto your horse?"

"I would," she replied as she stepped closer to the horse.

As she went to put her foot into the grooms' intertwined hands, Mr. Collier stepped closer.

"Dinah, don't do this," he murmured.

She stilled. "You called me by my given name."

"I did," Mr. Collier responded, unabashed. "I will tell you the truth, but you mustn't get on that horse."

Dinah turned to face him and gave a single nod. "All right."

Mr. Collier offered his arm. "Shall we take a turn around the gardens?"

She accepted it and allowed him to lead her towards the gardens. She found she was quite eager to learn the truth of the matter.

Once they'd stepped onto the gravel path, Mr. Collier began. "There is a radical group known as the Red Ravens, and they have threatened to kill you if I don't assassinate the prime minister."

Dinah gasped. "You cannot kill Lord Liverpool!"

"I am well aware, but while I am trying to formulate a plan, I need to ensure that you are safe."

"Why can't you arrest them?"

"It is not that simple," Mr. Collier said. "What if we

weren't able to arrest everyone in the group? You are still at risk."

"Aren't you, as well?"

Mr. Collier smiled, but it didn't reach his eyes. "I did not get to this position by being cowed by threats. My life is constantly in danger."

"That sounds frightening."

"It is my reality." He glanced over at her. "Now do you see the precariousness of the situation?"

"I do."

"Will you remain inside while I find a way to thwart the Red Ravens?"

Dinah removed her hand from his arm. "I will."

"I am relieved to hear that," Mr. Collier said, holding her gaze. "I don't think I can do my job if I am worried about you."

"Why not?" she asked boldly.

"I... uh..." He stopped speaking and cleared his throat. "It is my fault that you are in this position, and I feel responsible for you."

"Oh," she replied, disappointed by his response. "Is that all?"

"It is."

Dinah shifted her gaze away from his as she attempted to suppress her emotions. She had hoped that he would admit that he cared for her, but it appeared that was just wishful thinking on her part.

"Do you have another home you can reside in for the time being?" Mr. Collier asked.

"When we're not in London, we retire to my cousin's country estate in Dover."

Mr. Collier nodded in approval. "It might be best if you remove yourself there until I send word."

Dinah shook her head. "I can't leave London without Evie."

"You don't have a choice," Mr. Collier said. "Your life is in danger."

"I understand, but—"

"Clearly, you don't understand," Mr. Collier asserted. "These men will kill you, without hesitation or remorse."

"But what about my sister?"

Mr. Collier stopped and turned to face her, his boots grinding on the gravel. "I have a feeling your sister can take care of herself."

"But I can't take care of myself?" she asked. "Is that what you are saying?"

"I am."

Dinah tilted her chin stubbornly. "I am not some weak simpleton that you can bully around," she stated, her voice rising.

"I know, and I respect you more because of it."

"You do?" She eyed him curiously. What game was he playing?

"I do." Mr. Collier's face softened. "You are a brave young woman, and entirely too stubborn for your own good."

"Was that a compliment mingled with an insult?"

He grinned. "It was a compliment, and I rarely hand those out, so you should consider yourself fortunate."

"You may want to work on your compliments," she joked.

"Duly noted."

Dinah's eyes darted to his lips, and she quickly averted her gaze, hoping Mr. Collier hadn't noticed her brazenness. "I'm afraid I don't know much about you," she said.

"What do you wish to know?"

"Truly?" she asked. "You will answer my questions?"

"Assuming they are reasonable."

Dinah pressed her lips together, then asked, "What were you like as a child?"

Mr. Collier chuckled. "I was an absolute menace until my parents sent me off to boarding school."

"In what way?"

"I'm afraid to admit that I didn't think rules applied to me, and I had no fear of being hurt."

"That is a terrible combination."

"My parents would agree with you," Mr. Collier said. "They did everything to curb my enthusiasm, but I fought them at every turn."

"I must admit that doesn't surprise me."

Mr. Collier gave her a knowing look. "If I had to guess, you were the perfect child and followed all of your parent's rules."

"I was not perfect, mind you, but I did see the merit to being obedient."

"I don't believe we would have gotten along when we were younger."

Dinah smiled. "No, I suppose not," she admitted.

"But we are older now," Mr. Collier said.

The breath hitched in her throat. "That we are," she forced out. She had a hard time formulating words when he looked at her like that.

"Dinah…" His voice stopped. "Do you mind if I call you by your given name?"

"I would prefer it."

"Then you must call me Nathaniel."

"I will."

Nathaniel watched her for a moment before saying, "I have never given a young woman leave to call me by my given name."

"Me either." Realizing her error, she rushed out, "What I mean is that I have never given a man permission to call me by my given name. I have given loads of women permission to call me Dinah."

Nathaniel's lips twitched. "I knew what you meant, but I do thank you for the clarification."

"I just wanted you to be made aware." Why couldn't she

find something clever to say? Everything out of her mouth sounded absurd.

He looked into her eyes. "It would ease my mind greatly if you retired to the countryside until the threat on you has passed," he said softly. "I swear to you that I won't stop searching for your sister, and when I find her, I will ensure she is safe."

"I shall have to discuss this with my aunt, but I find that I am not as opposed to it as I once was."

"I would be happy to join you when you speak to her."

"That won't be necessary," Dinah replied. "She is a reasonable person."

"That is true," Aunt Nancy said, startling them both. "Perhaps you could continue your conversation over some tea in the drawing room?"

"I do thank you for the kind offer, but I'm afraid I have a previous commitment," Nathaniel replied.

"Then good day to you, Mr. Collier," her aunt said.

Nathaniel bowed. "Good day, Mrs. Carter." He turned towards her. "I will call on you later to continue this discussion."

"I shall be looking forward to it."

Aunt Nancy turned to Dinah as Nathaniel walked away. "Do you want to explain why it appeared as if you were about to kiss Mr. Collier?" she whispered harshly.

"We were not about to kiss."

"You could have fooled me," her aunt said as she spun on her heel.

Nathaniel stepped inside his townhouse and glanced around the entry hall. He counted nearly a dozen vases filled with red roses.

Balfour stepped into the entry hall with another vase of roses and placed it on an already full table. "Welcome home, my lord," he said. "I do apologize for not being here to greet you."

"Where did all these roses come from?"

"Two good Samaritans returned them," Balfour informed him. "It was quite a harrowing tale, if you must know."

"Do enlighten me."

"They encountered the ruffian who stole the roses from your mother's garden and demanded they be returned at once. When the criminal refused, they had no choice but to fight him and his band of brothers."

"Band of brothers?"

"The men said they fought nearly ten of the scoundrels but managed to come out unscathed."

"I see," Nathaniel said. "Did you tip these men?"

Balfour bobbed his head. "I did," he replied. "I gave them a generous one, since her Ladyship was so pleased by the return of her roses."

"If you ever see these two men again, please let me know. I would like to personally thank them."

"I will be sure to do so," Balfour said. "I wish there were more men like them in London."

Nathaniel let out a disbelieving huff. "Is my father home?"

"He is out, and your mother is receiving callers in the drawing room."

"Then I shall retire to the study," Nathaniel replied.

Balfour acknowledged his words with a tip of his head. "Very good, my lord."

As Nathaniel walked towards the rear of his townhouse, he shook his head at Worsley and Talbot's antics. He wondered if they had missed their calling in life by not working in theatre. Regardless, he would have a few choice words for them when he saw them next.

He went around his desk and sat down. On the top of the

pile of correspondence was a note from his father, directing him to sign a stack of documents.

Nathaniel dipped the quill into the inkpot and obeyed, then he put the quill down and reached for the next letter in the pile. He had just unfolded it when Haddington stormed into the room. "You found her?"

"I see that you spoke to Merritt."

"I did."

He set the paper down, giving Haddington his full attention. "Would you mind closing the door so this conversation can remain private?"

Haddington hurriedly turned around and did so. "Why didn't you tell me that you found Evie?"

Nathaniel gestured towards the chair that faced the desk. "Perhaps you should take a seat."

Haddington snorted but sat. "Merritt mentioned you found Evie, but he didn't have time to go into great detail."

"I found Evie holed up with Rutledge." Nathaniel didn't want to reveal Evie's role within the agency, even to his friend. If Merritt hadn't shared that information, it was not his place to do so.

"Yes, and he was injured while saving her," Haddington said, "I know all this. What I want to know is, how is she faring?"

"She appears to be well."

"When does she intend to return home?"

Nathaniel shrugged. "I'm not entirely sure," he replied. "She claims she is staying away to keep Miss Dinah safe."

"You don't believe her?"

"I'm not saying that I don't, but she is quite resistant," Nathaniel said. "I can't help but wonder what she is keeping from me, from us."

Haddington shot up from his chair. "Evie is many things, but she is not a liar."

"She followed me into the rookeries last night dressed in men's clothing."

"Why was she following you?"

"To see where I was going."

"Where were you going?"

"To the Rotten Rabbit for a meeting with the Red Ravens," Nathaniel revealed. "When I offered to escort her home, Evie told me she could see herself home."

"Evie?" Haddington repeated, his eyes narrowing. "Since when do you call her by her given name?"

"Since she gave me leave to."

Haddington walked over to the drink cart and picked up the decanter. "I know that Evie puts on a brave front, but I must wonder if she is frightened by her circumstances."

"Quite the contrary," Nathaniel said. "She appears to be ready for a fight."

After pouring himself a drink, Haddington picked up the glass and took a sip. "Regardless, I would like to see her for myself."

"I take no issue with that."

Haddington sat more comfortably on the settee. "How did your meeting with the Red Ravens go?"

"They believe me to be a Bow Street Runner and are threatening to kill Miss Dinah if I don't kill the prime minister."

"But not you?"

Nathaniel smirked. "Oh, they have threatened me, repeatedly, but it does little to affect my resolve."

"What do you intend to do?"

"I can't do anything until I discover what Barnwell's role is in all of this," Nathaniel responded. "I was able to convince Miss Dinah to depart for the countryside until this matter is resolved."

"Do you think it is safe for her to leave?"

Nathaniel rose from his seat and came around his desk. "I

was hoping I could convince Evie to travel with her to keep her safe."

"You truly believe that Evie can guard her sister?"

"I do."

Haddington took a sip of his drink. "I daresay that you are giving her too much credit."

"And I fear that you aren't giving her enough," Nathaniel countered. "After all, she has managed to elude the Red Ravens for this long."

"That is a far cry from having to fight them off, assuming the need arises."

"I need you on board, because I will need your help when I go speak to Evie."

"Why me?"

Nathaniel winced. "Evie doesn't trust me."

"How do you know this?"

"She told me as much."

Haddington chuckled. "She isn't one to mince words."

Nathaniel sat across from his friend. "No, she does not," he said. "I thought about putting Miss Dinah and her aunt in the townhouse with Evie and Rutledge, but that would force me to reveal who I am."

"Does Evie know the truth of who you are?"

"She does," he admitted. "Rutledge used my name in her presence."

"Do you not think Evie will reveal that to her sister?"

"Quite possibly, but she has assured me that she won't reveal that I am an agent."

Haddington nodded. "You can trust Evie."

"Will you come?" he asked.

"Do you even need to ask?" Haddington put his glass onto the table and rose. "I want to see Evie for myself and make sure she is all right."

"I should note that your being there might raise some questions for her."

"I am willing to take that risk."

Nathaniel rose from his seat. "I'll call for a coach." He walked over to the door and opened it. "Balfour!"

A moment later, his butler appeared by his side. "Yes, my lord."

"Will you see the coach is brought around front?" Nathaniel asked. "I have an errand to run."

"Yes, my lord."

Nathaniel turned his attention back to Haddington. "Merritt sent them to the townhouse in Cheapside."

"That's not too shabby."

"I need to have a word with the two agents assigned to guard them, because Evie managed to slip out of the townhouse undetected."

"That is quite the feat," Haddington remarked. "I must admit that I am relieved to hear that Rutledge is alive and well."

"As am I."

Haddington eyed him curiously. "May I ask about all of the roses in the entry hall?"

"Worsley and Talbot are idiots."

"No objections here, but would you be more specific as to why that is?"

"I will in the coach," Nathaniel replied as he exited the study.

Chapter Eighteen

The coach stopped on the busy street and Nathaniel let himself out, not bothering to wait for the footman to come around.

He turned to address the driver. "Wait here," he ordered. "We'll be back shortly."

"Yes, my lord."

Haddington came to stand next to him. "Shall we?"

As they started down the sidewalk, Nathaniel said, "I do hope that Evie will be reasonable."

"She will be."

Nathaniel glanced over at him. "How can you be so sure?"

"Evie is very protective of Dinah," Haddington replied. "Has been ever since they were little."

"That bodes well for us, then."

They approached a whitewashed two-level townhouse and walked up the three steps to the entrance. They knocked on the door and waited a long moment before it opened, revealing a familiar agent.

"Good afternoon, Ferrell," Nathaniel greeted.

Ferrell opened the door wide. "Come in before anyone

sees you," he said, ushering them in. "What brings you by today?"

"We were hoping to speak to Miss Ashmore," Haddington replied.

Ferrell frowned. "I do hope she is here."

"Why wouldn't she be here?" Haddington asked.

"Why, indeed?" Ferrell responded. "Miss Ashmore comes and goes as she pleases, not caring a whit about her safety."

Evie's voice came from the top of the stairs. "I do care about my safety, but as I have said on more than one occasion, I am more than capable of protecting myself."

Nathaniel glanced up and watched as Evie gracefully descended the stairs. She was dressed in the same worn dress that he had seen in the Bradford and her hair was neatly tied in a bun at the base of her neck.

Ferrell shook his head. "Good luck," he muttered under his breath as he walked off.

Evie stopped on the last step and smiled knowingly at Haddington. "Since you are here, I must assume that you are an agent, as well."

"I am, but I trust that you will keep this to yourself."

Evie clasped her hands in front of her. "You need not fear on that account."

Haddington returned her smile. "I wanted to come and see for myself that you are well."

"I am," Evie said. "Ferrell has been most accommodating."

"Somehow, I don't believe that is true," Haddington responded.

Evie laughed. "He hates me."

"It may have something to do with the fact that you sneak out when he is trying to protect you," Haddington pointed out.

"Perhaps," Evie replied with a wave of her hand, "but I can't change who I am to please him."

"No one is asking you to, but there are dangerous men afoot," Haddington said. "Everyone just wants to ensure that you stay safe."

Evie nodded. "I understand, but I can't sit idly by and do nothing."

Nathaniel interjected, "I believe I have come up with a solution that will benefit both of us."

Gesturing towards a room off the entry hall, Evie said, "Let's continue this conversation in the drawing room."

They followed Evie into the room and waited until she sat down before claiming their seats.

Evie gave Nathaniel an expectant look. "What plan are you proposing?"

Nathaniel decided just to be honest with her. "The Red Ravens have threatened to kill Miss Dinah unless I kill the prime minister."

"How could you let this happen?" Evie asked, her voice critical. "I left Dinah so she *wouldn't* be in any danger!"

"Unfortunately, Abrams saw us together at the rally and assumed that we had formed an attachment," Nathaniel explained.

"Which you have," Evie said.

"We have not," Nathaniel asserted. "We are just friends."

Evie didn't look convinced but thankfully didn't press him on that matter. "So how do you intend to keep Dinah safe?"

"It would be in her best interest if she retired to the countryside, with you accompanying her to keep her safe."

"You wish for me to go with her?" Evie asked.

"I do," Nathaniel said. "It would be far better if you were there than assigning an agent to watch over her. You have more access to her, whereas the agent would be restricted."

"You make a good argument, but what about Barnwell?"

"I intend to search his study tonight, in hopes of finding something that will connect him to the Red Ravens."

Evie leaned back in her seat. "Or I could just shoot him."

"We need proof of his treachery," Nathaniel said. "You can't go around shooting people that you don't like."

Evie's lips twitched. "It was with good reason that I shot Barnwell."

Haddington spoke up. "Just think of the scandal that it would have caused if you had succeeded in killing him," he remarked. "You would have spent the remainder of your days in prison, and Dinah would be ruined."

"That's assuming I would have been caught," Evie said, "which I wouldn't have."

"No plan is without some risk," Haddington stated.

"I planned everything out perfectly, but I did not anticipate that my sister would be at the rally," Evie said with a pointed look.

"She was there only to look for you," Nathaniel shared.

"I know, but now she is in harm's way because of it," Evie said.

Nathaniel shifted in his seat. "Not if we remove her from London, far away from the Red Ravens."

"Your plan does have some merit, but I would like to accompany you to search Barnwell's office tonight."

Nathaniel shook his head. "No, it is much too dangerous for you."

"But not for you?" Evie pressed.

"I am an agent," Nathaniel said. "This is what I am assigned to do."

"I am, too. I can prove useful to you—"

"My answer is no."

Evie pursed her lips, and Nathaniel braced himself for a fight on that matter. After a moment, she surprised him by saying, "I understand."

"You do?" What game was she playing?

"I do," she replied.

"It's a relief to hear you say that," Nathaniel said.

Evie sat silent for a moment. "I also believe it is time I

return home to keep Dinah safe," she remarked. "I will travel with her to our country estate and remain with her until we receive word that we can return to Town."

"With any luck, I should have this assignment wrapped up soon, and it won't inconvenience you too much," Nathaniel said.

Haddington interrupted, "I would be happy to accompany you while you travel to your country estate."

"I thank you for the kind offer, but there is no need," Evie responded. "I don't believe the Red Ravens will follow us out of Town."

"I hope you are right," Nathaniel said. "When do you intend to return to your family?"

"Tomorrow morning, and we'll depart shortly thereafter." Evie rose, causing the men to rise. "If you will excuse me, I need to ensure that Rutledge has clean dressings on his wounds."

"Of course," Nathaniel responded.

"I trust that you can see your way out," Evie said as she walked over to the door.

After she departed, Haddington turned to face him. "Evie is up to something."

"You believe so?"

"I do," Haddington replied. "She gave in entirely too easily when it came to searching Barnwell's study."

Nathaniel sighed. "I thought that, as well," he said. "I suppose there is a good chance she will make an appearance tonight."

"I would plan on it."

"What a vexing young woman," Nathaniel muttered.

Haddington chuckled. "I think she is quite brilliant."

"If our circumstances were different, I would most assuredly agree with you," Nathaniel said. "We should go. We have stayed here long enough."

The moon was high in the sky, casting an eerie glow over the empty street. Dressed in dark clothing, Nathaniel walked down the pavement, keeping his head low. He was hoping to go unnoticed in the affluent part of town by keeping to himself.

Up ahead, he saw Barnwell's townhouse, and he stepped into an alleyway. He followed it to the end and came out on the other side. He located Barnwell's back gate and quietly opened it. Once he was in the gardens, he hurried towards the rear of the townhouse.

He hadn't been in Barnwell's townhouse before, but he had been to one of the neighboring ones. If the layout was the same, the study would be in the back right corner.

All the windows were dark, and the only light came from the moon. He stopped next to a pair of windows that faced the gardens. He retrieved a razor from his pocket and scraped the putty away from around a small, square pane of glass before prying the glazing bars away. Once the glass was loosened, he removed it and set it on the ground, then stuck his hand in and unlocked the window.

He opened the window and cautiously entered the study. A desk sat back near the window and bookshelves filled the rectangular room.

Nathaniel opened the thick drapes to allow more light in before he headed over to the desk. His eyes roamed over the papers, but he found nothing that proved Barnwell's association with the Red Ravens. He reached for the top drawer of the desk, but it was locked.

He had just reached into his pocket for a long, thin piece of metal when Evie crawled out from under the desk, dressed in trousers and a white shirt.

"Do you want to use my hairpins to pick the lock?" she whispered, extending two towards him.

Nathaniel gave her an exasperated look. "What are you doing here?" he asked in a hushed voice.

"I figured you would need my help."

"And why would you assume that?"

Evie shrugged. "It was just a feeling."

Nathaniel took the hairpins from her hand. "Just stay there and try to avoid doing anything that would alert the whole household to what we are doing."

He turned back towards the lock and slid one of the hairpins directly into the lock, pushing on it slightly. Then, he pushed the other hairpin into the lock and moved it around until he heard a click.

He returned the hairpins to Evie and opened the drawer. He pulled out a ledger and a stack of papers.

"What can I do?" Evie asked.

Nathaniel handed her the stack of papers. "Look through these and see if you notice anything out of the ordinary."

Evie accepted the papers and started rifling through them. He picked up the ledger and walked closer to the window. He ran his fingers down the lines, looking for anything suspicious, and he kept seeing a repeat transaction for flowers. The odd part was that the amount always totaled the exact same amount of twenty pounds.

He closed the ledger and returned it to the drawer. "Did you find anything?" he asked.

Evie shook her head.

Before he could respond, they heard men's voices coming from the hall on the other side of the door. He quickly returned the papers to their original location and closed the desk door before grabbing Evie's hand and stepping behind a set of drapes. He put his finger to his lips as she looked up at him in surprise.

The door opened and the voices became louder, albeit

slurred. It was evident that these two men had been drinking heavily.

Nathaniel risked peeking out from behind the drapes and saw Lord Barnwell as he dropped down on the settee. The second man was holding a cane, and he immediately recognized him as the man who had come into the shop to speak to Abrams.

Lord Barnwell leaned his head back against the back of the settee. "With any luck, this will all be over soon enough."

"I daresay that you aren't putting enough pressure on him."

"Bah," Lord Barnwell replied. "He is doing exactly what I have instructed him to do."

"What if he betrays you?"

Lord Barnwell let out a deep chuckle. "No one would believe him. He is just a stupid plumassier," he said. "Besides, once this is over, he won't have to worry about anything."

"No, he won't."

"Go home, Abbott," Lord Barnwell grumbled. "I have had enough for one night, and I need to be up early for a meeting at the House of Lords."

"As you wish, my lord."

Abbott departed, and it wasn't long before the sound of snoring could be heard echoing through the room.

Nathaniel met Evie's gaze and gestured with his head towards the window. She nodded her understanding before stepping out from the safety of the drapes and placing her foot onto the windowsill. After she exited the window, he followed suit.

Once he was outside, he inserted the piece of glass back into its frame and closed the window. He remained low as he hurried towards the gate, pleased that Evie was following him.

It wasn't until they arrived in the alleyway that he let himself breathe a sigh of relief. They had been most fortunate that they had managed to escape undetected.

Evie's voice broke through his musings. "We now know with certainty that Barnwell is in league with Abrams."

"We do, and he has been paying him twenty pounds a month for years."

"How did you discover that?"

"It was in the ledger," Nathaniel revealed. "The line item said it was for flowers, but it wasn't hard to deduce."

Evie gave him an expectant look. "Do you have enough evidence to arrest him?"

"I'm afraid not."

"Whyever not?"

"It is nearly impossible for a member of the peerage to be found guilty by a member of his peers."

"So we let him get away with it?"

"I never said that," Nathaniel said. "It is *nearly* impossible but not *im*possible. We will just need to get Abrams to turn on him."

"How do we do that?"

Nathaniel smirked. "We arrest him and force him to talk."

Evie glanced over her shoulder before asking, "Does this mean Dinah and I should still leave Town?"

"I think that would be for the best," Nathaniel said. "Besides, it would greatly ease my mind if Miss Dinah was safe and far away from all of this."

"And me?" Evie questioned with an amused look.

Nathaniel cleared his throat. "Yes, of course. I meant you, as well."

"You will eventually have to tell her the truth of who you are, especially if you want a future with her."

"That isn't feasible."

"Why do you say that?"

"Because," he held up his hands, "I live in the shadows. What I do keeps England safe, and I refuse to do anything that might put her in harm's way again."

Evie arched an eyebrow. "You would just walk away from her?"

"It's what's best for her."

"And you get to decide that for her?"

Nathaniel crossed his arms over his chest. "What would you have me do?" he asked. "Tell her that I am an earl and work as a spy?"

"That would be a good start."

"I have deceived her and used her for information," Nathaniel said. "Why should she ever believe a word that comes out of my mouth?"

"Love alone is worth fighting for."

"Love?" he huffed. "Who said anything about love?"

"No one had to, but it's obvious," Evie replied, placing her hand on her hip. "I know you care about my sister, and you would be a fool not to fight for her."

Nathaniel ran his hand through his hair. "What exactly do you know about love?"

"I know what it is like to be alone, and it's not something I recommend," Evie said.

"Why are you encouraging me?" he asked. "You don't even trust me."

Evie dropped her hand to her side. "No, but Rutledge does, and I'm beginning to believe you aren't terrible."

"I shall take that as a compliment."

"You should, although I wouldn't become accustomed to it." Evie brought her hand up to her nose. "It smells awful here," she said. "Would you mind if we go?"

"I have no objections."

Chapter Nineteen

With the morning sun streaming into the windows, Dinah sat alone at the table in the dining room as she attempted to read the newssheets. She was tired after a fitful night of sleep, unable to stop pondering the situation with Mr. Collier. In her heart, she knew the truth of the matter—she had fallen in love with the Bow Street Runner.

What was she to do? She was starting to believe that maybe, just maybe, Mr. Collier might have some feelings for her. She didn't dare presume that he had fallen in love with her, but he had seemed as if he had wanted to kiss her.

Or was that just wishful thinking on her part?

Dinah folded the newssheet and placed it on the table. She hated being in this predicament. By following her heart, she risked being an outcast amongst Society, for they would never welcome a Bow Street Runner into their ranks.

Dinah reached for her teacup and took a sip. "What am I to do?" she muttered.

A footman stepped forward. "Miss?"

Dinah forced a smile to her lips as she returned the teacup to the saucer. "I do apologize. I was speaking to myself."

The footman tipped his head and stepped back.

A commotion could be heard coming from the entry hall, and Dinah rose from her seat, wondering what the fuss was. She walked out of the dining room and saw Evie embracing their aunt. She was wearing a threadbare blue gown and had pulled her hair into a tight bun at the base of her neck.

"Evie!" she shouted.

Evie smiled and closed the distance between them. As they embraced, she whispered, "I missed you, little sister."

"And I you."

Evie dropped her arms and stepped back. "How have you been faring?"

"Terrible," Dinah admitted. "I have missed you most dreadfully, and I can scarcely believe that you are finally home."

Aunt Nancy perused the length of Evie. "Dare I ask where you found that dress?"

"I bought it from a woman on the street," Evie shared.

"You bought a dress off the street?" Aunt Nancy asked in disbelief.

"I did," Evie said. "You wouldn't believe some of the items that people sell on the streets. I found some men attempting to sell socks. Can you imagine?"

"No, I cannot," their aunt muttered.

"Are you hungry?" Dinah asked.

Evie put a hand on her stomach. "I am, dreadfully."

"Then let's adjourn to the dining room and get you some breakfast," Dinah said as she looped arms with her sister.

They stepped into the dining room and Evie piled her plate high with food before sitting down next to Dinah at the table. Aunt Nancy sat across from them.

"Did you get enough food?" Aunt Nancy asked.

"I did," Evie confirmed.

"Good. Now you can explain where the blazes you have been!"

Evie smiled. "I have never heard you use such strong language before."

"I have never had to," their aunt responded, unabashed. "I suppose you have brought it out of me."

A footman set a cup of tea in front of Evie, and she eagerly reached for it and took a long drink. "I have missed this."

Tired of waiting to learn the truth about her sister's disappearance, Dinah asked, "Where have you been?"

All humor dropped from Evie's face. "I was forced to go into hiding when I overheard a conversation that I was never meant to hear."

"Why didn't you go to the constable?" their aunt asked.

"Constables are useless," Evie replied.

"I agree," Dinah said. "We notified a constable of your disappearance, and he was adamant that you had run off to Gretna Green to elope."

"With whom?" Evie asked.

Dinah shrugged. "It didn't seem to matter to the constable."

"Regardless, I didn't want to return home and put you both in danger," Evie said. "I stayed away to ensure your safety."

"Where did you stay?" Dinah asked.

"I rented a room at a boarding house," Evie replied.

"Which one?" Dinah inquired.

"It doesn't matter," Evie said dismissively. "I have returned home because I think it would best if we adjourned to our country estate for the duration of the Season."

Their aunt turned her attention towards the servants and ordered, "Leave us."

Once the footmen had left the room, closing the door behind them, their aunt asked, "Is this because of what happened at the rally?"

"Partially," Evie said. "There are men that are anxious to see me dead."

"And you think they won't follow us to Dover?" Dinah asked.

"I do not," Evie responded.

Dinah shifted in her seat to face her sister. "There is someone who can help us," she said. "He is a Bow Street Runner, and he will know what to do."

"How are you acquainted with a Bow Street Runner?" Evie asked.

"I hired him to find you," Dinah revealed.

Evie considered her for a moment, then said, "If we bring the law into this, then I could be arrested for my actions."

"Mr. Collier is only interested in speaking to you," Dinah asserted. "He has told me as much."

"You must be cautious about who you trust," Evie urged.

Their aunt interjected, "That is what I have been saying all along."

"If you must know, Mr. Collier has encouraged me to depart to the countryside, as well, because he worries that my life is in danger," Dinah said.

Their aunt gasped. "When did he tell you this?"

"Yesterday, when he came to call," Dinah replied.

"Yet this is the first I have heard of it," their aunt accused.

Dinah winced. "I intended to speak to you this morning over breakfast."

Aunt Nancy pursed her lips. "Based on what I am hearing, I think it will be best if we depart at once for the country estate. I do not think your cousin will mind, given the circumstances."

"I should say not," Dinah said. "He hasn't bothered to call upon us since we arrived in Town, not even after we sent a message about Evie's disappearance."

"I have heard he is quite busy with his mistress," Evie remarked.

Their aunt rose from the table. "I shall go inform Barnes that we will depart at once. We will go on ahead, and our trunks can follow us."

"I am amenable to that," Evie said. "Although I do require a soak before we depart."

"And we need to burn that dress," their aunt stated as she walked over to the door. "I will ask Barnes to see to heating the water for your bath."

"Thank you, Aunt Nancy," Evie responded.

After their aunt departed, Dinah shook her head. "I can't believe you left us."

"I had to."

"Did you also have to try to kill Lord Barnwell?"

Evie nodded.

"Why?"

Evie glanced over her shoulder before saying, "He is a bad man. He is not the man that we thought he was."

"How is that possible?" Dinah asked. "He has only ever been kind to us."

"You must trust me on this," Evie insisted.

"I do trust you."

Evie looked relieved at her admission. "I will tell you the truth of the matter as we travel to Dover, but for now, I need to get out of these clothes."

Dinah glanced down at the worn dress. "Did you truly buy that from a street vendor?"

"I did," Evie said.

"I cannot wait to hear about your adventure."

Evie huffed. "It was hardly an adventure; it was more survival."

"If I had been in your shoes, I wouldn't have survived," Dinah said.

Reaching over, Evie placed her hand over hers. "You are stronger than you give yourself credit for, Dinah," she stated. "I have no doubt that you would have thrived."

Dinah smiled. "How I have missed you."

Evie returned her smile as she removed her hand. "I find myself curious about this Bow Street Runner that you spoke of," she said. "Mr. Collier, was it?"

"It was."

"Why is it that you smile when you say his name?" Evie inquired.

"I do?" Dinah asked. "I haven't noticed."

Evie looked at her curiously. "It would appear that you had your own adventure while I was gone."

"I did it so I could find you."

"Was this the man that was with you at the rally?" Evie asked.

"It was," Dinah replied. "Reginald accompanied us, as well."

"I'm afraid I didn't see Reginald," Evie said, "but I would be remiss if I didn't tell you that you risked your reputation by attending the rally."

Dinah let out a disbelieving huff. "I do believe you lost the right to lecture me when I saw you trying to shoot Lord Barnwell."

Evie put her hands up in surrender. "You make a good point," she said, rising. "It is time for my soak. I need to get the layers of filth off me."

Dinah scrunched her nose. "You do smell awful."

"I have no doubt," Evie replied. "That is what happens when you live in the shabby part of town."

"I have so many questions for you."

"And I promise I will answer every one of them in due time."

Dinah rose. "I shall walk you to your bedchamber."

"I would greatly appreciate that."

Many hours later, Dinah stepped into the coach and sat next to her sister on the bench. The door closed and the coach merged into traffic.

She couldn't help but wonder if Mr. Collier would miss her while she was residing at her country estate. Did she dare believe that he would write her? That would be a bold move on his part, but she wouldn't mind.

The thought kept creeping into her mind that he might forget all about her, and it terrified her. It wasn't as if he had made his intentions known to her, and she was fearful that she could just be a passing whim to him.

Frankly, she didn't know what Mr. Collier would do. She had left a part of her heart with him, and she knew she would never get it back.

Evie nudged her with her shoulder. "You seem lost in thought," she commented. "Whatever is the matter?"

"I was just woolgathering, I suppose," Dinah admitted

Their aunt spoke up. "Were you thinking about Mr. Collier?"

"I was," Dinah replied, seeing no reason to deny it.

Aunt Nancy sighed. "I do wish you would recognize that he is below your notice. He isn't a worthy suitor for you."

"I am not entirely sure of that," Evie objected.

Their aunt frowned. "Not you, too?"

Evie half-shrugged. "It has been my experience that the heart wants what it wants, and you don't force these things."

"Even if your sister was the laughingstock of the *ton*?" their aunt asked. "Because that is precisely what would happen if she married a Bow Street Runner."

Evie glanced over at her. "What do you know about this Mr. Collier?"

"Not a lot, actually," Dinah replied. "But, more importantly, I know how he makes me feel."

"Which is?" her sister pressed.

"I feel protected and safe around him."

"Then you should rely on your instincts," Evie insisted.

Dinah eyed her curiously. "Since when did you care about feelings and love?"

Evie smiled. "I just want you to be happy, whatever path that may be," she said. "Although, the road to true love is never an easy one."

Dinah glanced down at her hands in her lap. "I never said I loved him."

"You didn't have to," Evie said. "I am your sister, and I can tell when you are hiding something."

Their aunt interjected, "Speaking of hiding things…." Her voice trailed off as she gave Evie a pointed look.

Evie laughed. "Fair enough, Aunt Nancy," she said. "What would you wish to know?"

"Why did you try to kill Lord Barnwell?"

All humor was stripped off Evie's face. "He is trying to start a revolution."

Dinah exchanged a concerned look with her aunt. "Lord Barnwell?" she asked.

"I didn't believe it at first, either, but I have since learned the truth," Evie pressed.

"Where did you discover this truth?" Dinah asked hesitantly.

"I met a man who enlightened me," Evie said. "He saved me from two ruffians that were intent on seeing me dead after I overheard their conversation."

"What did they say?" Dinah inquired.

"I didn't hear much except for Barnwell's name, but it was enough for them to follow me into an alleyway," Evie explained. "If it wasn't for him, I would be dead. He was injured while protecting me, and I kept watch over him in our room."

Aunt Nancy's brows shot up. "You were alone with a man in a room?"

"I was, but he was old enough to be my father," Evie said.

"That won't matter to the gossips if they ever discovered the truth," their aunt stated. "Do you not care a whit for your reputation?"

"Apparently not, especially since I've done far worse these past few weeks," Evie remarked. "I can assure you that it couldn't be helped."

"Pray tell, what else have you done?" Aunt Nancy asked stiffly.

"I also wore men's clothing to go undetected in the rookeries," Evie responded.

Their aunt's eyes grew wide. "Why were you in the rookeries?"

"I was following someone," Evie said.

"Who?" Dinah asked.

Evie waved her hand in front of her. "It doesn't matter now," she replied. "I have since learned that I find him trustworthy."

Their aunt removed a fan from her reticule and started fanning her face. "Your parents entrusted me with your safety, and they would be greatly disappointed with your recent exploits."

"I doubt that somehow," Evie said. "My father always told me to be true to who I was."

"And who is that?" Dinah asked.

"I'm still trying to figure that out, but I finally am on the right path to do so," Evie responded.

"By wearing trousers and shooting at people?" Aunt Nancy questioned.

"You assume that Lord Barnwell is innocent, which is an incorrect assumption," Evie expressed. "He is trying to stage an uprising so Whigs could be in the position to take power."

"That is quite the accusation," their aunt said. "Do you have any proof?"

"Not exactly," Evie replied, "but I know someone who is working on that."

"Who?" Dinah asked.

Evie's eyes grew guarded. "I'm afraid I can't say."

"Whyever not?"

"It is for your own good," Evie assured her.

Dinah tossed up her hands. "Why do people keep saying that to me?" she asked. "Mr. Collier said the same thing to me."

"He isn't wrong," Evie said. "There are some things I have learned that I wish I had never discovered in the first place."

"Shouldn't I be the one who decides that for myself?"

Evie adjusted the sleeve of her grey riding habit. "I know it seems unfair, but…" She stopped as the coach suddenly increased its speed. "Something is wrong."

Dinah watched as Evie opened the window and stuck her head out. "It would appear that we have some unwanted visitors," she announced as she returned to her seat. She reached into her reticule and pulled out a muff pistol.

"What are you going to do with that?" Aunt Nancy asked.

Evie tightened her hold on the pistol. "I thought it would be a good time to invite them to tea."

"Do be serious," their aunt chided.

"I'm going to protect our coach." Evie turned to Dinah. "Do you have your pistol in your reticule?"

"I do," Dinah confirmed.

"Get it out and hand it to me when I ask for it," Evie ordered.

"I can do that."

"I count three of them, but if I can hit two of them, then the other one might ride off," Evie shared. "I just have to wait until they get closer."

"Why?"

"Because the muff pistol is only accurate at close ranges," Evie said before she stuck her head out of the coach.

Time seemed to slow, but it was only a moment before Evie aimed her muff pistol and fired.

She leaned back in and announced, "I hit one, and he's falling back." She held her hand out as the coach started swaying back and forth. "Give me your pistol."

Dinah placed it in her outstretched hand and asked, "What can I do?"

"Just hold on," Evie said. "The driver is trying to force the other two riders off the road."

Evie braced herself before she leaned out of the window. The only noise Dinah could hear was the sound of pounding horse hooves as she attempted to keep herself upright.

Evie fired again, and she pulled herself back into the coach. "I hit the second rider in the arm, but he isn't falling back, and now I see a coach trailing us with additional men."

"What do we do now?" their aunt asked, her voice shrill.

"Let's hope the driver can lose them," Evie said.

The wheel hit a deep rut, causing the coach to jerk to the side, and they were flung to the floor in a sprawling heap.

"Good heavens!" Aunt Nancy exclaimed.

As Dinah helped their aunt to her bench, the coach tipped to the side and started dragging on the ground, hitting rut after rut.

"The wheel must have come off," Evie said. "Hold on!"

Dinah braced her hand against the side of the coach and hoped they lived to tell their story. The coach started slowing down, eventually coming to a full stop.

Evie turned towards her, her expression solemn. "You must be brave, Dinah."

"Why?"

"I don't have time to explain, but you must promise me, no matter what happens," Evie said.

"I promise."

Her words had barely left her mouth when the door was wrenched open, revealing a burly man with a ghastly scar on his chin. "Look what we have here," he declared, a sneer on his lips. "I will count this as a win."

Evie shielded her with her body. "Just take me. You don't need my sister or my aunt."

"You are right," the man agreed. "We don't need your aunt, but we were ordered to take your sister alongside you."

"There is no need—" Evie attempted.

The man reached in and grabbed her arm, yanking her out of the coach. "I don't want to hear it. If you don't be quiet, I will make you."

After the man handed Evie off to someone else, he put his hand into the coach for Dinah. "You will find that I am not a complete brute, assuming you come along like a good girl."

Dinah tentatively placed her hand in his, and he helped assist her out of the coach. "Thank you," she murmured as she stood next to her sister, whose arms were clamped to her sides by a burly man's viselike grip.

The man with the scar gestured towards the other coach. "After you," he said.

When Dinah didn't move fast enough, he grabbed her arm and forcefully led her. "You will find that I am much more hospitable if you follow my directions," he growled.

Dinah climbed into the coach and sat down. She had just situated herself when Evie was tossed into a heap on the floor.

Dinah leaned down and assisted her sister onto the bench. "What is going on?" she asked in a low voice.

Evie didn't have time to answer her question before the burly man entered the coach and sat across from them.

"You didn't think I would let you ride alone, considering that stunt that you just pulled," he said, eyes hard as stone. "You cost me two good men."

"They deserved it," Evie said.

Leaning forward, the man struck Evie across the face. "It is best if you remain quiet. You might make me angry."

Evie brought her hand up to her reddened cheek, but

thankfully, she didn't challenge the man. Dinah didn't think she could handle watching the man hurt her sister again. These had to be the dangerous men that Mr. Collier had told her about, and she shuddered at the thought of what they might do to them.

Chapter Twenty

Nathaniel sat at his desk as he read through the pile of correspondence, reports, and other paperwork he'd neglected lately. It was an exhausting but necessary evil. He knew that once he inherited his father's title, he alone would be responsible for the livelihood of hundreds of people, and that thought was rather daunting.

The long clock in the corner chimed, alerting him of the time. He truly hoped that Dinah and Evie were having an uneventful time as they traveled to their country house. Now that Dinah was safe, he could finally breathe a sigh of relief. He could complete his assignment without any more distractions. But he knew in his heart he would miss her. She was the one bright spot in this dreary place.

His father stepped into the study. "I'm glad to see you are working."

"Good afternoon, Father."

Stopping in front of the desk, his father asked, "Did you read the quarterly report that Mr. Bolton sent over?"

"I did," Nathaniel replied.

"What are your thoughts on it?"

"I agree with Mr. Bolton's assessment, and it would be best if we invested in new farm equipment," Nathaniel said.

His father nodded in approval. "I concur," he replied. "Do you intend to meet with Mr. Bolton today?"

"I do."

The words had just left his mouth when Haddington stepped into the room with a solemn look on his face.

Haddington tipped his head at his father. "Lord Montfort."

"Haddington," his father greeted. "It is a pleasure to see you."

"Likewise," Haddington said.

His father glanced between them. "If you will excuse me, I am late for a meeting."

After his father left the room, Haddington closed the door and announced, "We have a problem."

"Which is?"

"The agent that was assigned to trail the Ashmore's coach just returned and informed us that Evie and Dinah have been abducted."

Nathaniel shot up from his seat. "When did this happen?"

"It was about an hour outside of London."

"Did the agent attempt to stop the attack?"

Haddington shook his head. "He was outnumbered and would have been killed if he had interceded."

"That wouldn't have stopped me."

"Me either, but it was a good thing he didn't," Haddington said. "If he was dead, we wouldn't have known about their abduction until much later."

"What about Mrs. Carter?"

"She was banged up, but alive and free," Haddington revealed. "The agent spoke to her, and she was adamant that highwaymen took her nieces."

Nathaniel clenched his jaw. "I should have accompanied them."

"If you had, you might have ended up dead." Haddington put his hands on the back of the upholstered chair and leaned in. "Abrams is in Newgate, but he refuses to speak to anyone but you."

"Then I do not wish to disappoint him," Nathaniel said, coming around his desk. "With any luck, he will tell me where Dinah and Evie are."

"How do you intend to accomplish that feat?"

"I will ask nicely."

"And when that doesn't work?"

Nathaniel walked over to the door. "I will do what needs to be done to ensure Dinah and Evie are returned safely." He opened the door. "Shall we?"

Haddington pushed off on the chair and approached him. "Merritt wanted me to remind you that we need Abrams alive if we want to arrest Barnwell."

"I am well aware of what is at stake," Nathaniel said before he departed from the study.

"I hope you do not mind, but I took the liberty of asking Balfour to saddle your horse."

"Not at all. That will save us a considerable amount of time."

As they stepped into the entry hall, his mother stepped out from the drawing room. "There you are," she said in a cheery voice. "Do not forget about Lady Wycombe's ball tomorrow evening."

"I will try to make it, Mother."

"That is not good enough," his mother replied, giving him a stern look. "I expect you to be in attendance."

"Understood, but I must not tarry any longer. I have an important errand to run."

His mother smiled. "Go, then."

After they were mounted, they hurried to Newgate, skirting coaches along the way. They arrived and secured their horses before stepping inside.

A guard sitting behind a desk greeted them with an expectant look on his face. "What's yer business?"

"I am here to speak to a prisoner," Nathaniel replied.

"Which one?"

"John Abrams."

"When was he brought in?"

Haddington spoke up. "This morning."

The guard reached for a piece of paper and ran his finger down the names. "Abrams," he said, his finger stilling. "He is in a cell for the refractory. He attempted an escape when he first arrived, which did not end well for him."

"I am not surprised by that," Nathaniel remarked.

The guard leaned back in his chair, appearing to have not a care in the world. "Come back tomorrow and ye can speak to him."

"I have to speak to him right now," Nathaniel asserted.

"My hands are tied on this one."

Nathaniel reached his hand into his waistcoat pocket and removed a pound. He extended it to the guard and said, "I just need a few moments with him."

The guard accepted the money and slipped it into his pocket. "I think I can arrange that." He rose from his seat. "Follow me."

They followed the guard through the dark, narrow halls of the prison and he stopped in front of a cramped cell. "Abrams!" he shouted.

From the corner, Abrams rose awkwardly and grunted as he held his hands over his ribs. He made his way slowly over to the corner and met his gaze. "I knew you would come."

Nathaniel's eyes ran over Abrams' swollen eyes, nose, and lip. "I see your attempted escape did not come to pass."

"It was a foolish mistake on my part." Abrams spat on the ground. "Now that you are here, you can get me released."

"And why would I do that?" Nathaniel asked.

"Because if you don't, Miss Dinah will be killed."

Nathaniel stepped closer to the cell, his teeth clenched. "You will tell me where she is," he ordered.

Abrams chuckled dryly. "I will do no such thing. She is my ticket out of this place."

Turning towards the guard, Nathaniel barked, "Leave us."

"Ye have five minutes," the guard responded before he walked away.

Abrams watched the guard's retreating figure, then said, "If you don't have me released by the end of the day, then Miss Dinah will be killed."

"You wouldn't dare."

Abrams' expression grew hard. "Do not test me, or you will lose," he seethed. "As I have said before, you are not the first Bow Street Runner that has challenged us."

"You seem to forget one thing," Nathaniel said.

"Which is?"

"You have a sister."

Abrams' expression slipped slightly. "You will leave her out of this," he barked.

"I'm afraid you involved her when you had Miss Dinah and Miss Ashmore abducted," Nathaniel said. "If you don't tell me where they are, I will have her locked up for conspiracy to kill the prime minister."

"She has nothing to do with this."

"Neither does Miss Dinah."

"No jury would convict her," Abrams insisted.

Nathaniel smirked. "I can assure you that the case will never go to trial," he said. "Perhaps I will have her transported, as well. I'm sure she would do well as a lone woman in another country."

"That would be a death sentence."

With a slight shrug of his shoulders, Nathaniel responded, "I guess you have to decide what you are willing to sacrifice to keep your sister alive."

Abrams grabbed the cell bars and leaned forward. "You would do something so underhanded?"

"You can't even comprehend what I am willing to do to ensure that Miss Dinah remains safe," Nathaniel stated.

"But you are a Bow Street Runner. You are supposed to uphold the law."

"That is where you are mistaken," Nathaniel said. "I have no qualms about breaking the law to achieve my purposes, starting with your sister."

Nathaniel could see the indecision on Abrams' face. Finally, after a long moment, Abrams said, "If I tell you where Miss Dinah and Miss Ashmore are, you will leave my sister out of this."

"I give you my word."

Abrams released his hands from the bars. "Even if you are successful in saving Miss Dinah, the threat on her life won't end there. She will be hunted down and killed unless you kill Lord Liverpool."

"I will keep Miss Dinah safe."

"You are a marked man, as well," Abrams said.

"That means very little to me."

Abrams scoffed. "It should. This treachery will not go unpunished."

Haddington spoke up. "Is Barnwell calling the shots?"

"What do you know of Barnwell?" Abrams asked hesitantly.

"We know he is working with you," Haddington replied.

Abrams shook his head. "You know nothing."

The guard approached them. "Time's up," he said.

Nathaniel turned back towards Abrams. "Where is Miss Dinah?" he demanded.

"There is an empty warehouse on Mousley Street," Abrams said.

"If I discover that you are lying…"

"You don't need to say it. I understand what is at stake." Abrams smirked as he stepped back. "I wish you luck."

The guard gestured towards the hall. "It is time for you two to leave."

"I don't trust Abrams," Haddington remarked as they walked out.

"Neither do I," Nathaniel said. "It almost appeared as if he were eager for us to go to the warehouse."

"Do you think it's a trap?"

"I think it would be safe to assume it is," Nathaniel responded. "I believe it is time to round up more agents to help, and I know just the two."

Dinah sat on the cold, hard floorboards with her back against the wall as she watched her sister pace back and forth in the small, square room. They had been here for what felt like hours, and she was starting to lose hope that they would ever be rescued.

How would Mr. Collier even know where to look for them, assuming he even knew they had been abducted? Would he even care? Frankly, the only thing that she did know was that they were somewhere deep within the rookeries in a dilapidated building of some sort.

Dinah's eyes roamed the room, and she noticed the deteriorating blue papered walls. No furniture was in the room, and the only source of light came from a window in the corner. The stale air suddenly seemed very warm, almost oppressive, and she resisted the urge to fan herself with her fingers.

Evie walked over to the window and examined it. "The window has been nailed shut," she announced. "If we could pry the nails out, we might be able to escape out this window."

"How would we be able to do that?"

"We could climb down the wall," Evie replied.

"It sounds rather difficult."

Evie glanced over at her. "It's not," she assured her. "You just look for the bricks that are jutting out."

"How did you learn how to climb brick walls?"

"Father taught me," Evie said.

Dinah lifted her brow in surprise. "Father taught you?"

Evie nodded. "He did," she replied. "He also taught me how to throw a dagger."

"Why?"

"Because I asked him to."

"But why would you ask for such things?" Dinah pressed.

Evie let out a sigh before sharing, "Father was not who you thought he was."

"Who was he?"

Evie turned and leaned against the windowsill. "He was a spy."

Dinah let out a huff. "You can't possibly be in earnest," she said. "Father was anything but a spy."

"I know this may be difficult to hear, but Father was indeed a spy."

"How would you know this?"

"The man who saved me, Rutledge," Evie started, "it wasn't the first time I had seen him."

"Where had you seen him?"

"At our townhouse. He would frequently visit Father."

"That could just be a coincidence."

"It was more than that," Evie said. "Rutledge also confirmed it when we spoke."

Dinah pressed her lips together. "Why didn't he tell us?"

Evie gave her an amused look. "Spies tend to keep that to themselves."

Dinah leaned her head back against the wall. "I'm beginning to wonder if I ever knew Father or you."

"I am the same person."

"Perhaps, but you have another side of you that I know nothing about," Dinah said.

"It is better that way."

Dinah frowned. "Mr. Collier has said that same thing, but I am tired of being coddled."

"I am not coddling you."

"No?" Dinah asked. "Because it feels like you are."

Evie pushed off the windowsill and came to sit down next to her. "You must understand that everything I did was to protect you."

"It doesn't feel that way."

"If I had come home, I would have brought danger to you, and that was something I couldn't do," Evie said. "I thought by staying away I would keep you safe."

"You could have left a note."

"There is a lot I could have done differently," Evie responded, "but the truth of the matter was that I was making it up as I was going along."

The sound of scratching and scampering inside the walls caused her to shudder. She didn't dare think of the rodents that were all around her.

Evie noticed her shudder but didn't appear to have the same aversion, because she almost appeared calm, which was ludicrous. How could anyone be calm in a situation such as this?

"Rats are the least of our concern," Evie said, rising. "We need to try to escape, or else we will be killed."

"How do you know they will kill us?"

"We've seen their faces." Evie pulled her dress up and retrieved a small dagger that was strapped to her leg. "We can use this to pry out the nails."

Dinah rose awkwardly. "Why do you have a dagger strapped to your leg?"

Evie walked over to the window, then responded, "Because

I knew they would never think to look for it there."

"I should say not."

As Evie attempted to pry a nail out, she asked, "How did you become acquainted with Mr. Collier?"

"You want to discuss that now?"

"I just find myself curious," Evie said, letting out a small grunt.

Dinah came to stand next to her sister. "I saw Mr. Collier on the street near J.B. Abrams' shop and noticed that he was wearing a red waistcoat. I had the driver stop the coach and hired him on the spot."

"How did you know Bow Street Runners wore red waistcoats?"

"From the newssheets."

"I see," Evie said, "and Mr. Collier told you he was a Bow Street Runner?"

Dinah looked at her sister curiously. "I don't believe he came out and said it, but it was fairly obvious," she replied. "Besides, if he wasn't a Bow Street Runner, he wouldn't have taken the case."

Evie proudly held up a nail and announced, "One down."

"Can I help?" Dinah asked.

"You can," Evie said. "Rip the bottom of your dress and use it to see if you can remove the nails on the side."

Dinah reached down and tore off a section of her gown. Then, she fingered a nail and tried to pull it out. "It won't budge."

"Wiggle it back and forth," Evie encouraged.

While Dinah worked to remove the nail, she said, "Now that you have returned home, there is no need for Mr. Collier to come around."

"Is that what you want?" Evie asked.

Dinah pressed her lips together, delaying her response. "I don't know what I want."

"Yes, you do."

"Pardon?"

Evie shifted to face her. "You are clearly smitten with Mr. Collier."

"I am the daughter of a viscount and Mr. Collier is a Bow Street Runner," Dinah said. "A match between us would be impossible."

"I hadn't taken you for such a prude."

"I am not sure how to respond to that."

"There is more than meets the eye when it comes to Mr. Collier."

"How would you know that?" Dinah asked. "You haven't even met the man."

Evie hesitated. "I did meet him."

"When was that?"

"At the Bradford," Evie responded, "and then later when I was following him into the rookeries."

Dinah's hand stilled over the nail. "Mr. Collier said that you weren't at the Bradford."

"That's because I asked him to tell you that," Evie revealed. "I couldn't risk that you would come looking for me yourself, and I wasn't ready to come home yet."

With a frown on her lips, Dinah said, "Regardless, he should have told me the truth."

"We were both trying to protect you."

"From what?"

"From yourself."

Dinah huffed. "That seems unlikely, since you were the one who tried to kill Lord Barnwell."

Evie gave her a look, then asked, "If you knew I was at the Bradford, would you have come looking for me?"

"I would have," Dinah admitted.

"Precisely, and I couldn't risk you doing that."

"So you and Mr. Collier decided to work together to intentionally deceive me?"

"Protect you," Evie corrected.

Dinah looked heavenward. "I see it differently, and I doubt I can ever trust Mr. Collier again, knowing what I know now."

"It would be foolish to just give up on him."

"It would be for the best."

"You can always take the easy way out and walk away from him, but you would come to regret it. Maybe not today or tomorrow. But one day, you will wake up and realize what you gave up."

"Which is?"

"A chance at true happiness."

"And you would know this how?" Dinah asked.

A pained looked came to Evie's face as she turned back towards the window and slid the dagger under a nail. "I learned the hard way." Her words were so soft that Dinah almost didn't hear her.

"Evie—"

"We've wasted enough time," Evie interrupted. "We need to remove these nails before anyone comes back."

It was evident that Evie didn't want to continue this conversation, so Dinah focused on trying to remove the nail, which was a much harder task than she'd ever imagined. No matter what she did, the nail didn't seem to want to budge.

Knowing the precariousness of her situation, Dinah felt tears well up in her eyes, but she blinked them back. She didn't want Evie to think she was weak or that she couldn't rely on her. Although she wasn't feeling strong at the moment, and the fear of the unknown was starting to affect her.

Chapter Twenty-One

"You want to do what?!"

Not perturbed by Merritt's outburst, Nathaniel repeated, "I want to save Miss Dinah and Miss Ashmore."

"I understand that, but what you are asking to do is madness," Merritt said.

"I disagree."

Merritt pressed his fingers to the bridge of his nose. "You can't just walk up and demand their release. If you did do something so foolish, you would be killed before you finished speaking."

"I have no intention of using the main door."

"Then how do you plan to enter the building?" Merritt asked.

Nathaniel glanced over at Haddington, then responded, "We scouted the area, and we discovered a broken window on the first level of the warehouse. We intend to slip in that way."

Merritt lowered his hand and shifted his gaze toward Haddington. "I expect this lunacy from Hawthorne, but not from you."

"I do believe Hawthorne's plan will succeed," Haddington said.

LAURA BEERS

"Now I am dealing with two delusional agents," Merritt huffed. "All right, tell me the rest of the plan."

"We plan to bring two other agents along to distract the men in the warehouse," Nathaniel shared.

"What other agents are mad enough to go along with this plan?"

"Worsley and Talbot," Nathaniel replied.

"I should have known," Merritt muttered.

"They will create a ruse for being there, and we will sneak into the warehouse while the guards are occupied," Nathaniel explained. "We will find Miss Dinah and Miss Ashmore and depart from the building without anyone the wiser."

"You cannot possibly be that naïve," Merritt said. "When has a plan of yours ever gone according to plan?"

"I'll admit there are risks…"

Merritt scoffed. "I can't even count on my hands how many things could go wrong with this plan."

"Haddington and I counted five men guarding the girls," Nathaniel said.

"That you could see," Merritt countered. "There might be more."

"That won't be a problem."

Merritt leaned back in his seat. "I know you want to save them, but what you are suggesting is suicide."

"I disagree."

"Why don't I send in a team of agents to surround the building and come at them all at once?"

"What if Miss Dinah and Miss Ashmore are caught in the crossfire?" Nathaniel asked. "We don't even know where they are."

Haddington interjected, "We do believe they are being held in one of the rooms on the second level, but we can't be certain."

"That doesn't instill a great deal of confidence in me,"

Merritt said. "What are the chances I can talk you out of this plan of yours?"

"Not likely," Nathaniel replied.

"That is what I assumed." Merritt grew quiet. "Here is what I propose: we go along with your plan, but if you are not out in a reasonable amount of time, a team will go in after you."

"I can agree to that," Nathaniel said.

Merritt let out a sigh. "I was a lot like you when I was younger," he stated. "I used to go in, gun drawn, without weighing the consequences of my actions. But it all changed when I married my Eleanor. I realized that I had something to live for, and it changed my perspective."

"With all due respect, I would do anything to save Miss Dinah from those men, including giving my own life," Nathaniel asserted.

"I know, and that is what worries me," Merritt responded. "I don't want to lose one of my agents to stupidity."

"What would you have me do?" Nathaniel asked, his voice rising. "Leave them to their own devices and be killed?"

"I never said that, but I want you to understand what is at risk here."

"I do understand!"

Merritt shook his head. "Stop being pigheaded and listen," he declared. "You are not the only one who wants Miss Ashmore and Miss Dinah to be returned safely."

"It sounds like I am," Nathaniel mumbled.

Turning his attention towards Haddington, Merritt asked, "How do you tolerate being friends with him?"

Haddington smirked. "I'm beginning to ask myself that same question."

Nathaniel rose from his seat and walked over to the window. "We don't have time for this," he exclaimed. "I have to save Miss Dinah."

"What do you intend to do with Barnwell?" Merritt asked.

"We intend to pay him a visit after we have rescued the Ashmore sisters," Nathaniel responded.

"I understand that Abrams hasn't turned on Barnwell yet," Merritt said. "Without his testimony, the magistrate won't even issue an arrest warrant for him."

"I understand, but we haven't even begun with finding ways to make Abrams talk."

"With Abrams' testimony, it should be enough to discredit Barnwell with the Whigs," Merritt remarked. "He should be arrested and held at Newgate, but I sincerely doubt a jury of his peers would ever convict him."

"It is still the right thing to do. He is trying to start a revolution by having Lord Liverpool killed," Haddington said.

"Without hard proof, it is just hearsay," Merritt pointed out.

Nathaniel leaned his shoulder against the wall. "I won't let Barnwell get away with this."

Merritt pointed his finger at him. "You will not take matters into your own hands, and that is an order."

"It would be best if Barnwell just disappeared," Nathaniel said.

"I won't disagree with you, but you can't go around killing lords and not expect repercussions for your actions," Merritt warned, lowering his hand. "We may be spies, but we are still civilized in our conduct."

"Understood, sir."

Merritt watched him for a moment. "Just be patient. We will find a way to bring down Barnwell."

"I have never been one for patience," Nathaniel acknowledged.

"I am well aware," Merritt replied. "Go and get the rest of your team and bring them up to speed."

As Nathaniel walked towards the door, Merritt continued, "Use your time wisely, because we will be close behind you."

"Yes, sir," Nathaniel said before departing from the office, followed closely by Haddington.

Neither of them spoke as they hurried out of the building. Once they were outside, Nathaniel approached Worsley and Talbot. "Merritt agreed to our plan, declaring it 'brilliant'."

"He did?" Talbot asked.

Haddington interjected, "He thought it was sheer madness, but he is giving us an opportunity to rescue the ladies before the rest of the agents arrive."

"Then we'd best hurry," Worsley said as he reached into the cart. "Does anyone want a potato to eat on our ride over?"

"Who would eat a potato raw?" Nathaniel asked.

"I do, occasionally. It's a little bitter and leaves a chalky taste in your mouth," Worsley shared, "but it is better than going hungry."

Haddington shook his head. "It is a good thing you two are competent agents, or I have a feeling that Merritt would have already fired you."

Talbot reached into the cart, pulling out two pistols. "The cart allows us to carry more firearms," he said. "The building has never been more secure."

Nathaniel gestured towards the awaiting coach. "We have the ride over to discuss our plan at length."

"I have never ridden in a fancy coach before," Worsley said as he moved to step inside.

"Try not to dirty the seats," Talbot joked.

Haddington met his gaze with questions in his eyes. "Are you sure about these two?"

"I am," Nathaniel replied.

"Then I trust you." Haddington walked over to the coach and stopped. "And just so you know, I feel the same as you. I will fight until my last breath to bring Dinah and Evie home safely."

"Let's hope it won't come to that."

Haddington tipped his head in acknowledgement before

he disappeared into the coach, and then Nathaniel heard Worsley exclaim, "You sat on my potato!"

Nathaniel let out a sigh as he realized that he'd never had so much to lose. If something happened to Dinah, then he would never forgive himself. He would do whatever it took to ensure that she survived this and went on to have a long, happy life. It was what she deserved.

But he had a sneaking suspicion that he wouldn't be involved in Dinah's life from here on out, not when she found out the truth about him.

Dinah's fingers were red, raw, and bleeding as she pulled her hand back. She had been trying her best to pull this nail out, but she was having no luck. It was embedded deep into the wood, and no matter what she tried, it wouldn't budge.

She glanced down at the three nails resting on the windowsill. Her sister was having much more success than she was. It made her realize that no matter what she did, she would never be as good as Evie was. Her sister was everything that she wanted to be but couldn't manage to achieve.

Evie glanced down at Dinah's hands and said, "You should take a break."

"But not you?"

"I don't need one," Evie replied as she wiped the sweat off her brow with the sleeve of her traveling habit.

"I'm sorry I let you down," Dinah said as she rested her back against the wall.

"You did no such thing," Evie asserted. "Why would you say that?"

"I've failed to remove even one nail, and you have removed three."

"It is much easier with a dagger."

Dinah slid down until she sat on the cold, hard floor. "I am a disappointment."

Evie turned towards her and asked, "Where is this coming from?"

"I have done nothing with my life," Dinah declared.

"That isn't true," Evie said.

Dinah frowned. "You have more adventure in one day than I have in my whole life, and I am content staying at home."

"There is no shame in that."

"I have more handkerchiefs with my initials on them than I know what to do with," Dinah sighed.

"That is a problem," Evie said lightly.

Dinah met her sister's gaze. "How do you do it?" she asked.

"I am unsure of your meaning."

"How do you don a pair of trousers, sneak out of the house, and live an extraordinary life?"

Evie came to sit down next to her and put the dagger beneath her dress. "Not everyone would consider it extraordinary, you know."

"But I do."

"I suppose I have always wanted more out of life," Evie shared. "It's been that way since I was young."

"And I have always been boring."

Evie shifted to face her. "You have been anything but boring," she declared. "You are perfect just the way you are."

"You are too kind."

"It has nothing to do with being kind," Evie said. "I have never been content with what I have been given, and I'm always wanting more. Sometimes, I wish I could be more like you."

"How can you say that?"

Evie gave her a weak smile. "You were the perfect daughter," she said. "You always did what was expected of you without complaint, whereas I drove Mother and Father mad."

"And they loved you for it."

"No, they tolerated it," Evie stated. "They didn't quite know what to do with me. No one does."

"I don't believe that. Mother and Father adored you."

Evie rested the back of her head against the wall. "I have never quite fit in Society, and it has only gotten worse as I grow older."

"Sometimes fitting in isn't as great as it is made out to be." Dinah paused. "Do you think we will survive this?"

"I do."

"How do you have so much confidence?"

"Because I know that Mr. Collier will come after you," Evie said. "We just have to stay alive until he does."

Dinah glanced down at her hands in her lap. "I hope he does, but I do not dare to presume he would risk his life for me."

"I have only spoken to Mr. Collier a few times, mind you, but I've seen the way he looks at you," Evie said. "He is clearly smitten."

"Do you really believe so?"

Evie nodded. "I daresay that your problem is that you don't see how incredibly special you truly are."

"I don't feel special," she admitted.

"Then, dear sister, we need to change that," Evie said.

Her words had barely left her mouth when the sound of the door being unlocked echoed through the room. The door opened, and the burly man stepped inside.

His menacing eyes landed on them. "The boss wants to see you."

Evie rose and boldly declared, "If Abrams wants to see us, he can come in here to speak to us."

"Don't be daft," the man spat out. "That isn't the boss."

Rising, Dinah said, "We should do as the man says."

The burly man bobbed his head. "You should listen to your sister," he growled. "Follow me."

"It will be all right," Evie whispered as Dinah started towards the door. She wanted to believe Evie's words, but she wasn't sure how they were going to get out of here with their lives.

They followed the man down the narrow hall until they descended a flight of rickety stairs. They stepped into a large hall with three chairs positioned across from each other in the center of the room. Broken windows ran along the length of the hall, providing some light to the dark space.

"Sit down," the man barked.

Dinah obeyed, her back straight. If she was going to die, then she would do so honorably.

Evie sat down next to her, and her alert eyes roamed the hall. "How many men do you see?" she whispered.

Dinah took a moment to count the men that remained in the shadows. "I only see four."

"That is how many I count, as well, but we must assume that there are more."

A door in the distance creaked opened, followed by the sound of footsteps resonating throughout the hall.

The figure approached them, and the light hit his face, revealing Lord Barnwell. He stopped next to the empty chair and studied them. Finally, he shifted his gaze to Evie and said, "This is all your fault."

"My fault?" Evie repeated.

"If you had just died, then your sister would never have gotten involved," Lord Barnwell said.

"My apologies," Evie remarked dryly.

Lord Barnwell sat down and tugged down on the ends of his blue waistcoat. "You have always been an exasperating chit. Your parents indulged you when they should have beat the stubbornness out of you."

Not waiting for a response, Lord Barnwell continued.

"Your mistake was thinking that you could kill me, but you failed in that regard."

"I can assure you that next time, my aim will be true."

Lord Barnwell chuckled. "I'm afraid there won't be a next time. I intend to kill you and your sister."

"Dinah has nothing to do with this," Evie said. "You should set her free."

"That is impossible, because she knows too much." Lord Barnwell smirked. "Just as your mother did."

Dinah grew rigid. "Pardon?"

Lord Barnwell turned his attention towards her. "I didn't want to kill your mother. Quite the contrary, in fact, but I had little choice in the matter. I'm afraid your father was not who he claimed to be, and he associated with the wrong people. I had to kill him because he was on the verge of discovering who I truly was. If he had, my carefully laid out plans would have been ruined, and I couldn't let that happen."

"You killed my parents?" Evie demanded.

Lord Barnwell shrugged. "It was either them or me."

"I wish it had been you," Dinah said.

Lord Barnwell looked amused. "If your father had been smarter, he would have triumphed, but it appears that failure runs in your family," he stated. "Your father's mistake was asking too many questions, leading me to wonder what his true motives were. Either way, he deserved to die."

"I'm going to kill you," Evie hissed.

Lord Barnwell held his hands out, gesturing to the room. "Look around you. Right now, there are guards with pistols pointed at you. You wouldn't even be able to make it out of that chair without being killed."

"If that is the case, then why haven't you already killed us?" Evie asked.

"That is simple. I am using you for collateral." Lord Barnwell rose and walked over to Evie. He grabbed her hair and pulled back, forcing her to look up at him. "Not you, per se, but your lovely sister. You are just a bloody nuisance."

"I'm happy to oblige," Evie said.

Lord Barnwell released her and stepped back. "It shouldn't have come to this," he claimed. "If you had just minded your own blasted business and hadn't killed one of my men."

"In fairness, he was trying to kill me," Evie replied cheekily.

"You think you are so clever," Lord Barnwell mocked. "Yet you will die just as your father did, as a complete and utter failure."

"I wouldn't count me out yet."

Lord Barnwell scoffed. "Are you truly putting all your faith on a Bow Street Runner?" he asked. "Because that is who is coming for you." He paused. "Or should I say, for Dinah? After all, Abrams informed me that the man is quite smitten with her."

Dinah squared her shoulders but remained quiet.

Lord Barnwell stepped over to her. "What would your parents have thought of you being courted by a lowly Bow Street Runner?"

"He is not courting me," Dinah replied.

"I regret to inform you that he's only after your money," Lord Barnwell remarked. "He may say he cares for you, but he sees you as his ticket to a life he has only dreamed of. I'm afraid it is a tale that is as old as time. Once he has secured your hand in marriage, he will cast you aside and spend all of your money."

"I care not what you say," Dinah said.

Lord Barnwell put his hand on the back of her chair and leaned close. "I had such high hopes for you, my dear. You were the golden child, the one that was going to make your parents proud, but you squandered that chance the moment you sought out that Bow Street Runner."

Dinah pursed her lips together. "I had my reasons."

"You did, and now you are going to die because of it," Lord Barnwell said as he leaned back. "You would have been safe if you had remained in your gilded life."

"Someone is approaching," one of the guards near a window said.

Lord Barnwell nodded his approval. "It is time." He turned back towards them. "Tie them up, and be sure to gag them."

Chapter Twenty-Two

"Does everyone remember the plan?" Nathaniel asked as he eyed the warehouse.

Worsley raised his hand.

Nathaniel looked heavenward. "Yes, Worsley," he sighed.

"What you are proposing is madness," Worsley replied. "If you go in alone, you will surely be killed."

"Not if we stick to the plan," Nathaniel pressed.

Talbot spoke up. "Even then, it is a great risk to you."

"I am well aware, but I can't ask any of you to put your lives on the line," Nathaniel said.

"You don't have to," Haddington asserted from next to him. "I believe we all know what is at stake here."

Nathaniel bobbed his head. "If all goes well, we will soon be toasting our victory at White's."

"I've never been to White's," Worsley shared.

Talbot turned to him and swatted him on the arm. "That's because you ain't a gentleman."

"Neither are you," Worsley responded.

"Perhaps not," Talbot said, tugging on the lapels of his jacket, "but I have a certain amount of class."

Haddington frowned. "Are you two ever serious?"

"No," they replied in unison.

Nathaniel put his hand on Haddington's shoulder. "If something happens to me, I want you to promise me that you will get the ladies out."

"I promise," Haddington stated.

Worsley put his maroon cap back onto his head and turned towards Talbot. "Are you ready to start a brawl?"

"Am I ever," Talbot said, clenching his fists.

Haddington watched their retreating figures for a moment before saying, "I will be behind you. All you need to do is stall and avoid getting yourself killed."

"I can't promise that." Nathaniel started down the street and ducked into the alleyway adjacent to the warehouse. He walked over to the broken window that he had noticed before and looked inside.

Empty.

He pushed the window up slowly. Then, he crawled through the opening, being mindful to be as quiet as possible. Once inside, he pulled out his pistol and headed towards the open door. He stepped into the narrow hall and listened, but the only sound came from the rats scurrying in the walls.

With light steps, he walked down the hall, not knowing where the threats were lurking. The hall opened into a large room, and he saw Dinah and Evie were tied to chairs in the center, their backs to him. A guard was positioned near the opening, and Nathaniel came up behind him. He hit the man in the back of the head with the butt of his gun, catching him before he hit the ground.

Nathaniel laid the guard on the floor and removed the pistol from his waistband. He didn't see another guard, but he could hear a commotion outside. It appeared that Worsley and Talbot had indeed started a brawl in front of the empty warehouse or had otherwise managed to attract a rowdy crowd. With any luck, the remaining guards were preoccupied with that.

Staying low, he hurried towards the ladies and reached Dinah first.

Dinah's eyes grew wide as she looked at him, and she started mumbling something. He couldn't understand her with the gag that was in her mouth, so he removed it.

"What is it?" Nathaniel asked, crouching down in front of her.

"It's a trap," she said breathlessly.

Nathaniel gave her a reassuring smile. "I assumed as much."

"You did?" she asked. "But you came anyway?"

"I had no choice." Nathaniel removed a dagger from his boot and cut at the rope.

Once she was free, Dinah jumped into his arms, causing him to stumble back. He quickly righted himself and wrapped his arms around her. "It will be all right," he assured her.

"Thank you for coming," Dinah said, stepping out of his arms.

"You're welcome, but we are not safe yet." Nathaniel took his dagger and sliced Evie's ties.

Evie removed the gag from her mouth. "It's about time you got here."

Nathaniel chuckled. "It's good to see you, too, Evie."

The sound of slow clapping echoed through the hall. Nathaniel stood in front of the ladies as he turned towards the noise.

Lord Barnwell emerged from the shadows, followed by two guards with pistols in their hands.

Lord Barnwell stopped clapping as he stopped a short distance from them. "That was touching," he said. "It truly warmed my heart."

"These women are innocents and should be let free," Nathaniel declared.

"That is far from the truth," Barnwell remarked. "Miss Ashmore shot me in the arm. It was quite painful at the time."

"It is no less than you deserve."

Barnwell smirked. "What I find perplexing is that I set a trap for a Bow Street Runner, and instead, I caught an earl, the son of my political rival," he said. "Which leads me to wonder what you are about, Lord Hawthorne?"

Ignoring Dinah's gasp, he replied, "I am just here to rescue these girls."

"I doubt that." Barnwell shifted his gaze towards Dinah. "Based on the shocked look on Miss Dinah's face, I must assume that she didn't know who you truly were."

"That doesn't matter now," Nathaniel asserted.

"It does matter," Barnwell replied. "You lied to her. Why did you sully your hands to pretend to be a Bow Street Runner?"

"That is none of your business," Nathaniel growled.

"Were you bored?" Barnwell asked. "Did you hope to lift her skirt up?"

Nathaniel balled his hands into fists. "I did no such thing."

"Then what purpose did you have to deceive Miss Dinah?" Barnwell questioned.

"I have my reasons."

Barnwell scoffed. "A man of mystery," he said. "You are playing a dangerous game, pretending to be something you are not."

"And what of you?" Nathaniel asked. "You are trying to have the prime minister assassinated."

"With good reason. Once Lord Liverpool is killed, the people will rise up, and a revolution will begin."

"Why would you want needless killing?"

"The Tory party has ruled for far too long," Barnwell explained. "It is time for the prince regent to recognize that the Whigs are the way of the future."

"If I must guess, you believe that you should be the next prime minister?"

"I am the only sensible choice, and the prince regent will

recognize it when the time comes to appoint a new prime minister."

Nathaniel lifted his brow. "Your plan is far from flawless."

"I have been orchestrating this plan for years," Barnwell said, taking a commanding step forward. "You cannot understand the sacrifices I have had to make to bring this to pass, or the number of people that I have had to silence."

Evie spoke up from behind Nathaniel. "Lord Barnwell admitted to killing my parents."

Barnwell nodded. "That was an easy feat," he said. "Your mother was the last to die, and she pleaded for you and Dinah to be spared. It was pathetic."

"I would not antagonize her," Nathaniel warned.

"What is Miss Ashmore going to do to me?" Barnwell asked, holding his hands out. "Admit it. I won, and you all lost."

"That is not how I see it," Nathaniel said. "This fight has only just begun."

"There is no fight," Barnwell replied. "Although, this is not how I planned for the evening to go. I had hoped to convince you to kill Lord Liverpool in exchange for Miss Dinah's life. But then I saw who you were, and I realized that was an impossibility."

"You were never going to let any of us live," Evie claimed.

Barnwell nodded. "True. You all know too much," he replied. "It is a shame, really. Your bodies won't be discovered for quite some time, leaving people to speculate what has become of you. It will be most unfortunate for your aunt, because she won't be able to show her face in Town again once the gossips catch wind of this scandal."

"You are a horrible man," Dinah said.

Barnwell shrugged. "I have been called a lot worse." He turned back towards his guards. "Kill them."

"You made a mistake, Barnwell," Nathaniel declared.

Glancing over his shoulder, Barnwell asked, "And what was that?"

"You thought I came alone."

"My guards will have taken care of whoever you brought along on your misadventure," he responded, uninterested.

"Not these men," Nathaniel said. "They are trained agents who can hold their own."

Barnwell held his hands up and mocked, "And where are these so-called agents?"

Nathaniel glanced back at the doorway, wondering the same thing.

Lowering his hands, Barnwell chuckled. "That is what I thought," he said. "Your plan failed, and your time is up."

Barnwell removed the pistol from the waistband of his trousers and pointed it at them. "Which one of you should I kill first?"

As the words left his mouth, Haddington stepped into the room, his pistol not straying from Barnwell, and ordered, "Lower your pistol, or I will kill you."

Barnwell carelessly obeyed as he turned. "This is who you brought? Did you bring along more lords to die?"

Haddington walked further into the room. "I have no intention of dying today."

"No?" Barnwell asked. "Because I can't help but notice you are terribly outnumbered."

"Am I?" Haddington asked.

The sound of pistols cocking could be heard coming from the edges of the room, and Worsley and Talbot stepped out from the shadows, guns raised. The two of them moved to Barnwell's guards and took their weapons, then motioned the men toward the door.

"While you were babbling on, we were taking out your guards, one by one," Haddington explained. "I would highly recommend you surrender if you want to stay alive."

Barnwell narrowed his eyes. "I will not take orders from a pretentious dandy."

Haddington shrugged his shoulders. "Then don't," he replied. "Quite frankly, I am thinking of just shooting you so you'll stop talking."

"Even if you have me arrested, no jury will convict me," Barnwell said smugly. "I will be a free man."

Nathaniel interjected, "But you will be discredited and ostracized by the *ton*."

"They are a fickle lot," Barnwell replied. "I will be welcomed back in their ranks soon enough."

"I will never allow that to happen," Nathaniel asserted.

Barnwell brought his pistol up. "Then we have a problem," he growled.

"Lower your pistol, or I will shoot," Haddington commanded.

Nathaniel could see the fear in Barnwell's cold eyes, and he knew that he was desperately trying to stay in control of the situation, making him very unpredictable and dangerous. Putting his hands up in front of him, Nathaniel said, "You can walk out of here with your life if you don't do anything stupid."

"I had it all planned out!" Barnwell exclaimed. "And you ruined it!"

Evie stepped forward. "No, I did," she declared. "If you want someone to blame, it should be me."

"You are right," Barnwell said as he started to shift his pistol towards Evie.

In a motion Nathaniel barely noticed, Evie brought her arm back and threw it forward, releasing a dagger that hit Barnwell squarely in the chest.

The pistol slipped from Barnwell's hands as he fell to his knees. "What did you do?" he asked, disbelief etched on his features.

Evie slowly approached Barnwell and picked up his pistol. "It was either you or one of us, and I chose you."

Barnwell's eyes slid into the back of his head, and he dropped to the floor.

The silence was deafening, but it came to an abrupt halt when Worsley, who'd almost made it to the door with the man he was guarding, said, "Well, that was unexpected."

Dinah couldn't believe what had just transpired. Evie had just killed Lord Barnwell with a dagger, and Dinah couldn't seem to stop looking at his body sprawled out on the floor.

Nathaniel turned back to face her, concern on his features. "Are you all right?"

"No," she replied honestly.

"We should get you out of here."

He reached for her arm, but she stepped aside. "That would be for the best," she agreed.

"I would imagine that you have some questions for me," Nathaniel said as they walked towards the door.

"I do, but I don't know where to start." Dinah stopped next to Reginald. "Thank you for coming when you did."

Reginald smiled. "It was my pleasure."

She stepped closer to him and asked in a hushed voice, "Are you a spy, as well?"

His smiled dimmed. "I… uh…" His voice trailed off. "What do you know about spies?"

"I know my father was one, and I now know that Lord Hawthorne was not a Bow Street Runner, leaving me to conclude he is a spy," she explained.

Reginald met her gaze. "All you need to know is that our allegiance lies with the Crown."

"I understand," she said.

Evie came to stand next to them and whispered, "That is the polite way of saying that they are spies."

Dinah turned towards her sister. "You knew this entire time?"

"I did."

"And you didn't think to tell me the truth?"

Evie shifted her gaze towards Nathaniel before replying, "I didn't think it was my place to do so."

"What else have you kept from me?" Dinah asked. The stress of their situation had taken a toll, and now that the pistols were put away and Lord Barnwell's body behind her, Dinah's emotions rolled through her.

"Nothing," Evie replied with a slight wince.

Dinah let out a disbelieving huff before turning back towards Nathaniel. "And you..." Her voice trailed off. "You lied to me this entire time."

"I did, but it was for your own good," Nathaniel said.

"My own good?" she asked. "You led me to believe that you were a Bow Street Runner!"

"It was much safer that way."

Dinah tossed her arms in the air. "Obviously not," she declared. "I was abducted and held hostage by a delusional lord!"

"I know you are upset, but—"

"But, what?" she asked, cutting him off. "Do not trivialize my feelings by trying to justify your actions!"

"I have no intention to." Nathaniel gestured towards the doorway. "Can we talk about this in private?"

It was on the tip of her tongue to refuse him, but she heard the plea in his voice and realized she'd been shouting. "All right," she agreed before stepping into the hallway.

As she spun back around, Nathaniel came to a stop and said, "I know you are angry, but I can explain."

"Can you?" she asked, crossing her arms over her chest. "Because it seems like I don't really know you, my lord."

Nathaniel frowned. "I do not like you making use of my title."

"Were you ever going to tell me the truth?"

"Revealing the truth of what I do is not something I make a habit of," Nathaniel said.

"After everything we have been through, you still can't fully trust me?"

"Heaven help me, but I do trust you."

Dinah gave him an exasperated look. "You have a funny way of showing it, then."

Nathaniel ran a hand through his blonde hair. "You seem to forget that you were the one who mistook me for a Bow Street Runner."

"I did, but you could have corrected me at any time."

"For what purpose?" he asked. "Once I heard your plight, I knew that your sister was somehow involved, and I needed to find her."

"So you used me?"

Nathaniel sighed. "I could see how you could think that, but I think we benefited from each other's association."

"You repeatedly lied to me," she said. "How can I ever trust you again?"

"Please don't say that."

Dinah's eyes searched his as she asked, "Was any of it real?"

"It was." He took a step closer to her. "I am the same man, Dinah. Everything I did was to protect you."

"Yet you never thought to tell me the truth."

"I couldn't."

Dinah took a step back, creating more distance between them. "I don't know you."

"Dinah…"

She put her hand up, stilling his words. "I don't think anything more needs to be said between us."

"I disagree," Nathaniel said.

His words had barely left his mouth when the main door flew open and men started running into the building, their pistols drawn.

Nathaniel moved to shield her with his body. "Just make no sudden movements."

Once the hall was filled with agents, a tall, older man stepped into the room, a pistol tucked into his waistband. "Is the threat taken care of?"

Nathaniel nodded. "It is."

"Did you put Barnwell under arrest?" the man asked.

"We did not," Nathaniel replied slowly.

The man's face went slack. "You didn't kill him, did you?"

"I didn't, but Miss Ashmore did when it became apparent that he was going to kill her," Nathaniel explained.

"Miss Ashmore killed him?" the man asked. "How?"

"With a dagger, sir."

"Botheration," the man muttered. "Do you know how much paperwork I am going to have to do now to explain his death?"

Evie stepped out from the other room. "In my defense, Lord Barnwell was becoming unhinged, and he had every intention of killing me. I had no choice, Merritt."

Merritt studied Evie for a moment. "You remind me so much of your father."

"You knew my father?" Evie asked.

Merritt smiled. "We may have worked together on a few assignments."

"You should know that Lord Barnwell admitted to killing my parents," Evie shared.

All humor vanished from Merritt's face. "Then I am glad he is dead." He turned his attention towards Dinah. "I'm glad to see you looking well, Miss Dinah."

Not sure what to say, she stepped out from behind Nathaniel and muttered, "Thank you."

"I have a coach waiting out front that will take you ladies

home," Merritt informed them. "With any luck, your appearance in the rookeries will go unnoticed."

Nathaniel put a hand on Dinah's sleeve. "Would you like me to escort you home?"

"I do not think that will be necessary."

"It would be my pleasure," he pressed.

Dinah moved her arm and watched his hand fall to his side. "I think it would be best if we went our separate ways."

Nathaniel stared at her. "You don't truly mean that," he said, disbelief clearly evident on his features, "do you?"

"I do," she replied.

"If that is what you want," he hesitated, "I will respect that."

"It is."

Nathaniel tipped his head. "It has been a true honor getting to know you, Miss Dinah," he said, and disappeared into the next room.

Evie moved to stand next to Dinah and asked, "Are you ready to go home?"

"I am."

Merritt went and opened the door for them. "Allow me the privilege of escorting you to the coach."

After they were situated, Evie eyed Dinah with concern. "Do you want to talk about what just happened?"

"I assumed you overheard everything," Dinah replied.

"We did," Evie admitted. "Reginald and I were shamelessly eavesdropping."

"Then you know why I said what I did."

Evie pursed her lips, then said, "I don't."

Dinah clasped her hands in her lap. "How can I ever trust Lord Hawthorne again?"

"How can you trust me?"

"That is different."

"Is it?" Evie asked. "I lied to you, as well."

"But you never used me for information."

Evie shook her head. "You are faulting him for doing his job," she said. "That is hardly fair of you."

"How am I supposed to act?" Dinah asked. "Everything he told me was a lie."

"Not everything. He cares for you."

Dinah huffed. "That was probably an act, as well."

"Lord Hawthorne is not that good of an actor," Evie responded. "What does your heart tell you to do?"

"My heart has nothing to do with this."

"It should. You are making a terrible mistake in letting Lord Hawthorne go."

Dinah glanced out the window. "It is my life, and I'm doing what is best for me," she replied curtly.

"You are hurt—"

Dinah cut her off. "Of course, I am hurt!" she declared, her voice rising. "I just discovered that the man I love has been lying to me the entire time I've known him!"

"You love him?"

"I do," Dinah admitted, "but it makes no difference now."

"It should. Love doesn't come around very often."

"Please spare me the lecture on true love," Dinah said. "If Lord Hawthorne truly cared about me, he would have told me the truth."

"Dinah…"

"I do not wish to speak about this anymore. I made my decision, and there is no going back."

Evie put her hands up in surrender. "Fine. I will leave you be," she sighed.

Dinah turned her attention towards the window and tried to banish the look of hurt on Nathaniel's face from her mind. She had made the right decision. It wasn't as if she could trust him anymore.

Her heart ached as she realized that she would never love another as much as she'd loved him.

Chapter Twenty-Three

Nathaniel stared out the darkened window and tried again to banish Miss Dinah from his thoughts. He couldn't seem to stop thinking about her, despite knowing she wanted nothing to do with him. The sad thing was that he wouldn't have gone back in time and changed a thing. If he had, there was no telling what the outcome would have been. The slightest variance could have meant death for either one of them.

The most important thing was that Miss Dinah was home safe, where she belonged. How he wished that she recognized that she belonged with him, in his home! He had never felt this way about anyone before, but it was all for naught. It had been sheer foolishness on his part to let his guard down and fall in love. It was a mistake that he would be forced to carry for the rest of his life.

How had he let it come to this? Nathaniel would do anything to see Miss Dinah one more time. With any luck, she would be at the ball tonight, and he could get a glimpse of her.

His valet broke through his musings. "Which cravat would you care to wear this evening?"

"Just pick one," he muttered.

"As you wish, my lord."

Nathaniel allowed his valet to tie the cravat and help him into his black jacket.

"Will there be anything else?" the valet asked.

"No. That should be all," Nathaniel replied as he headed for the door. He exited his bedchamber and walked down the hall. As he descended the stairs, he saw his mother pacing in the entry hall.

She stopped and said, "There you are."

"Here I am."

"If Hugh doesn't hurry, we shall be late," his mother remarked.

Hugh's voice came from the top of the stairs. "There is no reason to worry," he said. "No one will even notice if we are not there when the dancing begins."

"I see that you finally decided to grace us with your presence," his mother remarked.

Hugh tugged at the lapels of his black jacket and smirked. "It takes time to look presentable for the ladies."

"Where is Father?" Nathaniel asked.

"His meeting ran late at the House of Lords. He sent word that he will meet us there." Their mother motioned towards the door, which Balfour was holding open.

They followed their mother out and stepped into the coach. Once the coach jerked forward, Nathaniel turned his attention towards the window. He truly didn't want to engage in mindless drivel, not when his life seemed bleak.

Hugh glanced over at him and commented, "I'm not complaining, but you seem more despondent than usual."

"I'm fine."

"It was merely an observation," Hugh said.

His mother watched Nathaniel closely. "Who is she?"

"Why do you assume my mood has something to do with a lady?" Nathaniel asked.

"You are not the only one who can be quite astute," his mother responded.

Nathaniel frowned. "If you must know, Miss Dinah Ashmore has rejected my advances."

"Miss Dinah," his mother repeated. "She would be a fine choice for a bride."

"She would, if she didn't reject me."

His mother waved a hand dismissively. "She will come around."

"I am not sure that is true," Nathaniel said. "She was quite adamant about it."

"Can I have a go at her?" Hugh interjected.

"Don't you dare," Nathaniel growled.

Their mother shook her head. "Do not mind Hugh," she said. "He is just trying to antagonize you."

"It's working," Nathaniel grumbled.

Hugh shifted in his seat. "Not only are the Ashmore sisters both heiresses, but they are also quite beautiful."

"I agree," their mother replied. "It is a shame that Miss Ashmore hasn't married yet. She is destined to become a spinster if she continues on the way she is."

"There are worse things," Nathaniel remarked.

"Not for a genteel woman," their mother responded.

The coach pulled up in front of a three-level townhouse in the fashionable part of Town. The coach dipped to the side as the footman stepped off his perch and opened the door.

Once they were standing on the walkway, Nathaniel offered his arm to his mother. "Shall we get this over with?"

"You never know," his mother started, "you might enjoy yourself this evening."

"That is unlikely," Nathaniel murmured as he led her into the townhouse.

They stepped into the entry hall and Hugh announced, "If you will excuse me, I am going to find the cards room."

"Please don't spend your entire evening in there," their mother said.

Hugh shrugged. "It depends on whether I am on a winning streak or not."

She watched Hugh walk off. "When is he going to stop wasting his life?"

"I don't rightly know."

She turned to face him. "And you," she began, "are you just going to let Miss Dinah walk out of your life?"

"She wants nothing to do with me, Mother."

"Convince her otherwise."

"And how do you propose I do that?"

His mother stepped closer and lowered her voice. "I do not say anything when you come home in threadbare clothing or when you leave at ghastly hours in the night. I don't pretend to know what you do with your time, but I am not a simpleton."

"I never implied that you were."

"What I do know is that it is time for you to settle down with the right girl."

Nathaniel rested his hand on her shoulder. "Thank you for your concern, but I assure you this is for the best."

"Do you love her?"

He dropped his hand to his side. "Mother—"

She spoke over him, repeating her question. "Do you love her?"

"I do," he admitted reluctantly.

"Then you must go get her."

Nathaniel's eyes scanned over the entry hall. "I don't even know if she is here tonight."

"She will be," his mother replied. "Mrs. Carter is a dear friend of Lady Wycombe."

"That doesn't mean Miss Dinah will come."

His mother arched an eyebrow. "I have never known you to give up so easily."

"I need to respect her decision and learn how to live without her."

His words had barely left his mouth when he saw his friend, Berkeley, approaching. "I haven't seen you in days," he said, forgoing niceties entirely. "Where have you been?"

"I have been busy with work," Nathaniel responded.

"I do hope when I inherit our ancestral estate that I won't spend nearly as much time on managing it as you do," Berkeley remarked.

"It is a necessary evil," Nathaniel said.

"Would you care to box tomorrow?"

Nathaniel nodded. "I would," he replied. "I find that I need something to hit."

Berkeley chuckled. "I am happy to oblige." He turned towards Nathaniel's mother and bowed. "How are you, Lady Montfort?"

His mother smiled. "I am well," she replied. "How is your father?"

"Not well, I'm afraid," Berkeley replied. "But with any luck, he will feel much better soon."

"I do hope so."

Nathaniel turned his head towards the door and caught sight of Miss Dinah. She was dressed in a very becoming pink gown with a low neckline edged with ivory lace, which gave slightly more coverage to her bodice. Her hair was piled atop her head and pearls were interwoven throughout. To say she looked beautiful would be an understatement, in his opinion.

Miss Dinah turned her head and their eyes met. It felt as if time stood still, and all Nathaniel could hear was the beating of his own heart. It was evident that she was not affected as he was, because she ducked her head and continued towards the ballroom as if nothing had transpired.

His mother's voice came from next to him. "It is time for you to go to her."

"It is too late."

Berkeley followed his gaze with a baffled look on his face. "Do you have an understanding with Miss Dinah?"

"No, I do not."

"You could do a lot worse for yourself," Berkeley said.

Nathaniel's mother gave him a small push. "Stop wasting time and go speak to her."

Before he knew what he was about, Nathaniel found himself walking towards the ballroom without a plan, which was unusual for him. He was not one to be unprepared, but he had no idea what he could possibly say to sway Miss Dinah in his favor. All he knew was that he had to try one last time. He knew he would always regret it if he didn't.

He scanned the ballroom, but he saw no sign of Miss Dinah. He did, however, see Mrs. Carter and Evie standing near the back.

As he approached them, Mrs. Carter frowned. She didn't seem pleased to see him.

He stopped and bowed. "Mrs. Carter," he greeted. "Miss Ashmore."

Mrs. Carter cocked her head. "So, you are Lord Hawthorne?" she asked critically.

"I am."

"I find it odd that you never brought that up all the times you visited our home."

"I had my reasons," Nathaniel replied.

Evie put a hand on her aunt's sleeve. "Do not disoblige Lord Hawthorne with questions," she said. "If you recall, he saved Dinah and I."

"That is true, but he did treat Dinah most terribly," Mrs. Carter insisted.

"That was never my intention," Nathaniel said.

"Then what was your intention, my lord?" Mrs. Carter asked, her brow lifted.

Nathaniel grimaced. "I did lie to your niece, repeatedly, but I am hoping I can convince her to forgive me."

"And why would she do that?"

Nathaniel took a deep breath before admitting, "Because I

love her. She may not need me in her life, but I need her in mine."

"You have a funny way of showing that."

"I do not deserve her forgiveness, but I will not stop fighting for her."

His words seemed to appease Mrs. Carter because a faint smile came to her lips. "She is in the gardens, my lord," she revealed. "You may want to lead with that last part."

Evie gave him an encouraging nod. "I believe Dinah needs you in her life, as well."

Nathaniel felt hope swelling inside of him. "If you will excuse me, I need to go beg your sister to marry me."

———

Dinah was tired of crying, but she couldn't seem to stop the tears that flowed down her cheeks. It had been this way since she had walked away from Nathaniel the night before. She kept reliving their conversation over and over in her mind, wondering if she had done the right thing by sending him away. He lied to her, used her, and yet her treacherous heart still wanted him.

Why had she let her aunt talk her into coming to this ball? She was sitting in the rear of the gardens on a bench, watching enamored couples walking along the paths. No one seemed to give her any heed, and she preferred that. She had no intention of enjoying herself this evening, not when her heart was breaking into small pieces.

Regardless, it mattered not. It wasn't as if they'd had an understanding between them. They had shared a few special moments, ones that she would always cherish, but Nathaniel had never declared his intentions. Perhaps she had just hoped for something that was never there? No, she had seen it in his eyes. He cared for her, she was sure of that.

Dinah let out a sigh. When had her life become so complicated? She'd thought she was content with what she had, but now she realized she wanted more. She wanted Nathaniel.

What was wrong with her? When had she become so fickle and allowed a man to have such control over her?

The sound of boots coming near drew her attention, and her heart lurched at the sight of Nathaniel approaching her. He was dressed in a black jacket with matching trousers, a white waistcoat, and cravat. His hair was slicked to the side, not looking at all like the disheveled man she had grown accustomed to seeing.

Nathaniel came to a stop, ensuring proper distance between them. He didn't speak right away, but instead watched her closely. After a long moment, he said, "You have been crying."

"I have," she replied honestly. There was no point in trying to deny it, nor did she want to. She wasn't ashamed to show her feelings.

"May I ask why you are alone in the gardens?"

Dinah half shrugged. "I'm afraid I am not in a jovial mood."

"I am of the same mind."

Glancing back at the townhouse, she saw that her aunt and Evie had stepped onto the veranda to ensure that they were being chaperoned.

Nathaniel followed her gaze. "I assume that your aunt was overjoyed by your return last night."

"She was," Dinah replied. "She'd been beside herself with worry, and the constable once again proved himself to be useless."

"They usually are. What did you tell her about the ordeal?"

Rising, Dinah said, "We told her the truth, minus the part that you were a spy. We also left out that Reginald was there."

"That was for the best."

"It was," she agreed, clasping her hands in front of her. "I would be remiss if I did not thank you for saving my life."

"You don't need to thank me. I would do it again, without the slightest hesitation," he replied, his voice soft, but firm.

Dinah offered him a wry smile. "Let's hope there is not another time."

"Quite right," he said. "Although, you were rather brave, given the circumstances."

"I didn't feel brave," she admitted.

Nathaniel took a step closer to her. "I wish you saw yourself the way others see you."

"How is that?"

"You are brilliant, and it makes everyone around you look dull."

Dinah fought the blush that she could feel forming on her cheeks. "You are being rather complimentary this evening."

"I am only stating the truth."

She felt her back stiffen. "The truth?" she asked. "Pray tell, what version of truth is that?"

Nathaniel frowned. "I deserve that, but I want honesty between us from here on out."

"What makes you assume I want to spend more time with you?"

"Don't you?" he asked.

Dinah held his gaze before admitting, "Frankly, I don't know what I want. You hurt me terribly by deceiving me for as long as you did."

"I know I don't deserve your forgiveness, but if you allow me, I will spend the rest of our lives making that up to you."

Dinah's voice caught in her throat, unsure of his meaning. "What exactly are you saying?"

"I want to marry you," Nathaniel boldly stated. "Whether it is tomorrow, the next day, or even in a year, I intend to make you my wife."

Her lips parted in disbelief. "How can you think I could possibly trust you after everything we have been through?"

"Because I love you, and I refuse to let you go without trying."

Dinah shook her head. "This is all too much," she said. "I don't even know who you truly are."

Nathaniel took another step towards her, closing the distance between them to mere inches. "I did lie to you about who I was, but I promise I will never lie to you again."

"Is that supposed to make it right between us?"

"No, but it is a start," he replied, his eyes showing vulnerability, "and it is the first step in a long journey for us."

Dinah tilted her head to look up at him. "It is not that simple," she said. "You are a spy."

"I am, and that probably won't change until I inherit my father's title." He paused. "But I would give it up to be with you."

"You are willing to stop working as a spy for me?"

Nathaniel grew solemn. His eyes held hers, a plea in their dark depths. "I would do anything for you, Dinah. You have stolen my heart, and without you, my life has no meaning."

Dinah could hear the sincerity in his voice, and her heart softened towards him, allowing her to admit, "I love you, too, but I'm scared."

"There is no reason to be scared," he said. "I will safeguard your heart. There is nothing that I will treasure more."

As Dinah stared deep in his eyes, she knew that he was her future. Admittedly, there was a lot she didn't know about him. But she did know two things—he completed her in a way that she'd never thought possible, and he had a place in her heart that no one else could ever have. But was she strong enough to trust her heart?

Nathaniel must have sensed her inner turmoil because he placed his hand on her sleeve. "You do not need to answer me now," he said. "My love for you will never diminish, and I will wait, for as long as it takes."

Dinah knew that he misconstrued her silence for apprehension. "There is no need to wait. I already know what I would like to do."

She watched Nathaniel swallow slowly. "Which is?"

"I don't want you to stop working as a spy," she said. "It would be terribly unfair of me to require that of you."

"But I would give it up—"

"I am well aware, but I fell in love with a spy, and I have no desire to change any part of you."

Nathaniel looked unsure. "Where does that leave us?"

"If you do not object, I would like to post the banns and be married in three weeks," she said plainly. "During that time, I will expect you to court me properly."

Nathaniel grinned broadly. "I have no objections."

"Good, because I want to go on carriage rides through Hyde Park during the fashionable hour, have bouquets of flowers delivered to my townhouse, and stroll through the museums."

"That sounds awful, but I am willing to do it."

"And you will do so without complaint."

His eyes dropped to her lips. "Will I be rewarded with a kiss if I do?"

"I am not opposed to that," she said, her voice breathless.

Nathaniel watched her closely as he leaned closer, giving her ample time to protest, but she had no desire to do so. His firm mouth brushed across hers, settling briefly, barely touching before deepening the kiss. She closed her eyes as she allowed it. She knew that she would always treasure this single moment when she first kissed the man she would spend the rest of her life with.

He leaned back but remained close. "I don't think I will ever tire of that."

"Nor I," she replied, relishing in his touch.

Nathaniel glanced over his shoulder at the ballroom before saying, "I'm afraid after our little display of affection, you will have no choice but to marry me."

Dinah followed his gaze and saw a crowd of people forming on the veranda, and it was evident that they had witnessed their kiss.

"Shall we go tell our families the good news?" Nathaniel stepped back and held out his gloved hand.

Dinah accepted his hand and was pleased when he brought it up to his lips. "I must admit this is not how I thought this evening would go."

"This is precisely how I hoped this evening would end." He grinned flirtatiously. "Although I did imagine it with more kissing."

"You, sir, are a rogue," she teased, feeling freer than she had in a long time.

"No, I am just a man in love."

As Nathaniel led her towards the townhouse, Dinah knew her heart was full. She had never thought she could burst from happiness, but that is the way she felt. Her journey to find love was not at all what she'd expected, but now she would spend the rest of her days holding onto it.

Epilogue

Three weeks later

"RAISE A GLASS TO FREEDOM," Berkeley said, holding his glass up, "because it is something that you will never see again."

Nathaniel shook his head, amused by his friend's antics. "Aren't you being a bit dramatic?"

Berkeley lowered his glass to the table and replied, "I don't think I am. No one wants to fall prey to the parson's mousetrap."

"You seem to forget that I do want to marry Dinah. She makes me a better man," Nathaniel said.

"That is debatable," Berkeley joked.

Hugh spoke up. "Leave him alone," he encouraged. "If Miss Dinah makes him happy, then who are we to judge?"

"Thank you," Nathaniel responded.

"Besides, I am hoping he will provide me with an introduction to Miss Dinah's older sister, Miss Ashmore," Hugh remarked.

Haddington spoke up from across the table. "And why would you want that?"

"Miss Ashmore is beautiful and an heiress," Hugh replied. "Any gentleman would be lucky to have her."

"I'm afraid you couldn't handle Miss Ashmore," Haddington stated.

"Whyever not?" Hugh questioned.

"She is much too clever for the likes of you," Haddington declared.

Hugh eyed him curiously. "I'm beginning to think that you want to keep Miss Ashmore for yourself."

Haddington visibly tensed. "We are just friends, nothing more."

Nathaniel took pity on his friend and decided to sway the conversation away from him. "Grenton has been awfully quiet this evening."

Grenton brought his gaze up, his brow furrowed. "What was that?"

"You appeared lost in thought," Nathaniel replied.

"I do apologize," Grenton said, pushing his empty glass away. "I'm afraid I have a lot on my mind."

"Anything you wish to share?" Nathaniel asked.

"Not at this time," Grenton responded.

Hugh took a sip of his drink, then said, "We could always discuss Berkeley's pending nuptials."

"That isn't funny," Berkeley grumbled. "My father is relentless on the subject."

Nathaniel pushed back his chair and announced, "Gentlemen, if I do not leave now, I will be late for a very important appointment."

With a knowing look, Haddington raised his glass and said, "Say hello to Miss Dinah for me."

"How do you know I am meeting with Dinah?" Nathaniel asked.

"Because you two have been inseparable since you got engaged," Haddington replied.

Nathaniel rose. "I do love spending time with her."

"I'm glad, since tomorrow you will be tied to her for the remainder of your days," Berkeley muttered.

"I have no objections to that," Nathaniel said. "You will all be there?"

"Do you even need to ask?" Hugh asked, leaning back in his seat.

Nathaniel pushed back in his chair. "Then I shall see you all tomorrow for my nuptials."

Berkeley gave him a pointed look before saying, "It is not too late to break the engagement."

"Why would I do that?" Nathaniel asked. "Dinah is the best part of me."

Haddington chuckled. "You are blinded by love, I see."

"I am, and I prefer it that way." Nathaniel stepped back from the table. "Enjoy the rest of your evening."

After Nathaniel exited White's, he hailed a hackney and rode the short distance to Dinah's townhouse. He exited the coach and headed towards the back of the gardens. He stopped at the gate and took a moment to admire Dinah as she sat on the bench. He noticed that she was wearing a straw hat with a blue flower sticking out of it.

Dinah met his gaze. "You may come in," she encouraged.

"I know, but I find myself admiring your beauty."

A smile brightened Dinah's face as she responded, "You do say the kindest things."

Nathaniel opened the gate and stepped into the gardens. He saw a maid was positioned a short distance away for propriety's sake.

As he claimed the seat next to Dinah on the bench, he said, "After tomorrow, we won't require a chaperone anymore."

"I can hardly wait."

Nathaniel glanced up at the flower on her straw hat and remarked, "I see you kept the flower I gave you."

"Of course," she replied. "I will treasure it always, since it was the first gift that you ever gave me."

"But it certainly won't be the last," he assured her.

"You will find that I prefer small, meaningful gifts over diamonds or jewels."

"I shall give you both."

Dinah gave him an amused look. "You have already spoiled me with all the presents you've given me these past few weeks."

"I enjoy spoiling you," he said, leaning back against the bench. "Are you packed?"

Dinah nodded. "I am," she replied. "It does seem surreal that I won't be living with my sister and aunt anymore."

"They are welcome to live with us."

"I know, but they intend to remain at the townhouse for the remainder of the Season."

Nathaniel reached for her hand and brought it up to his lips. "I do promise that I will make you happy."

"You already do." She lowered her voice. "My aunt does find it odd that we will not be taking a proper wedding tour."

"I promise I will make it up to you."

"You misunderstood me," Dinah said. "I understand what is at stake. We will celebrate once things have settled down in London."

"That could be years."

"It's a good thing I'm not going anywhere."

Lowering their hands, Nathaniel asked, "What did I do to deserve you?"

"I ask the same question about you."

Nathaniel shifted in his seat to face her. "My mother is overjoyed that she is gaining a daughter tomorrow."

"Your parents have been kind to me."

"That is because they know how much I love you," he said. "I did speak to your aunt about something important."

"Which was?"

"She agreed to let us move this bench to our townhouse," he shared. "I have found the perfect spot to place it, assuming you are agreeable."

Tears formed in Dinah's eyes. "That was most thoughtful of you."

"I know it means a great deal to you, and I want you to always feel close to your mother, no matter where you are."

"Thank you," she said. "I hadn't even considered that was a possibility."

"I want you to feel at home at our townhouse."

"It will feel like home wherever you are."

Nathaniel wiped away a tear that was rolling down Dinah's cheek. "I do hope these are happy tears, my love."

"They most assuredly are," Dinah replied. "I can't recall a time when I was ever as happy as I am right now."

Nathaniel leaned closer until his lips hovered over hers. "Just wait. Our journey has only just begun."

"And what fun we shall have."

The End

If you enjoyed A Treacherous
Engagement, check out the next book
in the series

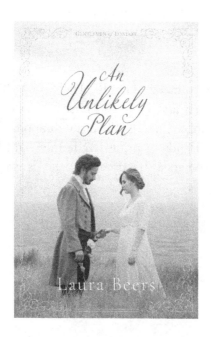

*He has to marry her to gain his inheritance, but she
wants nothing to do with him.*

If you enjoyed A Treacherous Engagement, check out the next book...

After his father is laid to rest, Aaron Berkeley, Earl of Graylocke, sets out to void the marriage contract that his father had in place for him. To his dismay, he discovers that he has no choice but to marry Lady Beatrice or else he will lose a vital part of his inheritance. To make matters worse, the contract stipulates that they must marry by his thirtieth birthday, which is only two months away. He resigns himself to the marriage, finding solace in one's cups.

Lady Beatrice Harford has been in love with Lord Graylocke since she was little. She is elated to finally marry him, and is determined to turn a marriage of convenience into a love match. When Lord Graylocke shows up drunk to their wedding, she is mortified, and has no choice but to call it off. Despite his pleas, she refuses to marry a man who would treat her so callously.

Aaron is determined, though. His usual flirting tactics backfire, however, and he finds himself working harder than ever to win Beatrice's hand. When she disappears, Aaron must work with his friends to bring her home—and back to him. But can he convince Beatrice that he is worth taking a chance on?

Also by Laura Beers

Proper Regency Matchmakers

Saving Lord Berkshire

Reforming the Duke

Loving Lord Egleton

Redeeming the Marquess

Engaging Lord Charles

Refining Lord Preston

Regency Spies & Secrets

A Dangerous Pursuit

A Dangerous Game

A Dangerous Lord

A Dangerous Scheme

Regency Brides: A Promise of Love

A Clever Alliance

The Reluctant Guardian

A Noble Pursuit

The Earl's Daughter

A Foolish Game

The Beckett Files

Saving Shadow

A Peculiar Courtship

To Love a Spy

A Tangled Ruse

A Deceptive Bargain

The Baron's Daughter

The Unfortunate Debutante

About the Author

Laura Beers is an award-winning author. She attended Brigham Young University, earning a Bachelor of Science degree in Construction Management. She can't sing, doesn't dance and loves naps.

Besides being a full-time homemaker to her three kids, she loves waterskiing, hiking, and drinking Dr. Pepper. She was born and raised in Southern California, but she now resides in South Carolina.